The Siren's Discord

First Printing, 2024

Illustrations

by

Dave Kippen

If you ever played mermaids as a kid, this book is dedicated to you.

Chapter 1

Sirena - Present

Sirena felt the water around her ripple in small waves. Her sister Maia, the new Queen of the Merpeople, was descending from her cave above Sirena's. Sirena watched as her sister's tail floated downwards, bringing the rest of her body to hover in front of the opening of Sirena's cave.

Sirena felt a prickling start underneath her skin and her heart went cold.

Maia's eyes were black and her skin gray. Blood trailed from her abdomen. A deep slice ran from throat to belly, her insides spilling out of her body and floating around her.

As the light of the Siren's power surged through her, Sirena screamed.

Chapter 2

Sirena - The Night Before

Years of loss and fear had ravaged her heart. Sirena had only known war, pain, and devastation in her brief life. Hopelessness was creeping in; complete hopelessness that their situation could ever improve. After years of fighting, life in Coralis had only become more complicated with the loss of their home, and their future looked bleaker with each passing day. Most days, Sirena wondered if they would even have a future.

The icy cold water rippled through her fingers as Sirena waved her hands in front of her, feeling for the edge of the cave she had called home for a few weeks. Gone was the sunlight and the beauty of the Sunlight and Twilight Zones of the ocean. An icy darkness replaced the light that would wake her in the morning, causing her bones to hurt. Her fingers ached constantly from the frigid temperatures that she dwelled in, and she flung magic sparks to keep her fingertips from freezing.

Three weeks. That's how long they had been in the Bathypelagic Zone, the Midnight Zone, of the ocean. She shuddered against the cold but also at the thought that they could live here for an indeterminable amount of time. Sirena had not been a mermaid that loved the sunlight or bright sunny colors that other merfolk sported on their tails, and when they plunged further into the depths of the ocean, she had thought she would enjoy the darkness. She was quickly learning that her body didn't love the cold of the lower layers of the ocean. For the first few days, she loved the darkness. The solitude and calm of the water had seemed rejuvenating after decades of fighting.

She was cold and constantly on edge. The dark, cold-loving Siren that she was, she still needed warmth that didn't come from her own magic. Tapping her magic to stay warm was exhausting, and she tried to build thicker skin for the last few days by withholding her magic. She was wildly unsuccessful, lasting only mere hours at a time before the cold won out.

Predators were different here as well. No more dodging sharks or whales. Instead, she was battling with malformed squids that appeared to have grown multiple heads or sea crabs that had nothing better to do than grow to four times the size of any merperson she had ever seen. They were so low in the Midnight Zone that she could see shadows of the terrors that lurked only a few feet lower than her as she hovered over the Abyss. When she closed her eyes, she would see the three headed squid that had attacked her pod within the first few hours that they had been in the Midnight Zone. She shuddered again, whether from the cold or the memory, it didn't matter. She hated it here.

Their beautiful territory, with caverns, ledges and cliffs, adorned in schools of colorful fish and plants, seemed like a distant memory. Dark jagged rocks and the caves that they dwelt in surrounded them and were little more craters in the rocks. Again, she told herself; it had only been three weeks. What were they going to do if they had to spend decades here? She couldn't imagine another three weeks.

Maia, her older sister, was ruler of all the merfolk and the Queen of the Sirens. They had known that this day would come, but it still seemed too soon to Sirena. Sirena was a young mermaid, only fifty years old when her father passed away several years ago.

Killed by humans. She was without her mother, too. The merfolk were a matriarchal species and her mother had been Queen and ruler of the merfolk territories. The Sirens ruled the species and others that were closely related, including the Water Nymphs and the Undines.

Their mother, Malee, was the most beautiful mermaid that Sirena had ever known. Kind but firm and fair in her ruling, the merfolk well loved her. Her black hair had framed her heart-shaped face and her jet-black tail had gold and ruby swirls throughout. The swirls started wide, lazy at the top by her waist, and circled closer together until they convened in alternating red and ruby tips at the base of her fin. Malee had been breathtakingly beautiful and among the most dangerous Sirens to have ever existed. There were legends from before Sirena was born that her mother had taken out entire armies with a few notes of her Siren song. If her mother had perished at the hands of humans, Sirena was certain that the rest of the merfolk didn't stand a chance.

Malee had only sung once above the ocean where Sirena had heard her. A fleeting attempt to buy her children time to retreat into the safety of the ocean. The act of a mother's love had bought them only seconds, and it had been enough. Maia and Sirena had got to their territory to warn the other Sirens of impending danger.

A few moments later, Maia was glowing and shaking and the power of the Sirens transferred to her. Malee was gone.

Sirena's memory kept the few notes that her mother had let out, and she hoped that she never forgot that sound. She hadn't even had time to process what she had heard or the idea that she was an orphan when Maia had shouted orders to the mers around her. Down to the depths. Sink to the Midnight Zone. Three weeks ago.

Sirena had been born into war times, as had her older brother Apollo. Maia was the only one of the three siblings that knew what life had been like when mers had sunned themselves carelessly on rocks above the surface. The times when they had roamed the waters freely and without regard to their surroundings were a legend to so many of the younger mers.

Maia was over two hundred years old, leaving quite the age gap between her and her siblings. The merfolk had a hundred years of open water and carefree attitudes, which Maia remembered, and Sirena would often ask her to share stories from her childhood or tell her what life had been like before humans hunted them. Maia would sigh and tell her what she could remember, and Sirena, never tiring of the stories, would listen to the same memories again and again. What a different world it had been back then.

Asterios, their father, had been five hundred years old when he died and Malee was only a few years older than that when she passed three years later. Merfolk mated for life, and her parents had been fiercely in love with one another. She had watched as her mother's physical and mental health showed their age over the last few years. Merfolk could easily live to be eight or nine hundred years old, but war and losing her mate had broken her mother's spirit. She had seen the hurt, the exhaustion in her mother's eyes when she sacrificed herself for Maia and Sirena. Malee, the Queen of the Sirens, had sacrificed herself out of love but also out of weariness and despair.

Fury ignited sparks within her and she let them loose from her fingertips as she thought about the war. Using her magic not only warmed her fingertips, but it also released some of the rage that she felt. Humans had killed both of her parents and so many of her kind. Because of them, she didn't know a loving and safe world. She knew of broken hearts, blood, tears and lived in constant fear of what was hunting them. Maia's pre-war stories had been the only thing that had given her hope for a better life.

She scoffed at the idea that some humans thought they were the predators. Human ideas that Sirens could lure them to their death with their song seemed absurd to Sirena. That they had lured men and sailors to their death with their voices was laughable. The few notes she had heard her mother utter were the only notes she had ever heard from a Siren. Those few seconds of music did nothing more than pause the hunters for a moment or two. None of the Sirens were singing; their songs were ineffective against the human hunters.

Could she sing herself? She didn't even know.

Humans had learned how to plug their ears; her mother had told her. They had learned how to ignore the songs of the Sirens. After decades without their song, the Sirens had lost their ability to sing. As the humans became more self-centered, they became more difficult to distract. Malee had told Sirena that Sirens had never killed humans for sport, but they had defended themselves. When humans stopped listening, Sirens stopped singing and their ability to escape their captors disappeared.

Hunters learned how to weaken other species of merfolk that didn't sing. Silver did the trick to some. Merrow mermaids naturally sought the love of humans and had become easy targets. The discovery of the merpeople's magic by the wrong human started the one-hundred-year war on the mers. The war had raged on until a few weeks ago, when Maia had said enough was enough. Their mother had died defending her people and her children, and Maia felt she was out of options.

And so, they plunged into the icy dark and dangerous blackness that was the lower layers of the ocean where humans couldn't travel. It was here that Maia thought she could determine what they would do next. Sirena thought again to the giant three headed squid that filled her thoughts. They may have escaped the hunters, but fresh horrors filled the waters here. Ones that they couldn't see chased them in the darkness.

In these last few weeks, there had been tension between the mer clans. There had even been tension in Sirena's own small pod. Pods comprised family and friends within a clan and Sirena's had always been close, but lately they were strained, too. Long bouts of cold and darkness could put a damper on one's mood, she had discovered.

Kassia and Cali were close friends and part of Sirena's pod. In recent days, she had watched as Cali had become more withdrawn. Her tail that was once deep but yet vibrant shades of green and blue had lost its depth and had a slight gray tinge to it. Never one to partake in drama, Cali had remained in the Siren's territory while the rest of her pod made frequent trips to the surface on rescue missions to track down and bring home captured merfolk. Kassia, who was more outgoing and wielded a beautiful dark pink tail with circles of orange and cherry colors, had grown frustrated with her friend, and was finding her difficult to communicate with. The red in her tail had become darker, almost blood red. After the last time they argued about something irrelevant, her tail had become so red it was nearly black. Cali and Kassia barely spoke and Sirena wondered how much longer until they were all at each other's throats.

Her own tail, once a deep black with the same shimmering gold swirls as her mother's, was dull. Where the shimmer and sparkles were, her tail was matte black and her gold swirls were more of a copper, bronze color. While Sirens could change their appearance to suit their mood, their tail would reveal their authentic emotions when depressed, scared, or angry. Sirena had always been one to wear her emotions on her tail and she scowled at the bronze streaks, trying to change them back to gold without luck. No matter how hard she tried to convince herself that everything was going to work out, she couldn't lie to herself. She was miserably sad.

Catalina and Nova, two other members of her pod, were different. They weren't Sirens. Catalina, Cat as they called her, was from the Encantado clan. Her clan lived off the coasts of South America. The few that were left. The Encantado were among the smallest clans of the merfolk, and many of them had perished during rescue missions. Their true forms were that of dolphins and once humans had discovered that, life hadn't gone well for them. Humans that knew the truth about merfolk no longer released dolphins caught in fishing nets until they proved they weren't Encantados. Their torture tactics had resulted in thousands of Encantados being captured and probably even more dolphins dying. Sirena had never seen Cat transform into her dolphin form. Cat was self-conscious about her true form as she had grown up around the always stunning Sirens. While Sirena loved her friend and was sure that Cat's dolphin form was beautiful, she couldn't deny the relief she felt that her friend most likely didn't even know how to shift. It was safer that way.

Those that remained in the Encantado territory dispersed themselves thin throughout the oceans or took up residence with the Aicaya, the mer clan that took in the orphaned and abandoned merfolk. Cat always had the option of finding her remaining Encantados or joining the Aicaya but she told Sirena she had made her home with the Sirens.

Nova was most certainly a Merrow mermaid, but they knew almost little to nothing about her background. Sirena had found her only a few years ago, wandering the oceans with no memory of who she was. Empathy rarely found its way into Sirena's heart, but she had felt it that day and brought Nova home to the Siren's territory. Sirena didn't want to banish the poor mer into a life of exile when she didn't even know who or what she was, despite the blame put on the Merrows for the start of the Human Wars. There was something about Nova that had drawn Sirena in and she had fought to keep her in the Siren's territory. The Sirens' advisors had protested but the privilege of being a royal eventually won out. Sirena's parents had given in and Nova was there to stay.

Sirena was close to her older brother and while Apollo had his own friends and she had hers, their individual pods were really one larger pod. Sirena considered Theo and Xan, Apollo's friends, as part of her pod, too. They grew up together and treated her like a sister. Both were loyal to the royal family and had been leaders of the rescue missions multiple times over. They were strong Siren warriors, the best of the Siren's, and she had learned almost everything she knew about the surface and rescuing other mers from them.

Her head resting on the wall of the cave, Sirena ran through the members of her pod. They'd been bickering and squabbling these last few days. The stress of the wars weighed on them as they adjusted to their new surroundings. She had snapped at Xan earlier in the day and had retreated to her cave for the night while still angry. He was struggling with how many mers were on the surface, fighting for their lives or living in captivity, and Sirena had defended the decision of the council, and Maia, to end rescue missions. Xan's intentions were good and if she was being honest with herself, she didn't like the idea of leaving mers on the surface, either. Risk lives by going to the surface to rescue trapped merpeople or save themselves and leave those on the surface on their own. She didn't know what the best solution was and so she supported her sister, the new Queen. She would apologize to Xan later, but her emotions had gotten the best of her. Sirena had needed a moment to collect her thoughts.

Chapter 3

Sirena - Present

Her arms were glowing, and the throbbing pain that was shooting from the top of her head down to the tip of her fin was unbearable. A quick glance downwards confirmed that her entire body was radiating light, like she had only seen once before, when Maia took over as the ruler of the merpeople.

She stared at her hands for a second. Beams of light were shooting upward from her palms before they faded into the distance. Sirena's magic had already been some of the strongest among the Sirens, and she felt white-hot power surging through her veins. The force of it was enough to make her sink to the floor of the cave opening. Her heart felt as if it would burst from her chest and she could see her veins turn black as power and magic forced their way through her body. She sat there shaking, willing the pain to subside.

Movement to the right of her caused her to swivel her head stiffly against the pain that seared through her. As she peered into the shadows created by the light emanating off of her, she felt sounds struggling in her throat; the words sounding as though they were coming from someone else.

"What is this? Help me…" she heard herself saying.

Coming into focus was Sophie, one of two royal advisors and a lifelong friend of her mother's. Her mouth was moving and forming words, but Sirena couldn't hear her, the ringing in her ears blocking out any other sounds.

"Please, help me," she pleaded again, not knowing if she was making any noise at all or shouting at the top of her lungs. Sirena tried to raise her hands to ears, to make the ringing tolerable, but the magic streaming from her hands only amplified the sound as her hands got closer to her ears. Screaming in frustration and pain, she writhed at the bottom of her cave.

Nova and Theo emerged from the shadows, each grabbing her by an arm. They held her in place as she thrashed against their grasps. Nova grabbed Sirena's face and stared into her eyes intently. "Breathe," she said.

Her gills responded to Nova's command, lightly opening and closing along the sides of her neck as she filled them with water and pulled the air into her lungs. The tingling and throbbing in her chest slowly subsided, and she felt the panic calming itself with each breath. She continued to stare into Nova's eyes, holding onto her friend's gaze to quiet the pain that was surging through her. Despite breathing through her gills slowly, her mouth was open in shock and her eyes felt as though they were bulging out from her face. Is this what Maia had felt? She hadn't done more than slightly glow. Maia must have been stronger than she was because Sirena felt as though she was moments from her last breath. Sirena felt as though she was dying while Maia had been directing the other mers. Sirena felt embarrassment trickling through her and fought harder to get herself under control.

Theo still held her by the arm, but was talking to Sophie. Others had appeared and formed a half circle around the entrance of the cave where Sirena still sat. Glowing and shuddering under the force of the power that had taken control of her. She shook her head to get the ringing that was pulsing through her brain to stop. It quieted only slightly.

"Maia," the only word she could get out.

"She's dead."

Sirena turned to see the glowering look from Orinn, the other Siren advisor. "And we're stuck with you."

"No, no, no. This isn't possible. What happened?" Sirena was looking between Nova and Theo, frantically searching for answers. She put her hands up to her ears as if that would stop the throbbing and ringing in her head.

A deep sigh shot out from Orinn as she crossed her arms over chest. "We don't know. Why don't you tell us?"

Orinn was normally pale, but she looked more ghostly than usual, making her athletic frame appear trimmer and leaner than normal. Her tail was the typical Siren black but unlike others with spirals or circles of color, the tip of her fin looked as though dipped in crimson red blood and then hung upside down as streaks of red, closer at the base of the fin, dispersing wider as they met the top of her tail by her waist. Sirena had always thought that her tail fit her harsh and uncaring personality. When humans thought of evil Sirens, Orinn was who she imagined they thought of.

Catalina was among those in the circle that formed around her. "Give her a minute. She's still glowing, for tail's sake!"

Sirena returned her gaze to Nova's calm face and held her friend's hand as she fought to calm her racing heart. "I don't know what happened. Maia floated past me and the next thing I knew, this… this..." she was holding her arms out to the sides and looking down at her tail and torso, at the body that was still shimmering and shaking.

Nova tossed her a sympathetic look, her long red Merrow hair floating in the waves that she created. Her friend sat next to her and threw her arms around her shoulders as Theo loosened his grasp on Sirena's arm, but didn't let go.

Sophie and Orinn were side by side, watching Sirena's every move. She thought about speaking again and then decided against it. Burying her face into Nova's embrace, allowing the comfort of her friend to soothe her nerves and the pain flowing through her.

"We need to notify the other clans. Xan, find the Water Nymphs, preferably Ozara, and have them spread the word. Except for the Morgens. We need to take care of that ourselves," Sophie quietly dismissed Xan who nodded in agreement but kept his focus on Sirena until Sophie coughed loud enough that he finally took action.

Sirena's stomach went cold. Leander, leader of the Morgen's, was Maia's mate. He remained in his territory and had planned to do so until his clan settled in the Midnight Zone. She would need to be the one to tell him. As the new leader of the merfolk and Queen of the Sirens, it would be her responsibility. The thought of it made her choke as ugly sobs escaped her.

Nova tightened her grip. "It will be fine. Everything is going to work out, lass." Lass, the term of endearment, was the only Merrow language that Nova ever used. She rarely used the word, or others like it, as she couldn't remember who she was or where she had come from.

"Get up," Orinn's voice was cold, harsh.

"I said give her a minute," Catalina's voice was equally cold while she stared down Orinn.

Sirena felt her body lifting itself more upright as Nova moved with her. It took her a second to realize that Nova was moving her. Theo had let go of her but extended an arm in her direction as though he expected her to float face forward. Staring at the space below, looking for signs of Maia and seeing none, Sirena finally felt her voice returning.

"The Water Nymphs will tell the rest of the clans. I will tell Leander myself. Sophie and Orinn, you remain in the territory to oversee the clan in my absence." Sirena felt her breathing return to normal as she tried to accept her new role. She felt uncomfortable giving orders, making her voice quiver.

None of the merpeople spoke or even moved. Filling the silence, she asked a question that she dreaded the answer to. "Where is she? Where did her body go?" Sirena was staring below her again.

"Vanished. She vanished quickly. Royals don't last long," Orinn said.

Sirena, her eyes focusing on what was in front of her, saw her pod and the two royal advisors, but no one else. She scanned again. A few other Sirens, but not Apollo.

"Where's my brother?" she muttered

Chapter 4

Apollo

Apollo found his captors had fallen asleep and so he went back to work trying to free himself of his heavy silver cuffs. Silver didn't control Sirens like they did other species of mermaids, the Selkies specifically, but the thickness and heaviness of the cuffs and chains certainly did their job keeping him immobile.

He had been sleeping and before he knew what happened; he felt ice run through his veins and darkness surrounded him. There was no way for him to tell where he was or for how long he had been gone. He knew Maia was gone, though. He had heard Sirena screaming and saw light blazing off of her, illuminating the

Siren's new den. That was the last thing he remembered before his world went black.

Apollo looked around his prison, seeing if there was any familiarity of scenery he could make out. Gray rock surrounded him. No vegetation, no light. He felt his way around on the floor underneath him as far as the chains would let him move, but there was nothing but stone. His captors sat facing each other at the only exit to the cave. Even if he could get free, he didn't know if he could get past them; he felt weak and drained. He didn't know what or who they were.

Two figures shrouded in black cloaks sat at the entrance of his enclosure. Merpeople didn't wear cloaks, but they didn't want him to know who they were. He tried to make out features, tails, anything that could give him a clue what they were, but he was at a loss. They had attempted to hide their identities. They didn't want him to know who they were. Maybe he was getting out of this situation. The coldness that he had felt before he lost consciousness told him that magic was at play and if that were the case, there was no way he'd find out who the two creatures were. It was even more unlikely that he'd be able to escape. He had magic, most Sirens did, but nothing more than sending some energy in the way of his opponents. He could probably knock down the guards, but that would be the end of that and probably the end of him. Sirena had been the one with the gift of magic.

Hand to hand combat had always been his strength so long as his captors weren't magic powered… maybe he could escape.

Sirena was the leader of all the merpeople and the Queen of the Sirens. That was a reality that was going to take some time to absorb. Maia had been a natural leader and knew that she would be the ruler of the merpeople since she was born, named after their mother for that very reason.

Malee had passed, only three short weeks earlier. Maia had been the Queen for a few weeks and now she was gone. Apollo felt his heart grow heavier as the realization of the loss hit him again. Only he and Sirena remained the last of their small family. Asterios, their father, had been gone for several years, but the grief over that loss felt fresh, the wounds being ripped open again as he mourned his mother and sister. His emotions cycled from grief and despair to rage and revenge. He used his rage to break free of his restraints while his captors were sleeping, but when they were awake; he had to subdue his emotions. They had punished him for any sign of disobedience or rebellion. He looked down at a gash that ran along his forearm. He wasn't healing as quickly as normal.

Maia had driven them all down to the Midnight Zone, but didn't have a plan beyond that. Or if she did, she hadn't shared it with her siblings because neither he nor Sirena had any idea what they were to expect. Maia had spent her days roaming their unfamiliar territory and meeting with the council members of the other clans. Well, mainly Leander, as far as Apollo knew.

There were those that were going to blame Sirena for Maia's death. Leander was going to be furious. Maia had been his mate for close to a century. He knew Sirena hadn't been at fault. He may not be there to see the aftermath, but he knew in his heart that Sirena would never hurt Maia, and she certainly wouldn't have done it to gain rulership.

Describing Sirena as indifferent to the royal family and their responsibilities was the best way he knew how to explain her behavior. Growing up, she didn't seem to care that they had responsibilities, nor did she care much when leaders from the other clans were in their territory. Sirena went about her life, doing whatever interested her. During her younger days, she explored with Catalina. It hadn't been until Sirena was in her early forties that she had gone on rescue missions and training with the rest of the Siren warriors. Sirena was a young mermaid, only fifty-three years old. Apollo wasn't much older than sixty. They had spent much more time together than either of them had with Maia.

Maia was over two hundred years old, and Sirena used to tease Maia that she had lived a whole life before they had been born. She was right, though; Maia had been around for over a hundred years before they were born, and she was wiser and more mature than he and Sirena were. She had spent her entire life preparing for the day that she would become Queen. Maia's life had differed from theirs and while they loved each other, they had different paths in life. Maia would lead the merpeople. She would have her own family, and her oldest mermaid would be next in line. Apollo and Sirena would continue on with their royal responsibilities, being Maia's advisors and being the intermediaries between the other clan leaders and Maia when needed.

Going to the surface and fighting with humans was probably the only royal responsibility that Sirena enjoyed. Both Apollo and Sirena had been leaders of rescue missions or members of other rescue teams. They had been to the surface more times than he could count and had rescued hundreds of mers but it was never enough. There were always more captured the next day and the day after that. Apollo had told Sirena that their rescue missions were their most important responsibilities because they were saving innocent lives, and Sirena she'd only continue the missions because she really despised humans. She hadn't cared whether it was a royal responsibility. Sirena was simply angry that the humans controlled their lives.

They both thought they would continue those missions and leading rescue teams and not have to worry about ruling the Sirens. Not unless something happened to Maia before she had children of her own. Then the responsibility fell on Sirena as the next mermaid in line. They had never considered this. Never planned for it. Sirena was unprepared and on her own. He didn't know if she had even met many other clan leaders. Did she even know much about the merfolk council?

He pulled himself from his thoughts and stared through the darkness at the shackles on his wrists. He should be at Sirena's side, helping her determine what happened to Maia, and restoring peace to the clans as they recovered from the Human Wars. They should figure out what they were going to do, because staying in the Midnight Zone wasn't the answer.

Apollo had argued with Maia shortly after she gained rule. Maia thought she had ended the immediate threat to the merpeople when she ordered the merpeople to sink to the Midnight Zone of the ocean, hovering over the Abyss. She felt the merpeople would be out of the reach of humans. When he had asked her how long she thought they needed to stay in the depths, she had simply said that the average human lived to be about eighty and there were kids on the ship that had taken Malee so, at least a hundred years to be safe. When he had tried to protest, she had simply brushed him off and said she'd handle it later.

The clans had done as told when she made her order. The Mami Wata were already in the Abyss, having moved themselves at the beginning of the wars. People criticized them for abandoning their people, but in hindsight; they were the wisest clan. The

Ningyo, Morgens, Aicaya, Ceasgs, Kelpies and Selkies had all followed the orders. The Encantados were so few that the Water Nymphs relayed the orders as they came across them, but they truly didn't know how many Encantados remained, or even where they were.

Maia had ignored that the Merrows even existed. Merpeople blamed Merrows for causing the Human Wars. Their love of humans and their desire to marry them and leave the merpeople forever were what got them into trouble. The wrong human took advantage of their knowledge of the merfolk and they had all paid the costly price for one mers love affair. Malee had banished the Merrows from the merfolk. No longer were they a part of the council and therefore, Maia had felt justified leaving them to be picked off by the humans. Apollo had disagreed with this decision as well, but she had reminded him of his place and he had backed down.

Trappers traded merpeople of all kinds for sport. Besides the Encantados; the Ceasgs, Kelpies and Selkies suffered the worst. Ceasgs brought good fortune to those that were in their presence. Humans bought and traded them for high dollar amounts but reaped rewards and riches beyond their wildest imaginations because of the fortune their enslaved Ceasgs brought them. There were stories of Ceasgs tossed in bathtubs for years, confined and forced to bring about the next latest and greatest advancement in human technology.

They shoved Kelpies, Selkies and Encantados into zoos and circuses, forcing them to entertain as both mermaids and their true forms of hippos, seals, and dolphins. There was a zoo that kept Kelpies in their hippo forms around the clock because they had lost theirs. To an untrained eye, you couldn't tell the difference, and if Apollo had learned anything during his time on the surface, it was that humans were stupid and selfish. Even if they could tell the difference, their entertainment was more important to them than the life and dignity of another.

Sirens, Morgens and the Ningyo (with the help of Siren magic) shapeshifted and went to the surface on rescue missions to retrieve captured merpeople. The sheer volume had put the Sirens' magic to the test they needed to expel to shapeshift the others and bring their captured folk home. Separate missions resulted in the capture and killing of both Malee and Asterios. Trying to put himself in Maia's place, part of him understood why she had pushed the merfolk into the Midnight Zone. Well, all besides the Finfolk.

Ah, the Finfolk. The underbelly of the oceans. The leprechauns of the sea. They bartered with everyone to get what they wanted and what they couldn't bargain for they took by force. He had never trusted the Finfolk despite the Merfolk Council, writing them off as useless and harmless. Eevi was their leader, and he'd met her once, maybe twice. Asterios had told him once that the Finfolk were too busy chasing shiny objects to get involved with the drama of the merpeople. The Finfolk rarely attended council meetings and his one encounter with crossbreed had left him hoping that it had been his last.

He suspected they were his captors. Some sort of ransom to get whatever they could out of the Sirens and preying on Sirena's inexperience and immaturity, perhaps. Apollo didn't think that they had anything to do with Maia's death, but was certain they'd capitalize on it if they could.

As his mind spun with details of his situation and all the mermaids that could be responsible for it, he knew one thing was for sure. He needed to get out of his captor's grasp. His magic wasn't working and he couldn't blast the cuffs off. He had no choice but to rely on one simple and possibly ineffective option.

Apollo clutched a small stone in his right hand and set to work, chiseling on the cuff on his left wrist. The slight scratching noise it made seemed to echo through the cave and he kept his eyes on the guards. Neither of them stirred. It wasn't much, but every scratch put him ever so slightly closer to home.

Chapter 5

Sirena

An eternity passed before Sirena finally felt the surge of ice through her veins subside. She had regained control of her body and the panic dissipated, but the cold in her veins had overstayed its welcome. Perhaps it had been more shocking than the Siren's power invading her, but either way, she was relieved to feel mostly normal again.

Her pod had given her a few moments to collect herself before they set off to find Leander and inform him about Maia's death. Xan had gone to find the water nymphs, and Theo and Nova were looking for Apollo. Cat had stayed with her a few minutes before Sirena had told her she needed some space. A few moments to collect herself was all she needed. Then she would gather her pod, find Leander, and inform him about Maia. Finally, she would find out what had happened to Maia. Orinn and Sophie had stared at her so intensely she had felt guilt despite knowing she had done nothing wrong.

A scream ripped through their territory, startling her, and Sirena raced toward the noise. Sirens scattered and fled the area. She pushed herself through the swarms of merfolk swimming against her as she made her way towards whatever danger was waiting for her. Not seeing anything other than terrified merfolk, she alternated, swimming higher and lower, trying to get a look at what the disturbance was. Fortunately, she didn't have to search for long.

A white ghost of a mermaid, a Rusalka, was floating in the center of the territory.

Sophie and Orinn were on the opposite side of the territory from her, staring at the Rusalka as well. Looks of shock and fear filled their faces. They banished the Rusalka off the coast of

Eurasia and prevented them from leaving. But one had escaped, or so it appeared.

"Xan! Theo!" Sirena screamed throughout the territory. Xan and Theo were going to be her best allies against whatever this was.

Xan appeared alongside her in a few moments, and she could see Theo close to Sophie and Orinn. She nodded at Theo and the three of them began closing in on the Rusalka, forming a wide circle around it. The Rusalka merely floated in place, not moving or making eye contact. As it stared blankly into space, Sirena ran through every piece of information ever told to her about the Rusalka.

Grimly, she realized she knew very little.

Rusalka, trapped souls of merfolk that had met tragic ends, could not leave their territory. They were little more than spirits, but appeared very much in the flesh to anyone looking at them. Ghost white with chalky hair, gray-white tails and black talons for fingernails. They were the creatures of nightmares. When humans described monster merpeople, Sirena was sure this is what they envisioned. The Rusalka and Orinn. She hated both of them.

Xan moved closer to Sirena, a few strokes ahead of her, putting himself between the Rusalka and Sirena. She felt her heart simultaneously flutter and sink as her friend moved to protect his

Queen. Before she had time to contemplate the absurd thought that she was the Queen, the ghost moved.

The Rusalka rotated itself forty-five degrees to bring their gaze in her direction. As it raised its hand, Sirena tried to speak to it but found her voice gone for yet the second time. Fear rippled through her as she told herself to maintain eye contact and to return the icy glare. The Rusalka continued to stare at her, but could not reciprocate the eye contact.

From the raised hand of the Rusalka, icicles shot through the water in her direction. They were about the length of a medium-sized anglerfish and as sharp as a human dagger. Xan shoved her quickly to the side as the Rusalka remained facing the area they had previously occupied. Not making their way through the water far, the icicles dropped towards the Abyss, spearing two mermaids that were attempting to flee. Sirena made a go after them, but blood spilled from both of them as their bodies quickly turned gray and sank to the lower level of the ocean.

"What in all the oceans is going on?" Xan whispered to her, still holding her by the shoulders as if he was going to steer her through the ocean.

Finding her voice again, Sirena called out to the Rusalka mermaid, "Stop! What are you doing here?"

The Rusalka simply turned to face them again and continued to shoot its ice daggers in their direction. "Seashells,"

Sirena muttered under her breath as Xan once again pulled her out of harm's way.

Looking to her left, then her right, she saw a large enough boulder off to their right. "Let's hide behind there," Sirena whispered in Xan's year.

Xan placed his body between the Rusalka and Sirena and with an arm around her waist, they swam behind the rock. The Rusalka never moved. Never turned towards them. She looked at Xan with wide eyes as he nodded. He understood. It was blind.

Theo seemed to understand too, as he made eye contact with Xan and then Sirena. The three of them nodded at each other in agreement. There had been enough rescue missions where they had to remain in the shadows, sneak in and get another mermaid out without making a sound or being seen. With the Rusalka's sense of vision missing, they simply had to get close enough to it without it hearing them.

Could it sense movement? As if he could read her mind, Xan whispered, "I don't think it can feel us either. It would have felt our waves as we swam by it." They were mere meters away from the ghostly mermaid and, as she examined it more, Sirena could tell that where most Rusalka still had eyes, this one had empty, dark sockets.

Theo nodded in their direction again and the three of them started towards the Rusalka, Theo from where he had been hovering by the advisors and Xan and Sirena from their hiding spot. Xan moved only slightly to his left to create a circle around the Rusalka, still keeping Sirena in his reach. She noticed Theo was doing the same.

Within seconds, they were surrounding the Rusalka. Her fingertips vibrated, and she lifted her hands, Theo and Xan doing the same. As their Siren magic electrified their hands and lit up the dark waters, the Rusalka remained motionless, its arms lowered.

This ghost had been a Siren. Long chalky hair streamed down its back and the once black tail was patchy with spots of Siren black poking through the gray and white decay that adorned the tails of a Rusalka mermaid. Her heart sank. They assigned this former member of their clan to come here and kill. Two Sirens had died at the hands of this ghost. Maybe three if the Rusalka had killed Maia.

She looked from Theo to Xan, realizing with horror that they were waiting for her signal. As their Queen, she gave the orders to strike. In a planned rescue mission, there was always one assigned leader. She was a leader only once, but this felt different. Swallowing hard and taking a sharp breath in through her gills, she nodded ever so slightly to them.

All three released streams of their magic, beams of black and gold shot from their fingertips and into the Rusalka. For a moment, nothing happened, and she widened her eyes in fear but didn't dare stop. Xan held her gaze, silently telling her to keep her magic flowing.

After one more heartbeat, the Rusalka started to flicker and melt. A slight eruption of gray ash began at the temple of the Rusalka. The ash spread down the face and neck of the mermaid, lazily spreading towards the tip of its fin. Chalky gray flesh caved inwards, causing the chest and abdomen to crumble. Within the next second, the rest of the mermaid had disappeared. A trail of black particles floating in the water between the three of them. Her heart caught in her throat as she glanced at her friends.

Theo looked equally shocked, but Xan had a slight smirk forming as his upper lip tucked up ever so slightly in one corner of his mouth. His wavy, dark brown hair fell over one eye and as he brushed it out of his face, he tail-flipped his brother congratulations. The brother's tails were the inverse of each other with Xan's tail black with gray fins and Theo's a dark charcoal with black fins. Theo gave her a half smile and Sirena let the breath out she was holding in.

As Xan smirked at her and celebrated, she felt relief that their spat yesterday was in the past. Before she could revel in Xan's attention, Sophie and Orinn were upon them, hovering while their eyes blazed with an emotion Sirena couldn't identify.

"Take your pod to the Morgens. Inform Leander and ask for his help. We have to pay the Rusalkas a visit," Sophie spoke in her quiet but firm tone of voice.

Sirena quickly replaced her relief at Xan's forgiveness with dread as she thought about talking to Leander. Also, she was sure that she was supposed to be giving orders, not receiving them. Before she could protest Sophie's orders, Orinn interrupted her thoughts. "I'm going with you."

She looked at the mermen in front of her, and they shrugged. Shrugging, she nodded her head and turned to get the rest of her pod. Hesitating for a moment, Sirena turned to Xan and Theo. "Where is Apollo?"

The brothers paused, looking sideways at each other for a moment before Theo finally spoke. "We can't find him."

"What do you mean, you can't find him?" Sirena tried to control the crack in her voice, but could hear her emotions coming through.

"We've looked, Sirena. We didn't find him. I'm sorry to add more to your growing list of issues," Xan spoke sympathetically.

Feeling numb, she looked at the brothers, seeing the worry on their faces. "Is he…?" she couldn't bring her to say the words.

"We don't know," Theo whispered. "Well, then I guess we are overdue for a visit to the Rusalka territory," Sirena replied as she gestured towards where the Rusalka ghost had disintegrated.

Adrenaline and anxiety pulsed through her, and she turned to gather the rest of her pod.

Chapter 6

Leander

Jolting awake, Leander looked around him. Seeing nothing but darkness, he settled down in his resting spot. Uneasy, but seeing no evidence to suggest there was trouble, he tried to convince himself everything was normal. That nagging feeling in his mind was still there, though, and he grew restless.

He left his hiding spot that overlooked his unfamiliar territory, deciding to make a round to check on his people. The

Morgens were located to the west of North America rather than directly south of the Sirens. Previously, the Scottish clans of the Ceasgs, Kelpies and Selkies were in the small ocean space centered between Greenland, Africa and Eurasia. The ease with which humans breached their territories resulted in the complete abandonment of that area. The Morgens didn't have the luxury of roaming the outer edge of the entire continent of North America, as the clans that inhabited that area were at war with each other. His heart felt heavy. Not only were there the humans to worry about but the merpeople were also fighting with each other.

Once his mate was the Queen of the merpeople, he'd leave his territory in the hands of his most senior advisor, Ajax. Without a next of kin, there wasn't anyone to leave his clan to, and he felt anger at the humans again for this. He'd lost his sisters and brother to the humans at the start of the wars. The humans took his sisters first, leaving the territory to him. When he lost his youngest brother, there was an emptiness that he could never fill. However, hatred had filled that void well over the last several years and he had made several trips to the surface to slaughter unsuspecting humans purely for revenge and his own entertainment. The relief he felt after each kill was only temporary and after a few days had passed, he would feel as hollow as before. He hadn't shared his secret missions with Maia, deciding it was better that she didn't know.

As he patrolled his territory, he watched as many of the lower ranking Morgens slept in their pods out in the open. Only he and his advisors, Ajax and Neo, had actual caves to stow away in. Neo's cave was more of an overhang that covered a ledge and the merman barely fit his body in there. Neo, the lower ranking of his advisors, was his cousin that he had kept around out of loyalty to his parents. Most days, he had wanted to pass him off to the Aicaya. Since Neo was his cousin, the handoff of power to him was also possible, but there was not a chance in all the ocean that he would leave his people to Neo. The young, immature and bumbling merman got on Leander's nerves more days than not and there was absolutely no way he could, in good conscience, leave his clan in that situation.

His family would have protested his decision if they knew as it would end their centuries long reign, but he didn't care. What Ajax did with Neo once Leander was off with the Sirens, he didn't care about that either. Maia had made her orders only weeks ago, and he planned to get his people settled and leave shortly. Ajax was older than Leander and there wasn't a doubt he could have handled the transition, but both Leander and Maia had felt that it was best that he stay for a while to make it easier on the clans.

Their courtship had begun over a century ago when he took over as the leader of the Morgens, inheriting his territory from his second eldest sister after she passed. Asterios had come to the

Morgen's territory to speak with him and offer his condolences, bringing along Maia. What first began as mild flirting grew to regular trips between the territories. Maia came to visit him under the guise of traveling with her father to build relationships with other clans and he visited the Sirens, frequently stating that he needed to learn from Asterios and Malee as he had not received mentorship for his new role. In hindsight, he didn't fool anyone, but they didn't care either. Leander was the leader of the Morgens and an appropriate mate for Maia, so the advisors and rulers of both clans let the relationship play out.

Leaving Maia a few weeks ago to plunge his people into the Midnight Zone had been the hardest thing he had done to date. She had held back tears in front of her people, but when they were alone; he saw how hard the transition had been for her. Maia had told him before he left that while she knew the day would come, no one had ever prepared her for how hard it was to lose both parents. He could see the determination on her face as he had hugged her goodbye. She was going to lead the merpeople to safety, even if that meant dropping them lower in the ocean than they had ever been.

"Hi Leander," an exuberant voice sounded behind him.

Leander sighed, but didn't turn around. Neo was hovering behind him, following him for who knew how long.

"Everything alright?"

He was not getting out of this. "Yes, I couldn't sleep, either, so I'm stretching my fins."

"Me either, but probably because I have to fold in half to fit on my shelf. You know, if Ajax would let me share his space… there's plenty of room."

"That's not my decision. Why don't you bother him? See how that works out for you?" Leander turned around to leave again, dismissing Neo.

Neo smirked as he said, "He told me to talk to you about it."

"You're welcome to sleep out in the open like the rest of the clan. You're not the senior advisor and you're only an advisor because my parents would come back from their watery grave and beat my tail if I sent you to live with the Aicaya. I'm doing you a favor. Take it or leave it."

Neo gave a small laugh, unbothered by the hostility he'd experienced from Leander. It was a daily occurrence. "Sure, whatever you think is best. Oh, wise and ruling leader."

Fighting the urge to tail-whip Neo until he fell to the Abyss, Leander turned towards the slight flutter of movement he saw to his side. Neo turned in that direction as well, confirming Leander's suspicions that there was indeed someone or something headed towards them. His fins twitched in anticipation as his fight response kicked in.

He instinctively put an arm across the front of Neo's shoulders and shoved the merman behind him in a protective gesture. This, of course, drew a response from the always difficult Neo.

"Thanks cousin. Toss me to the Aicaya. Make me sleep on a shelf but also protect me from the fishes." Neo tossed his hands up in frustration as he rolled his eyes.

"Shut your mouth."

Leander was gazing into the darkness as waves shifted the surrounding water.

They both stared as the movement grew more apparent and there was a slight chatter of voices. Whatever was in front of them could talk. Leander hated this pitch-black darkness of the Midnight Zone, but he respected Maia's decision and he wouldn't deny that he agreed with her. What else were they to do after a hundred years of fighting? The council had been pushing Malee to make the same decision for years.

As he was about to unleash a warning growl on whoever was quickly approaching him, he saw the slight glint of golden hair and bright blue tail next to several darker figures. He squinted, willing his eyes to adapt to the darkness. The darker figure next to the shiny one was definitely a Siren. Dark blue and black tails with black hair flowing lined up next to the shimmering hair and it took him only a second longer to recognize the face of the Siren that was barreling towards him. Sirena and her pod were swimming quickly through his territory. "Sirena?" He hesitated a second after he called out to her. "What are you doing here?"

Breathless, she paused and stared at him for a moment. Leander looked at the other faces in the crowd. Xan and Theo. Catalina and Nova. Sirena's closest pod members. There was one other Siren that he wasn't sure who she was, but there was no mistaking Orinn.

"I'm sorry. I…" Sirena's eyes dropped below her. She was quiet for a second longer before she tried to speak again. "Maia. I don't know what happened. We don't know what happened," she was gesturing to her pod.

"What…?"

Sirena didn't speak, but gave him the most pathetic look he'd seen come from anyone, let alone a Siren.

Leander stared at her for a second before erupting in anger. "Speak Sirena! Now! Where is she?"

"She's gone."

And with that, Leander roared across the ocean. His eyes flamed and flashed with his anger and he stared at Sirena. He had once thought of her as a younger sister, but seeing her, he could see the sparkle of a newly made Queen of the Sirens and the rage boiled within him. He could feel the water rippling around him as he shook with anger. Sirena stared at him. The coldness and distant look that he had once appreciated from her only stoked the fire in him.

"That's not good enough. You don't get to show up here and tell me my mate is dead and you're the Queen and have nothing to offer me."

To her credit, Sirena looked sick to her stomach. The rest of the Morgens were rising and peeking around ledges, tripping over each other to see what had gotten their leader so upset. Neo had gone rigid and, for once, probably for the first time in his life, he had remained quiet.

"I don't know what happened. Truly. I will find out. There was a Rusalka in our territory and…"

"Rusalka?" Leander roared. "Don't make up stories!"

"She's telling the truth," Orinn offered. Her face showed a look of confusion.

"I don't know what happened, but there was a Rusalka in the territory. Xan and Theo helped banish it, but I don't know how or why. There shouldn't be any way for them to leave their territory, yet they were there. Orinn and Sophie don't know either. I'm here to tell you about Maia, but I'm also here to ask you for help. This has never happened before and no one knows what to tell me and I came to you and…" Sirena faltered and rambled.

Leander felt pity looking at this utter child before him. Hovering there with her friends and an old, angry advisor. She looked even younger than she was.

Neo cleared his throat. "My mother told me once that only magic held the Rusalka in their territory. Well, more of a curse. It's a curse, not magic. Are curses magic? I think they are a type of magic. I guess I don't know," Neo paused, looking up in thought. He drew in a sharp breath from his gills and continued. "Because their souls passed in tragedy, a curse placed long ago traps them in the Rusalka territory. Maybe something changed and their souls are no longer trapped."

Leander, who was used to tangents from Neo, simply ignored him but he shook his head when he saw Sirena watching him intently. She was a child, after all.

"Who placed the curse? I guess I don't really understand how it works?" Sirena's face twisted with confusion.

Orinn chimed in, "Desdemona, the overseer of the Rusalka, was the first mermaid to exist. She met a tragic end, killed by her mate, and in her death, she promised to resurrect the souls of any merperson that had met a similar end to hers. The legend is that she was successful and the Sirens, unable to reverse her curse on lost souls, trapped them in the region that they lived in. And like I said - *the legend*- says this." Orinn emphasized her last words with a huff.

Still confused, Sirena looked to Leander for confirmation. He simply shrugged at her.

Neo clearly took offense to Orinn's dismissal. He crossed his arms, uncrossed them again, and looked at Orinn. "Right. A curse by Desdemona on lost souls and a curse by the Sirens to keep those souls trapped. Curses," he muttered under his breath.

"How would one break that type of curse?"

Leander still hadn't spoken, simply watching the Sirens work this out in front of him. Why this discussion hadn't happened before they showed up in his territory was baffling. Sirena was a pup, but Orinn should have known better. They looked pitiful and out of sync, he almost felt bad for them. Almost. The only Siren he had ever really cared for was Maia. He looked at Orinn, revealing his disapproval that they hadn't talked before coming here and babbling like idiots. Orinn rolled her eyes and shot a look of annoyance in Sirena's direction. Leander smirked slightly and nodded.

"It's a legend and not a curse. For all we know, the Rusalka have been able to leave their territory from the beginning of time and they just hadn't until today." Orinn tossed her hands in the air, clearly done with the banter.

Sirena replied with a simple, "Oh."

Neo interrupted again, "No, it's a curse. The Mami Wata would be the ones that would know how to break the curse. Or reinstate the curse. Whatever the issue is, they're the ones you need. They're the ones that actually placed the curse at the Siren's orders."

Orinn rolled her eyes again and Leander felt himself amused at this interaction.

"Why the Mami Wata?" ignoring her own advisor, Sirena was staring at his halfwit advisor.

"They create curses and they break them. They're the witches of the sea. The *legend*," he emphasized pointedly, "has it that Bia, the leader of the Mami Wata, was the one that set the curse on Desdemona and the rest of the Rusalka. Not the Sirens. Sirens don't create curses, but they were the ones that wanted something done about the angry lost souls roaming the oceans. The Mami Wata cursed their souls for eternity, binding them to that territory," Neo leaned back, obviously happy to set the record straight.

Neo, ever the wise historian. Leander was the one that rolled his eyes this time.

"Sea witches," Sirena's wide-eyed stare made her look even more childish. "No one has seen them since the start of the wars."

She had returned her gaze to Leander, and he returned it, wondering what more she could want. Most likely she didn't know, but he would not float in place and wait for her to figure out her life. "What do you think you want from me?" he could feel the ice in his voice.

"I… We… We are going to the Rusalka territory," she gestured to her pod. "I hoped maybe you would—"

"I'm going to stop you right there. I'm not going with you."

"Oh, I, um."

"No."

Sirena was wringing her hands, looking at Xan and Orinn. The Merrow that she insisted on having in her pod was as close to Sirena as she could get. Her aqua green tail with her blue tipped fins, floating in place as she placed a hand on the back of Sirena's arm. The Siren that he didn't know her name and Catalina flanked Sirena's other side. Catalina was a stockier mermaid, not thin and athletic, like the Sirens and Merrow in front of him, with a purple tail that had a slight blue iridescence to it. Encantado mermaid, that's what she was. He scowled at Sirena again. This Siren, a pup, with her pieced together pod. The two lost mermaids that Sirena had saved looked misplaced amongst the Sirens with their dark tails and features. They all looked as clueless as the next.

Xan spoke to him this time. "Leander, if not you, then an advisor or senior Morgen? Can you monitor our territory? Sophie is overseeing while we're gone, but she may need some help to quiet the masses with Apollo missing and Sirena seeking the

Rusalka. Things are a bit shaken up as well with the Rusalka attack. It would mean a lot to us if you could help us. Maia may be gone, but the Sirens and Morgens have had a long-standing partnership."

"Apollo is missing?" Leander felt concerned. Two of the royal Sirens were gone and Sirena was the only one left behind. Anxiety was creeping through him.

"We can't find him," Sirena spoke softly as she stopped wringing her hands long enough to raise her palms upward and outward, showing she had searched. "He's not in our territory and the Rusalka in the attack didn't exactly speak."

He looked at Orinn, and she slightly nodded, confirming. Sighing, he looked at Sirena. The last royal of the Sirens. Leader of all the merpeople. Sirena. He had been most indifferent to her, finding her young and pretending too hard not to care about royal matters and responsibilities. Yet she was on every rescue mission Asterios would allow her on.

Sirena had called him a Greek god once, and it hadn't been a compliment. Thinking about that day when she had eyed him up and down and told him that his dark hair and skin blended into his deep blue tail. Said that he was too common and boring. She had called him a blowfish and huffed away. All because he had told Asterios he didn't want his young, untrained pup on a rescue mission to find Ajax. He felt a bubble of laughter in his throat.

That was the one time he had actually found her endearing, when she was tide roaring mad at him. A pleasant change of pace from her dark, sulking Siren persona.

"Neo can go with you."

Sirena looked cautiously at him while Neo exclaimed his protests. He raised a hand to silence Neo. The merman obeyed, but he still huffed.

"Thank you and… I'm sorry," Sirena said to him, her eyes cast downward ashamedly.

Leander knew she was referring to Maia, but tried to his slight grin as he said, "Me too." This was one way of getting rid of Neo. Turning to look at Neo, he motioned for him to join their pod.

Neo raised an eyebrow and cautiously said, "It will be an honor to accompany you on your journey. But we're going to the Mami Wata first. I'm not swimming into Rusalka territory blind."

Leander felt validated that he made the right call. Good riddance to them.

Chapter 7

Aiko

Aiko rolled a large pearl in her hands, admiring not only its beauty but its dramatic increase in size over the last few months. Sirens had natural born magic. At birth, their mother gave the Ningyo an item that possessed their magic. Separate the mer from their item and their magic was gone and you could control them. The magic that your mother gave you at birth was the magic you had for life. Aiko had received a pearl from her mother, no bigger than a small seashell a year ago. The pearl had significance to her as Ningyo, devoid of emotion, cried pearls when they could muster up enough feelings to cry. The pearl gifted to her was the single pearl tear that her mother had cried as she gave birth to Aiko.

Ningyo had power similar to the royal Sirens. The ability to blast streams of power to destroy or change items, the power to heal herself or others and to change physical appearances. Despite having the ability to mimic the power of the Sirens and other merfolk, their power was minimal. A Siren could blast holes through caverns and destroy half the ocean if they wanted to. Aiko and the rest of the Ningyo could put chips into rocks. It would take her weeks to do the damage a Siren could do in mere seconds. Truth be told, the only magic she cared about mimicking was that of the Mami Wata. Curses and spells were far more interesting than shooting magic from her hands. She did, however, enjoy changing her appearance when it served her to do so.

Most merpeople could change their own appearance at will. Encantados could shift to dolphins, Kelpies to hippos and Selkies to seals. Sirens, Morgens, Merrows and Ningyo could change their own appearances, but only the Sirens could transform others. The Sirens gave the Merrows their legs and let them go to the surface. They could blame the Merrows all they want, but the Merrows couldn't have done it without the help of the Sirens.
The Rusalka controlled the territory, while the Ningyo controlled most of the Western region, except for the small territory

maintained by the Aicaya. The Eastern region was a mess as the Morgens had lost a large space of their territory when the Ceasgs, Selkies and Kelpies moved out of their ocean caverns between Eurasia and North America and out to the coast off of North America. Their sliver of territory they had before hadn't been safe any longer and they moved, putting a strain on the relationship between the Sirens and Morgens.

Other clans taking over parts of his territory did not make Leander feel thrilled. As part of the mercouncil, Aiko had been present for all the conversations and knew how unpopular the decision had been. She hadn't really cared at the time as she didn't care for any of the other clans, but when the Aicaya had moved south of her territory, then she had a problem. Apollo had been of zero help to her. Her mate had simply said it wasn't his decision. When she pushed the issue further, he had told her that the Aicaya were a small clan and it wouldn't affect her or her people. She had given up and dealt with it but once Maia had ordered them to the Midnight Zone, Aiko felt like the walls were caving in. Much like she had felt when Apollo ended their partnership.

Aiko used the pearl in her hands to turn her blue, black and gold swirl tail into solid green and then into solid blue before returning to her usual colors. She flicked her fin and the last of the bright blue that had been lingering transformed into her lazy swirl pattern.

"All the power in the world and you use it to play dress up," Sakura was leaning on the entrance to Aiko's home. The rest of the merfolk may live in caverns and dark caves, but not Aiko. She had used the power of her pearl to create a beautiful stone structure for herself and Sakura.

Sakura floated over to her and planted a kiss on Aiko's cheek. Her second in command and mate, Sakura, had been with her for all the territory discussions and when Maia had declared the order to sink to the lower layers, she was the one to convince Aiko it would be a pleasant change. Sakura's blood red tail matched her dark lips and was a beautiful contrast to her jet-black hair. Sakura was striking to look at and if you weren't careful, she'd use it to her advantage.

Aiko adjusted her position on the stone she perched on and briefly placed her head on Sakura's shoulder for a second. Sighing, she turned her focus to her mate and asked, "What would you do with the power?"

"Ha! Probably similar to you for a while. Change my living conditions, my hair and tail. Afraid that someone would find out what I was up to. How much power I actually had and how I got it. But then, at a certain point, I don't know that I'd care."

"Only three of us know."

"Only three of us know," Sakura agreed, nodding her head. "Your plan is in motion; in case you weren't aware."

Aiko lifted her gaze from her pearl to meet Sakura's eyes, raising an eyebrow.

"The Rusalka are loose and they're terrorizing the Sirens. Sirena and her pod are on their way to the Rusalka territory as we speak."

Aiko felt her heart race and her stomach went cold. "Sirena? Sent by Maia instead of Apollo? Or is he with her?"

"Oh, no... Maia is dead. Seems your plan worked a little too well," Sakura grinned mischievously.

"What?"

"The water nymphs were here, well Cara anyway, and she gave me her little rhyme and dance. Maia's dead, Apollo is missing and Sirena is traveling to the Rusalka territory to lock them back up," Sakura was positively gloating.

A look of disbelief spread on Aiko's face as she absorbed what Sakura had said. "No one was supposed to die! I let the Rusalka loose. I was going to use it as leverage to get out of rescue missions and to pull out of the council!" Disbelief had turned into panic.

"And the thing with Apollo. That's on you too," she winked at Aiko.

"I was only trying to scare him. To get even with him for leaving me in the middle of a war. I didn't mean to kill his sister."

Shrugging, Sakura didn't lose her excited tone when she said, "You let the Rusalka loose. What the shell did you think was going to happen?"

Her mouth was not moving but noises still escaped her throat as Aiko tried to put into words the sheer panic that she was feeling. She paced her underwater home, light shining from her hands and pearl as she illuminated the space in front of her in the always too dark Midnight Zone. Maybe Cara had been wrong.

"What did Cara say?"

Sakura rolled her eyes. "I don't remember exactly."

"Try." An order, not a question.

Sakura squinted her eyes and twisted her mouth to the side as she attempted to recall what the water nymph had said. Finally, she said, "I think it was something like…"

Once there was a Siren who lived in the sea

For only a few short weeks, a ruler was she

First the father, the mother, then the eldest sister

No one left but the little and the mister

Sakura sat back and looked at Aiko. Proud of herself. Aiko understood that this meant Maia was gone, but how did she know Sirena was off to the Rusalka? She hated the ridiculous rhymes and songs the ocean nymphs used. They didn't even rhyme most of the time. "And how do you know Apollo is missing and Sirena is traveling across the ocean?"

"I saw a Finfolk mermaid on my way over here. She saw them as they passed by her. With everything so blasted dark down here, no one can see anything and here they are blabbing away about their problems," Sakura added a slight giggle. "They're on their way to the Mami Wata."

Aiko blankly stared at her, blinking.

"Oh, for tail's sake, Aiko," she rolled her eyes. "They went to Leander first, and that blowfish sent Neo with them. The Finfolk mermaid heard him telling the pod all about the sea witches and spells and that they needed to resurrect whatever curse they placed on the Rusalka centuries ago."

"Neo?"

"Neo… the son of a Mami Wata and a Morgen. He's an advisor to Leander. He knows all about the sea witches and their curses. His mother told him all about them, or so he said. That's what the Finfolk tell me."

Aiko remained silent for a moment and finally conceded that her plan had spiraled some, but there was nothing left to do but see how it played out. "Apollo is *'missing'* then and Sirena is off ghost hunting and Maia is…" she trailed off. Maia, she actually felt bad for her.

"Yes. It's going even better than we planned!" Sakura clapped her hands together in excitement and her eyes gleamed in the light cast by the pearl Aiko was still holding. "What's our next move?"

"There is no next move. This isn't what I had planned. I was going to put the Rusalka back into place to get us out of the council and on our own. I don't know what Sirena will do. Maia would have let us out."

"Sirena will call a council meeting."

Aiko could have been mistaken, but she swore Sakura genuinely showed excitement about the idea of a mercouncil meeting. "Certainly. After they contain the threat, that means I lose my bargaining token."

"Maybe, but you still have your power."

"The Mami Wata will help Sirena," Aiko said in a whisper.

"Sure," Sakura showed her agreement, unshaken at Aiko's panic.

"It's a temporary setback."

"Yes, you'll think of something else. For now, enjoy the absolute downfall of the Sirens," Sakura's excitement was shining.

As her nerves calmed down a bit, Aiko had a revelation. Maia might have discovered that it was she who handled Apollo's sudden vanishing act but, Sirena wouldn't. She was too young, too inexperienced. Aiko and Sirena didn't know each other well and, hopefully, Aiko wouldn't even cross Sirena's mind. She settled into her seat and, despite hating their terrible riddles, she waited for an update from the water nymphs. In the meantime, she'd have to prepare herself to ask Sirena to let her merpeople out of the council and out from under the rule of the Sirens.

Chapter 8

Sirena

Surveying the members of her pod, Sirena looked from face to face, silently hoping one of them would step up and lead their journey. She had only led one rescue mission, the one her mother had given her life to save herself and Maia. The ambush from the humans hadn't been her fault, but she still felt responsible.

Xan, Theo, and Apollo were the usual leaders of the missions, Apollo taking over for Asterios when their father hadn't survived his last mission. She was used to following their lead, and she desperately wanted Xan or Theo to take over, but when she looked at both of them, they merely hovered in place, waiting for her direction. No judgment or wariness came from either of them. Neither had blamed her for Malee's death. Xan had reassured her over the last several weeks that they all knew the risks of the missions and that Malee had done what she had trying to save them. Sirena was sure they weren't blaming her for Maia's death, either.

Gathering her thoughts with absolutely no clarity about what she should do, Sirena cleared her throat and turned to her pod.

"I don't really know what we'll accomplish by heading into Rusalka territory without being prepared. The Rusalka were confined to their territory for centuries, yet something is different now." She paused, not wanting to speak her quiet thoughts aloud, whether the curse was broken or... Deciding she shouldn't hold information from her pod; she finished her thought. "Or, involvement from the humans that have released the Rusalka, we need to be prepared. I've never been to the territory and I would guess that none of you have either."

Glances exchanged among the pod members confirmed that most of them had never set a fin in the territory. Theo and Xan both gave her a slight tilt of their heads, indicating that other than the missions she knew about, they had not been to the Rusalka territory much either. Nodding, Sirena continued.

"Then I guess we need to think through our options. If Neo thinks the Mami Wata were involved in the original curse, then I think we need to go see them first."

"The Mami Wata are in the Abyss and heavily warded." Orinn crossed her arms over her chest and stared down at Sirena.

"Oh," Sirena uttered the sound before she could think of what to say next.

"You know, they plunged themselves into the Abyss the second that the humans attacked. They've been there since before you were even born. Since before, you were even a thought," Orinn said harshly.

Sirena felt herself at a loss for words for a moment and didn't know what to say. Warded. Abyss. Sea witches that had plunged to the second lowest layer of the oceans and cast protections and spells to keep everyone and everything out. She did not know of wards or sea witch magic. Her magic, Siren magic, was all that she knew, and she had to admit she had never tested her magic. She was untrained and certainly not a match for curses and spells cast by centuries old sea witches.

"I know enough about them and the wards," a voice broke her thoughts. Neo was staring at Orinn.

"Stay out of this," Orinn tossed her words angrily over her shoulder as she turned to Sirena.

"No. My mother was a Mami Wata. My father is Morgen. I'm half Mami Wata, half a sea witch. My mother told me about her people. About *my* people." Neo's tone was defiant as he spoke to Orinn.

He turned and looked at Sirena with an intensity that made her shiver. "I can help get us through their wards. I don't have the magic that you do, but I think I'll at least be able to recognize the wards. You'll need to speak with them once we're through; they don't care for me. I'm a crossbreed to them but, you're a Siren and their ruler. You can persuade Bia to help you."

"Bia?" Sirena asked.

"The leader of the Mami Wata," Neo offered without judgment. Sirena suddenly recalled Neo, referencing Bia earlier. She remembered her mother mentioning Bia and the Mami Wata as well. Her cheeks flushed with embarrassment, and she was grateful for the darkness surrounding them. She wished she had paid closer attention to things.

"Even if we get through the wards, what are we asking them? I want to make sure I understand. The Mami Wata cast a curse on the Rusalka? Or they used a curse to create borders around the territory? I don't know the history," Xan asked Neo the questions that Sirena had wanted to ask but was too afraid to. Xan shot her a small wink and her stomach fluttered. He was throwing her a rope, asking for the information that she should have known, being a part of the royal family. Neo spoke before she could wallow in her guilt.

"Centuries ago, when the territories divided the territories, everyone established their settlements. Everyone but the Rusalka. They still haunted the seas; they tormented sailors and fishers and the other merfolk. The Sirens had enough and I don't need to tell you all about Siren magic. You can sing and shoot energy from your hands, but that doesn't keep an unruly group of merfolk in check. The Mami Wata and Sirens came up with a plan to assign the last remaining water space to the Rusalka, the part of the oceans that no one else wanted. The dark, underwater mountains and treacherous caverns with no bottoms. That's where they decided the Rusalka belonged."

Neo looked slightly sad as he told the story, but he paused for a moment and met Sirena's gaze before he continued.

"Bia cursed their souls, keeping them in the assigned territory. Any merperson that meets a tragic death is bound to that territory. Rather than wandering the seas looking for those who wronged them," Neo's eyes drifted away from Sirena and into the darkness past her.

"A curse on souls rather than a boundary, then. Do we need Bia, or the Mami Wata, to place another curse?" Xan asked Neo, this time genuinely looking for the answer.

"I would assume so unless one of you is also a Mami Wata?" Neo shrugged, coming back from his distant stare.

"No, but you are," Sirena looked at him.

Neo blinked, the realization of what she said setting in. "I have minimal power; about half the amount of magic as a Siren, and maybe not even that. I'm more Morgen than I am Mami Wata."

"I guess we have to ask Bia then. Maybe you can still cast curses. What does your mother say about it? Or maybe she can help?" Sirena tried not to let her desperation show.

"My mother is no longer here and I don't know what I can do. My mother told me about our people's history as a child, but I've never used my magic. Other than my healing abilities. She's long gone, so she won't be able to help." Neo grew quiet and distant again.

"Sorry." Xan tapped him on the shoulder and shot Sirena a look that made her throw her hands up. She had no way of knowing.

"Your childhood bedtime stories are endearing, but they're only that. Stories," Orinn's voice dripped with cruelty. She ignored the depth of information Neo had shared and instead glared at Neo.

Sirena felt her heart clench in her chest. Having lost her own mother and sister recently, she despised how Orinn was staring down the only person in this pod that had given her any direction.

“Stop. That’s enough.” She glared at Orinn. She felt Neo shift his gaze to her. Xan stiffened next to her, but she didn’t care. “If Neo thinks we need to talk to the Mami Wata, then we’ll go talk to them. Does anyone else have another plan? Another idea? How about you Orinn? What are your thoughts?”

Orinn simply hovered in place, not backing down and not removing her crossed arms from her chest. But she also didn’t offer an answer, and Sirena had to fight her smirk. She should be concerned that not even her senior advisor knew what to do and instead, she gloated Orinn was as clueless as the rest of them.

When no one else answered and she had felt Nova and Cat giving her silent applause, she nodded her head in acknowledgement that it was done. They had a plan. Whatever it was, it was something.

“Neo, lead us to the Mami Wata. And… maybe tell us what you know about the warding they have in place, would you?” Sirena couldn’t hide a small smile this time as Orinn turned and sauntered a distance away from the group.

Neo’s shoulders lifted slightly as he focused his gaze on her and returned her smile. He was smaller than Xan and Theo, but not by much. His curly, dark hair tousled as his paler skin complemented his vibrant emerald green tail. His fins had tips in royal blue, and when she looked up at him, she noticed his eyes matched the same shade of blue. He acted younger than her, but the lines surrounding his eyes suggested he was older than he let on.

She eyed him cautiously. Asking him to lead them brought him up to the front of the pod alongside her, but she felt him still deferring to her rank. He was waiting for her to signal the start of their journey. Holding in her sigh of frustration, Sirena tilted her head to him to show that they should begin their travels. He took her lead and started out, but kept pace with her. Nova came up to her other side and Catalina wasn't far behind her. As Sirena stole a glance at her friends, she noticed a glimmer of a smile on Nova's face, and she knew Nova had caught her trying to give up leadership to the Morgen. Sirena felt Nova's hand pat her on the fin, and she ever so slightly tilted her head to look towards her friend.

Giving her a slight lift of an eyebrow and a shoulder raise, Sirena mouthed, 'Can you blame me?'

Nova's gaze showed she understood as she shot her friend an empathetic smile.

Turning her gaze in front of her, she followed Neo as he led them through the darkness.

Chapter 9

Apollo

"Get up. We're moving," his captor demanded, poking Apollo in the ribs.

Apollo opened his eyes but didn't move. "Going where?"

"That's for me to know," jabbing Apollo again.

Apollo rolled over onto his side and ignored him. He couldn't move, anyway. Not with shackles on his wrists, holding him in place. Get up? Move? How?

His captor was impatient and poked him in the fin, this time with a spear.

Apollo yelled out as his blood billowed out from the bottom of his tail. It was a flesh wound, but painful. He sat up and stared at his prison guard. There was nothing to see. A cloak covered their head and their tail stayed hidden. Other than a slight sign of a fin poking out from a cloak, there was nothing to see. No identity.

He stared at the gash in his fin. He wasn't healing. Why wasn't he healing? Closing his eyes, he tried to shove his energy into his fin to heal it. Nothing happened.

Without his magic, he couldn't heal. No magic, no healing.

Straining his neck, he bent as close as he could to see the damage. Would he bleed out? The tip of his fin was hanging. The bastard had tried to slice off a tip of his fin. A minor flesh wound but permanent cosmetic damage if he couldn't heal himself soon.

If they kept moving him, Sirena and the rest of the Sirens would never find him. He watched as he was unchained from the cave walls and followed in line with his captor. It was night, and the ocean was dark. There had been days where he could see some sunlight, so he knew they were closer to the surface. They weren't hovering above the abyss like Maia had ordered.

He tried to remember how many times he'd seen the daylight fade. He couldn't remember.

No one would find him unless they ventured out of their required zone and closer to the surface. He suspected they were in the high Twilight Zone. The Sirens wouldn't venture up here. The most he could hope for was a Finfolk or water nymphs. If he could be that lucky, what would they even do against whoever had captured him?

The captor to his right waved his hand and magically released the chains from the rock wall, where they attached behind his head. Magic like that was limited to Morgens, Sirens, and maybe an elite Ningyo. His stomach fell.

Was he captured by his own people? That couldn't be the case.

Who killed Maia?

Who was holding him captive?

It wasn't the Sirens, it couldn't be. Maia and Leander had been a couple, so the Morgens couldn't be responsible, either.

Knowing that his logic was severely flawed, Apollo went through everyone he knew that could have something against him and the Sirens.

Every clan shed blood during the Human Wars, and the only reason they weren't still fighting with humans was because Maia plunged them all into the Midnight Zone. Clans had been angry when she called off the rescue missions. Any merperson captured was on their own. The Sirens, Morgens and Ningyo were no longer braving the humans to retrieve the lost.

There were Sirens that were angry too. They had family on the surface as well. The Ceasgs were violently angry, but they didn't have magic. Not magic that could remove chains or subdue a Siren, anyway. He could throw confusion into the mix of emotions that he was experiencing.

The captor that had removed his chains stared at Apollo's fin for a moment and then looked at his partner. They drew their hoods over their faces so no one could recognize them.

"We're supposed to deliver him alive and intact. You broke the rules." His voice was completely flat.

"Well, things change sometimes. He's intact and alive. The tip of a fin is nothing."

"He's royalty. You shouldn't have done that."

"He'll live. I agreed to bring him alive and not to mar his pretty face. I did nothing of the sort," the unknown captor justified his behavior.

"Bring me where?" Apollo inserted himself into the conversation.

They ignored him, attaching his chains to a large iron plate fastened around the largest captor's waist. Dragging him out of the cave, they continued their squabble quietly.

Apollo watched as his blood left a small, dark trail behind them. If the humans didn't get them from being so close to the surface, an ocean predator would. A shark would be on their tails in no time at this rate.

"We should go back until I stop bleeding. I'm going to attract sea creatures," Apollo stated the obvious to them.

They ignored him again. Their conversation had ended, and they didn't seem interested in talking to him. Opening his mouth to speak again, he thought better of it and turned his focus to his surroundings.

They were in the Twilight Zone, but where, he had absolutely no idea. He had spent sixty years traveling these oceans and he couldn't pinpoint even a region. There weren't any fish, coral or plants. Open water and rock formations surrounded them. Everything looked the same to him and the further they got on their journey to nowhere, the more the scenery repeated itself.

Confusion, panic, fear, rage. With the endless line of rocks on either side of him, he had nothing to distract him from his thoughts and emotions.

If Maia was gone, and he was being held captive, a terrible thought occurred to him.

His only hope of survival was that Sirena was out looking for him.

If she was alive.

Chapter 10

Sirena

They had been swimming for what felt like days, but she knew it had only been hours. Taking over the Siren's power, fighting a Rusalka and spending hours traveling to the Morgen's territory; the last day had been a wave of emotions and constant movement. She hadn't rested for even a moment; the urgency of the situation had kept them on the move. The anxiety of talking to Leander alone had tapped her energy.

A thought struck her as odd when she thought about the encounter with Leander.

"Did anyone else notice that Leander got over Maia's death incredibly quickly?" She looked at her friends, not knowing what Neo's reaction would be.

Catalina came to a halt, stopping Theo, who had been bringing up the rear of the pod.

"Absolutely I did," Kassia spoke up for the first time since they'd left the Siren's territory. Normally outspoken, Kassia had seemed frustrated when they left their territory and her sulking had not gone unnoticed by Sirena.

Grateful that Kassia was talking again, Sirena engaged her in conversation. "He was angry, but it dissipated and then he seemed… indifferent? Is that the word I'm looking for?"

"Apathetic, cold. All of those things. I can tell you that if it was me and I had been told my partner was gone, I would be inconsolable. Heartbroken," Kassia placed a hand over her chest and looked at the other mermaids to her right, Nova and Cat, for confirmation.

Nova nodded in agreement, and Cat merely looked at her as she processed the conversation.

"If it was my mate that was killed, I'd be out avenging her death. I'd be out with us," Xan interjected himself into the conversation. Sirena's stomach fluttered a bit, and she caught Cat's glance for a moment.

"Right! That would be the right response. Instead, he acted as though he didn't care and he sent his advisor with us. I mean nothing by that, Neo, by the way. It's odd," Kassia turned to Neo. He responded with a raised hand, brushing her response off without offense.

"It's odd," Sirena mused. The group had now come to a complete stop. "Do we think he was involved?"

She had forgotten that Neo was with them for a moment. Her eyes widened, and she turned to him and he shrugged. No answer to her question.

"Why would he want Maia gone?" Xan mused.

"I don't think he was involved, but I think you're overestimating his care for Maia," Neo was deadpan.

Xan furrowed his brow and looked at Sirena and then at Neo. "What?"

"I don't think he was involved. I do not know, but I think Maia was a political move for Leander. He's all about appearances. Leander cares for Leander and anyone else he keeps around is purely for convenience or usefulness," Neo spoke bluntly. Then, realizing that his words might hurt Sirena, he turned towards her and muttered a quick, "Sorry."

"How long were they together again, Sirena?" Xan asked her.

"Around the start of the wars and for as long as I've been alive. I've never cared much for him," Sirena said. She saw Xan noted her tone, and that Neo's insight did not surprise her, and dropped it.

"Whether he cared for her or was playing politics is irrelevant at this point. Leander couldn't have lifted the curse on the Rusalka and killed Maia," Orinn interrupted, not hiding her annoyance.

"Ah, so you acknowledge that it's a curse." Neo didn't even try to hide his gloating.

"Regardless of what's happening with the Rusalka, I don't think that Leander had any involvement. I think that with the rapid shift in Siren leadership and the transferring of power so many times in a short period, something has shifted in our realms. Maybe the Mami Wata need to be involved or maybe we need to reinforce the rules with the Rusalka," Orinn's frustration was building.

"That's assuming that it was the Rusalka that killed Maia," Xan added.

"What?" Sirena pulled away slightly from Xan, shocked.

"We're assuming the Rusalka killed Maia, but what if they didn't?" Kassia clarified Xan's statement.

Shock ran through Sirena slightly, as she hadn't even wanted to consider that anyone else had harmed her sister. It had seemed straightforward when the Rusalka appeared in their territory. Maybe she hadn't wanted to admit to herself that it was possible that there was more to the situation. Rusalka on the loose and a killer in their midst. She had been in power for one day. One day.

"I can't even think about that," Sirena dismissed the thought.

"I don't think Leander was responsible but, I think you'd be setting yourself up for disaster if you don't consider all possibilities," Neo offered his opinion to Sirena. Xan and Theo had filled him in on the events prior to their arrival to the Morgen territory.

"Thanks for that," Sirena answered curtly, trying to shut down the conversation.

"Think about it, Sirena. The Rusalka couldn't see you when the three of you surrounded it. We're supposed to think that it swam up to Maia and killed her in her sleep? Maybe the Rusalka was a distraction. Apollo is gone too, after all," Kassia spoke softly, but her words struck a chord with Sirena.

She felt her back bristle at the mention of Apollo. Xan and Theo stiffened, too.

"I know he's gone," her voice came out colder than she had expected.

"I'm sorry, Sirena, but I think we need to keep our minds open to all possibilities. You even said it yourself. Maybe humans are involved. Maybe they can get to the Midnight Zone." Kassia kept her soft tone as she looked at a fuming Sirena.

"Maybe we should find a spot to rest for a while. I'm exhausted and hungry. I'm sure you all are too," Sirena spoke to the group, but still stared at Kassia. She knew she meant well, but suggesting others were involved scared her more than she wanted to admit. If it was only the Rusalka she had to deal with, she could handle that. Quarantine them again in their territory, find Apollo and return to their own territory to determine what comes next. Fine, she would do that. But, suggesting that there were other merpeople playing a bigger game or humans involved, she wasn't prepared for that. Being honest with herself, she hadn't prepared for any of this.

"There are sea critters around here. I'll snag some. Theo will help," Xan nodded at his brother. Theo showed his agreement.

Grateful that Xan decided without looking at her for direction, Sirena felt her heart lighten slightly. "We'll rest on those rocks over there, she pointed only a few meters to her right."

"How far are we from the Mami Wata, Neo?" Nova asked.

Neo peered around at the darkness around him and scrunched his brow for a second before answering. Sirena felt his frustration. She also felt lost. They weren't used to the Midnight Zone yet.

"I think a day, maybe a little less. We should get close to their territory in the Midnight Zone and then descend to the Abyss. I think that's our best option for dealing with their wards," Neo shared his thoughts, but Sirena could tell he was guessing. No one had been to the Abyss, other than the Mami Wata.

"All right. Then we rest for a bit before we hit the wards," Sirena motioned her pod towards the rocks off to their side.

***

Her eyes felt heavy as she settled onto a smaller rock. With her back pressed up against another, she could feel coldness setting into her fingers and nose as she stopped moving. When was she going to get used to this cold? If it was this cold here, the Abyss was going to have floating ice. Sighing, she fought to keep her eyes open as the others floated in around her.

Kassia was hesitantly sitting down to her left, looking at Sirena cautiously. "I'm not mad," Sirena said to Kassia, patting the space next to her. Kassia floated her way over to her, casting a glance at Neo, who had positioned himself on the other side of Sirena.

"I'm sorry. I didn't mean to imply anything," Kassia apologized.

Her eyes closed, head resting on the rock behind her, she dismissed Kassia's apology with a wave of her hand. "You're not wrong. I'm not prepared to handle any other option other than this being the sole work of the Rusalka."

"I know." Kassia looped her elbow through Sirena's and briefly rested her head on her friend's shoulder. Sirena pressed her head slightly down on top of Kassia's. After a moment, Kassia sat up straight again but kept her hold on Sirena's arm, offering Sirena comfort.

Nova and Cat filtered in on the rock underneath Sirena and she could feel their presence. She didn't know where Orinn was, and she didn't care. She was tired and Neo still had to prepare them for the Mami Wata wards. Racking her memory, she tried to remember anything that she might have been told about them but, admittedly, her family hadn't talked about that clan in years. The Mami Wata disappeared when the wars started, while the Sirens were busy saving the rest of the merpeople from captivity and harm, so no one ever really spoke about the Mami Wata.

"How old are you, Neo?" Sirena asked, not turning towards him.

"Does it matter?" he asked her.

"I guess it doesn't, but I'm trying to determine how much you know about the Mami Wata and how much is experience rather than hearsay," she still hadn't opened her eyes.

"Oh," he said, understanding her question. "I was born before the wars started, but not much before. When they started, I was six or seven, maybe, so I don't remember life before the wars at all, really. My parents lived with the Morgens rather than the Mami Wata. They should have lived with my mother's clan, but my father was Leander's sister's advisor before she passed. Leander is technically my cousin."

Sirena opened her eyes, following the lineage. Neo had been young when Leander took over as leader of the Morgens. She nodded for him to continue.

"Humans killed my parents," he shuddered. "I took my father's place as advisor to Leander when I got older. My parents were captured at the same time as Leander's sister," Neo said. Sirena remembered, distantly, the situation that resulted in Leander taking over as leader of the Morgens. The memory was cloudy as she had only heard the story and not lived it, but she remembered her father telling her about the transitions that the Morgens had gone through.

Neo gathered himself and continued, "My mother didn't practice magic like the Mami Wata did, and I don't know how she met my father. She never talked about it. I guess I never asked. I had wanted to learn everything I could about the sea witches, so I asked about spells and magic and she told me what she knew. She was non-practicing, though. I'd guess that most of what she knew came from hearsay."

Sirena felt slightly uneasy that neither Neo nor his mother were practicing Mami Wata and yet here he was, leading them into the most dangerous part of the ocean to meet sea witches she had only heard legends and rumors about. However, his honesty was comforting, even if it wasn't what she wanted to hear and it's not like she had merpeople lining up to help her.

Orinn snorted from somewhere above Sirena and she saw Orinn had perched herself on a higher rock above the rest of the pod. She ignored the terse, under the breath comments from the old mermaid and turned to look at Neo.

"What did your mother tell you about the wards?" she spoke softly, encouraging Neo despite the Siren advisor's protesting.

Neo paused before answering, concern lined his face. "It's heavy magic. We won't be able to swim into their territory freely. My mother told me they change them frequently, so that no one can learn them and get past them more than once."

Sirena groaned and rubbed her temples.

"It could be anything from creatures from the Abyss to magic so thick we can't swim through it," Neo trailed off a bit.

"Thick magic?" Nova questioned and Catalina sat up too, both looking at Neo inquisitively.

"My mother had tried to go home once, not long after I was born, to see her parents. To introduce them to me, I think. She said that there was thick magic, like the surrounding water turned into mud. She had to turn around. To keep trying to swim through it, she would have drowned. Her gills couldn't get air and she didn't have the strength to get through it," Neo said.

"How do we get through?" Nova looked at Sirena.

"Like I said, they change them. Thick water might be the least of our problems," Neo answered.

"We hope that all of you Sirens can blast through whatever comes our way." Cat playfully patted Sirena's fin, but her eyes showed her concern.

Sirena nodded and settled against the rocks, closing her eyes again. She would deal with whatever the Mami Wata threw at them. Tomorrow.

Chapter 11

Orla and Alanna

Orla tossed her long blonde hair over her shoulder and peered into Alanna's face as she slept. She would not let her sleep much longer, she needed to talk to her. Orla, who was the leader of the Merrows during the Human Wars and their subsequent exile, passed on the leadership to Alanna. Malee had insisted, in fact.

Malee's exile meant no more protection from the Sirens and no more inclusion in anything mermaid related. She didn't care what happened to the Merrows and Malee had made it known that the Merrows were free targets to any other clan that was angry at them. Other clans could do whatever they wanted to Merrow mermaids and there were no repercussions, no consequences, no Rusalka prisons.

Orla was bitter and angry with the Sirens, not emotions that she let herself feel often. She still didn't believe her merpeople were responsible for the wars, nor did she believe they deserved to be punished for the crimes of a few. Certainly, there had been other clans that had taken part in the merfolk's downfall. The other clans had fed each other to the humans to escape persecution themselves, causing things to spiral out of control. To put the blame on her and her merpeople seemed unfair and misplaced. However, she wanted to be part of the merfolk again and to have allies in the Siren ranks.

Alanna differed from Orla, and that's why Malee had insisted that Orla hand the reins down to her younger sister. Alanna hadn't been interested in humans, ever. When Merrows were floating to the surface and chasing after humans, Alanna had turned them into Malee and Asterios. She had caused strife in her own clan, and many of the Merrows were angry with Alanna. As a result, Alanna rested in abrupt shifts and asked Orla or one of her other closest friends to watch over her. Alanna was constantly looking over her shoulder and Orla pitied her. The other clans harbored hatred towards them and Alanna was unpopular, even within her own clan. She was an outcast within the outcast.

Malee's removal of protection for their clan had been difficult for the Merrows, but it had been downright devastating for Alanna. She lived in constant fear. Orla stuck her face in her sister's again to determine if she was sleeping or only lying there.

"I'm awake, you creep. You can back off," Alanna was emotionless in her tone and kept her eyes closed.

"Sorry, I can't always tell." Orla shook off the terse words.

Alanna sighed and sat up. She swept her long, red hair from one side to the other and curled her dark teal fin underneath herself, looking at Orla. "Was there something you needed?"

"No, well..." she hesitated for a moment, "I heard some rumors that the Finfolk are still making Merrow deals. I don't know who since we're all spread out, and it's hard to keep track of everyone but, there are whispers of it," Orla tried to match Alanna's emotionless tone. Alanna responded better when Orla was more subdued.

"Let them go," Alanna said.

"You're not concerned that we'll start another war? Next time, the Sirens will throw us both in Rusalka territory," Orla said, with an odd eagerness to her voice.

Alanna looked tired, frustrated and older than her years. She was younger than Orla by several years, but she looked much older these days. Being the leader of the clan that was held responsible for the deadliest time in merhistory, and being the sister of Orla, had worn on her. "You said it yourself. It's a rumor. You don't even know who. We don't even know where half the clan is. What would you like me to do?"

"I think it might be a good idea if you showed more of a presence to the clan. Maybe even reach out to the Sirens, extend peace. We have been living in exile for years. Maybe show the clan you're trying?" Orla's tone pinched, like she was nervous.

Alanna's red hair changed to a golden hue and then to shades of red, blue, and black. She was getting angry. Orla winced when she saw the variety of colors streaking through Alanna's hair.

"Appeal to the clan. Show presence. Reach out to the Sirens. Try to be a ruler. Any other brilliant advice?"

Alanna's tail deepened in color as well. Her strawberry red hair and teal tail were gone and instead she had returned to her deep blue and black tail and multi-colored hair, her usual. She was rare in her coloring and wasn't a typical Merrow with fair features. Alanna was insecure that she didn't look like the others, so she would shift her colors to the more common Merrow ones, but when she was angry, she reverted to her natural state.

"I'm sorry. I'm trying to help."

"I don't know what you want me to do. Outside of our territory, the other clans are killing each other. The Ceasgs, Selkies and Kelpies are eliminating each other one by one. They want to kill us too, you know. They've succeeded because we don't know what's going on. Because we're *exiled* from the merpeople. The clans are tearing themselves apart. And why? Because some of us decided they loved humans more than our own families. You want me to talk to the Sirens and beg them to let us back into the fold? Why?!" Alanna's eyes flashed red. She was completely in her natural state and Orla felt it was difficult to make eye contact with her.

"I want you to talk to them. I want you to get into their good graces. The Sirens used to let us go to the surface and fall in love and be human. They used to protect us. Our clan is resorting to the Finfolk. You know this isn't the answer!" Orla had raised her voice too.

Alanna remained silent for a few moments before she spoke.

"How long?" she asked when she finally spoke.

"How long for what?"

"How long have you been in love with a human?" Alanna was calm, but fired up. Her hair and tail were dark with anger.

Orla said nothing and looked down at her hands.

A slight cough sounded at the entrance of the cave that Alanna and Orla had been arguing in, and Alanna knew it could be none other than the water nymphs. She turned to have her suspicions confirmed as Ozara and Yara were lingering in the entranceway, staring at her like they hadn't ever seen mermaids argue before. She ignored the timid look on Yara's face and turned her attention to Ozara, the eldest ocean nymph. "Yes?"

While Yara squirmed ever so slightly to see Alanna's dark tail and fury emanating from her, Ozara maintained eye contact and simply stated,

"I have a message for you and your kind."

The Oceanids, water nymphs, hadn't brought their messages in years. Hadn't so much as spoken to them other than an occasional wave as they passed through Merrow territory. Alanna made a motion as if to say hurry and Ozara flinched ever so slightly but continued.

"I have a message for you and your kind
A new Siren ruler has taken hold
Of all young and old"

Shock ran through Alanna. Orla didn't move, but Alanna felt her shrink away slightly.

"Excuse me?"

"*Though not here, should I be*
I do this as much for you as for me ..."

Ozara's voice softened slightly as she looked at Alanna and then at Orla. She was anxious.

Certainly, she should not be here. They exiled the Merrows.

"They are in the zone of the Midnight
Where the humans know not how to fight."

Disbelief spread through her body as Alanna muttered a few words. "What happened to Malee?"

A slight tilt of her head and then, like that, Ozara was gone, leaving Yara to glance between the two one more time before disappearing herself. Alanna hated the terrible way the ocean nymphs communicated. They could speak normally; she was sure of it, but they always opted for cutesy riddles and rhymes. She much preferred the sea and river nymphs to Ozara, her sister and daughter. However, it was a relief to see any of them. It had been years since she had spoken to anyone other than a Merrow.

For a long moment, neither sister moved. As Alanna felt her rage fizzle out and confusion take hold, her Merrow form replaced the darkness that had temporarily crept into her tail and hair.

"I told you it was time to talk to the Sirens."

Alanna sighed and whirled around to look at her. "Fine, we'll leave shortly."

Chapter 12

Sirena

When Sirena had woken after only a few brief hours of intermittent sleep, she felt worse than she had prior to trying to rest. The rest of her pod remained asleep, so she had let them rest for a while as she thought through her current situation. Never, ever, had she thought she would be the ruler of the Sirens. The Queen of the Merpeople.

Sirena had always thought that she would be a part of the rescue mission pod and maybe one day be an advisor to Maia, and that had been her best hope for the future. Being born into conflict, she didn't have a peaceful world to envision. Maia had often talked about how she longed for the days that she could sun herself on the surface again. When Maia had plunged them into the icy darkness weeks ago, Sirena had felt the defeat in her sister and she'd be lying to herself if she said she hadn't felt defeated too. Maia had given up her hope and her dreams of the future and then she was gone, having never seen the world return to normal.

How many more merpeople would lose their hope before this was over?

Sirena surveyed her pod again and thought about the trust and respect that Xan and Theo had given her immediately. Theo and Apollo had trained her on rescue missions and she went on many missions with Xan, following his leadership. They had seen her mistakes, her insecurities, her hesitations on missions, and yet they fell in line the moment she became their leader. No questions asked. Xan had pushed back on Maia daily since she had plunged them into the Midnight Zone. The day before she died, he engaged in an argument with her when she ceased rescue missions. Xan had fought with Sirena that day, too. That Xan and Theo followed her should have given her confidence, but even two warrior Sirens acknowledging her rule didn't comfort her.

Perhaps the worst emotion of all was the incredible guilt that she felt. It had washed over her when the Siren's power had taken control over her. She felt waves of it continue. Guilt over what happened to her mother had been constant for the last three weeks, but she felt guilt over Maia's demise, too. She couldn't see her vision blurring and whether that was grief or guilt, she didn't know, but it was awful. There had only been minutes between Maia's death and the Rusalka attack and less than an hour between the attack and their departure for the Morgen's territory.

The guilt that hit her the hardest? She didn't miss Maia, not even slightly. She was furious at her. So angry, in fact, that if Maia came back, she'd kill her herself. Maia plunges them into the darkness to rot and then gets herself killed weeks in? Did she even fight to stay alive?

She realized Xan and Theo supported her, even though Xan had openly expressed his frustrations with Maia. Theo had grown more quiet than usual and had retreated from the pod a bit; much like Cali. Maybe that was the source of this overwhelming guilt. Her friends trusted her. They had hope again. She had absolutely no idea what she was doing and here she was, leading not only her pod but the entire merpeople. People wanted their lives to improve. They wanted to live again without fear of being hunted.

They were being hunted by their own kind with a ruler that didn't have a hope or vision. They were at the mercy of a Siren that had preferred rescue missions and her friends over learning about the other clans or the history of the merfolk. Xan had saved her in front of the group when he asked questions about the Mami Wata. He knew the answers to the questions he asked; she knew he did. Xan, who spent so much of his young life rescuing and defending other clans, had absolutely studied their history and knew the events that had gotten them here. The truth of it was, Sirena didn't have foresight into what she might need to know in the future because she had never really seen a future for herself. Her entire life had been a struggle. She had lost friends, family and she had lived under the watchful eye of her parents, never getting to stray far.

The first mission that she went on that didn't include Asterios had been exhilarating, but yet when they returned, Theo had taken a verbal lashing from Malee and Asterios for every misstep that Sirena had made. He endured it and never pressured her with future missions. He did, however, stop giving them every detail when they returned, instead giving them the highlights and painting Sirena as a brave and knowledgeable Siren warrior. When she started teaming with Xan, he did the same, having learned from his brother's mistake. As much as she loved the missions and had found purpose amongst the chaos, she had never felt like the successful warrior the brothers had made her out to be.

Sitting a moment longer with her guilt, Sirena tried to shove it down into the pit of her stomach and think about the tasks at hand, but one last fleeting thought popped into her mind. The look that Nova gave her yesterday when she had tried to let Neo take over leading the pod. She had thought Nova was playfully chastising her and after she reflected a bit; she knew what that look had meant to be.

Disappointment.

A fresh wave of guilt ran through her and she sighed as she thought about the day ahead. She hoped that Nova's disappointed look was the last she'd received for a while, but given she had absolutely no understanding of what lay ahead of them, she doubted it.

Chapter 13

Apollo

Listening carefully, Apollo was sure that they were on the surface. At some point, they decided to not only bind him but also blindfold him. He couldn't tell where he was or where they were going for most of their trip, but he was sure he was on the surface. Endless rows of rock formations had been better than hours of silence and blindness.

He could hear his captors talking again. As they spoke, he could hear the snake-like whistle to their voices. He hadn't heard the whistle when they spoke before, but he heard it now.

The Undines. Soulless mermaids.

The soulless creatures, barely passable as mermaids, had been responsible for the mermaid trade. When Merrows introduced humans to the mermaid species, the Undines had taken advantage of greedy humans and had captured and traded mermaids for their benefits. They traded other mermaids for souls. Souls that granted them life on land.

Their desire to achieve a soul fueled Undines. The only creatures of the sea that were immediately destined to an afterlife of misery if they died without a soul, they were relentless in their pursuit of freedom. They had two paths laid out before them to gain their souls: either being granted a soul from a human or finding a human that loved them and marrying them, binding their soul to the soulless Undines.

As vile looking creatures, it wasn't too often that they found someone to marry them. Which meant that they often convinced an ignorant human to trade their soul for a chance to swim in the ocean. They traded their soul and human form for what they believed was going to be a beautiful life in the sea. Giving up their soul to an Undine meant a tragic ending. The revelation they would suffer forever in the realm of the Rusalka shocked humans, as they realized they would experience only misery, loneliness, and despair.

Undines had become crafty and took human souls by force when they wanted. Difficult as it was, some attempted the forced soul trade but many more favored taking other merpeople hostage to gain their better eternity.

Apollo cringed at the thought of being handled by Undines. He had always thought of them as the bottom feeders in the ocean. Their upper halves, while still resembling humans, were a ghostly white and their faces looked as though they had melted. When he had been to the surface during a rescue mission, there had been a candle in the home of a human. The first and only time he had ever seen a candle. Their faces looked like the melted candle wax that had spilled on the table when he unknowingly stuck his finger into the flame.

Their webbed hands were thick and grotesque and, like the Finfolk, they looked sticky to the touch. Asterios had told him once that they were indeed sticky and their skin was part of what they used to trap unsuspecting merfolk. It was like glue.

While the rest of the mermaids had long, flowing hair, the Undines had small stubbles that lined the top of their faces in short, jagged peaks. The crowns of their heads were bald. Their look was complete with snake-like tongues that could act as a poison dart to kill or severely weaken their victim. Whether you died depended on how much poison the Undines injected you with. An Undine had temporarily paralyzed him in the past and he certainly held a grudge against their kind for it. That must have been how they subdued him so quickly when they captured him.

The flesh wound in his fin was aching and still bleeding, albeit slowly. To be a victim of the Undines yet again was infuriating, and he felt a fresh wave of resentment and anger flood him. How long had it been since he had been taken from the rest of the Sirens? From his last living relative? How long had Sirena been the Queen of the mermaids?

His sense of time was completely gone.

He felt waves lapping against the sides of his body and tail. They were definitely at the surface. Icy fear surged through his body. Mermaids had plunged deep into the oceans to avoid humans after the wars for a reason. Safety right now was in hiding. Until mermaids were out of the thoughts and minds of humans, until they were myths and legends, they needed to remain hidden. They wanted him alive and intact and they were at the ocean's surface. The plan for him was a trade. What other reason would there be to take him to the surface?

A royal merman. A trade that would yield souls for as many Undines as they could line up.

If Maia was gone and he was being traded, Sirena was most certainly dead or being held captive. Whoever was behind this wanted the royal Sirens out of the picture. They were being eliminated. Fresh grief surged through him. He'd lost his entire family. Sirena was his closest sibling and his closest friend.

Any hope that he had was evaporating. Maybe the Siren advisors would look for him, but it was unlikely. Sophie and Orinn had always been difficult. They advised the Siren rulers and stayed neutral; that was their job. He suspected they were the ones that had been behind the idea of ending rescue missions. Not that he disagreed with the decision, but that left him on his own. There would be no rescue from the advisors or council.

One last shred of hope flitted in his heart. Maybe Theo and Xan. He had worked with them on several missions and they were loyal to a fault. If they were still alive. They loved Sirena and if she was gone, there was no doubt in his mind that they were both gone. Both mermen would give their lives for her. Apollo struggled with his thoughts, his hope diminishing.

Apollo lifted his head to a sound in the distance. Despite his current lack of vision, he felt his other senses kick in and there was certainly movement and sound off to the distance, beyond where he and his captors were swimming. With their continued murmured speech, they didn't hear or feel the presence. He wondered if they were being deliberately obtuse. The surrounding presence was heavy, and he felt the weight of the dark as they continued to drag him.

"Did you hear that?" he tentatively questioned his captives.

A hard thump landed in the middle of his chest. Apollo lifted his head ever so slightly and felt air rush into his lungs through his nose versus his gills. He choked a few times. They were on the surface.

Apollo felt fear rushing and pleaded with his captors again. "There's someone out there. You need to listen to me."

"Don't leave another mark on him. You've done enough damage," the snake whistle sounded again.

Another thump, this time to the side of his head. They continued on for what felt like hours, but was probably a matter of minutes. Apollo heard the noise again and felt something surrounding him, encapsulating him. If they hadn't been dragging him, he wouldn't have been able to move on his own. Nausea tore through his body and this time; the darkness came from behind his own eyelids as his body went limp.

Apollo had one fleeting thought before his mind stilled. Undines didn't have magic. How were they using magic on him?

Chapter 14

Sirena

They had been swimming for about an hour when Sirena realized she hadn't heard a sound from Neo. She hadn't known him for more than a few days but, from what she had seen, he was typically much more conversational than he had been this morning. They were leading the pod with Orinn, Nova, Kassia and Catalina in the middle. Xan and Theo were trailing the pod, keeping an eye out for anything that could come up from behind them. Xan had insisted.

Neo met her eye as she tried to steal a glance at him. Caught, she asked him, "Is everything alright?"

"Yes," he replied unconvincingly. "Is everything alright with you?"

"Ye-."

Before she could complete the short word, she was laughing.

"I'm absolutely not alright," Sirena shared between inappropriate bouts of nervous laughter. "I'm a mess."

She laughed until she cried, tears streaming down her face. Neo laughed with her but also at her, as she couldn't contain herself. Her body convulsed in fits of laughter, and every time she tried to calm herself, she'd start up again.

When she had calmed down, she noticed Neo had moved in closer to her and spoke in a lower tone of voice.

"Are you scared?" he asked.

"Of the Mami Wata and the wards? Not particularly," Sirena said.

"No, I mean to be the ruler of all." Neo opened his arms wide, gesturing to the oceans.

"Oh, that. Terrified. Absolutely terrified," she swallowed another bubble of nervous laughter. Neo watched her as she choked on a chuckle.

"And do you always laugh when you're terrified?"

"It seems to be a fresh development. Who would have guessed?" She threw her hands up in the water and smiled at him.

"Fear does strange things to us," he returned her smile. "I'm sure having a crossbreed guiding you possibly to death doesn't help that much at all." His voice softened again.

"You know more about the Mami Wata than we do, and maybe having you with us will help when we break through the wards and find them," Sirena reassured him.

"Maybe. I don't think they'll know me, but maybe," he had returned his gaze forward.

"And don't call yourself a crossbreed. Most merpeople aren't full-breeds any longer, anyway. If Maia would have lived, her children would have been half Siren, half Morgen, and no one would have said a word about that," Sirena said firmly.

"I guess I didn't think about it that way. Leander always reminded me I was a crossbreed, so I guess it stuck with me a bit," Neo spoke bitterly, remembering Leander's comments.

"Leander was a blowfish. Did he ever tell you I called him that once? To his face. So conceited," Sirena rolled her eyes. "He was awful," Sirena rolled her eyes, thinking about the leader of the Morgens.

"Ah, you're the one that called him that," Neo said, recalling the conversation with Leander. "Didn't you also call him a Greek god?"

"Yes, but I didn't mean it how you think I meant it. He was an arrogant prick. Like the Greek gods in our stories. And he thinks he's the most gorgeous merman to swim the oceans." Sirena was laughing a bit again, but more controlled this time.

"I remember him telling me about that encounter with you. He was blowing seashells mad," Neo was the one laughing this time.

Sirena smiled as she appreciated hearing that her comment had gotten under Leander's fins a bit. Good. She still felt unsettled about how quickly he seemed to process Maia's death. She'd point that out to him in the future, now that she was his ruler.

Neo interrupted her thoughts. "Why is your name, Sirena? Isn't that 'siren'? Your parents named you 'siren'?"

Sirena let out a soft laugh as she said, "It's my nickname from Cat. We were so young that no one has called me by my real name for decades. Sirena Oscura, she called me."

Neo waited inquisitively for her response.

"It means the dark mermaid," she laughed.

"Ah, ok. Because you're a siren. Clever," he said in a tone that indicated he didn't actually find it all that clever. Sirena picked up a hint of disapproval, perhaps.

"I liked Sirena better, and it stuck. Even my parents called me Sirena."

"And what is your real name, dark mermaid?" Neo teased her.

Wrinkling her nose and closing her eyes, Sirena said, "Alcina. Alcie for short."

"Alcie? What's wrong with that?" Neo looked confused.

"Nothing, I guess. They named Maia after our mother, Malee, because she was going to take over for her one day. Apollo and I had 'A' names, after our father Asterios, because we weren't in line for leadership."

"Until you were in line for leadership," Neo beamed at her with pride radiating off of him.

"I guess. No one ever thought… I never thought…" Sirena trailed off.

"But here you are, kicking ass," Neo beamed at her.

"Ass?" she laughed. "You've been to the surface," she stated, noting the human language.

"A few times. Twice maybe," he said admittedly. "But it's one of Leander's favorite human words, so I've picked it up."

"What's he really like?"

"Leander?" Neo asked.

Sirena nodded. She was curious what Leander was like outside of his interactions with Maia. If she was being honest with herself, she may not have liked him, but knew he couldn't be all bad if her mother had approved of him.

"He's… difficult. What you saw of him yesterday, that's fairly typical. He's harsh and distant. We don't get along; he doesn't get along with many but he loved Maia. I'm sorry about my comments yesterday. I was harsh and angry with him. He cared for Maia, whatever his political reasons were for being with Maia, those were secondary," Neo said gently.

Sirena nodded her appreciation for his assurance. "How come we've never met? Ajax has always been around when we've visited the Morgens or at council meetings, but I've never seen you?" Sirena asked.

"Leander kept me around and made me an advisor out of respect for my parents. My dad was his sister's advisor. I mentioned that. We're cousins. Second cousins, actually. My dad was a cousin to Leander and his sisters and brothers. However, the first chance he had to get rid of me, he took. As you well know," Neo said sadly.

"Do you have any family left?" Sirena matched his quieter tone.

"No, Leander is all that I have left."

"I understand that feeling. I think I'm the last one left in my family, too."

Sirena couldn't handle the look of pity that Neo gave her. She shook it off and focused her sight forward again.

"Apollo is still out there. We'll find him," Neo reassured her.

She showed she agreed, but her heart broke. Out of all of her family, Apollo was the one that hurt the most. She had always felt like she was on the outside looking in with her parents. They were so wrapped up in the war and making sure Maia was knowledgeable about their affairs that often Apollo and Sirena found themselves together. Apollo was almost a decade older than her and he would often joke about how he had raised his pup already and that he didn't need children when he settled down with a partner. He would tease her, but he also watched out for her and had never made her feel like a burden when they were growing up. Something that she couldn't say about Maia.

"My sister is gone and never coming back and I should be sad, but all I can think about is that if I never see Apollo again, I don't know how to process that," Sirena sputtered out. She recoiled at the shock of her sudden outburst of truth.

"I think that's fair. It seems like you and Apollo were close. Xan and Theo were talking about some rescues the four of you went on. You spent more time with them," Neo said.

"That's true," Sirena agreed.

"I don't think anyone will judge you for anything you think or feel. I think everyone is grateful that they aren't you," Neo laughed.

She gave a small chuckle at that. "Thanks, I wish I wasn't me too."

"Nah, you're right where you're supposed to be," he smiled.

"You don't even know me," she argued.

Neo laughed at her again, his dark curls bobbing in the water. "That is true, but I know cranky old merpeople and that they like to make life difficult for younger ones that they think might challenge them." He nodded his head in Orinn's direction. "I also know of Xan and Theo. They saved quite a few of our clan. Leander has mad respect for them, and Apollo. He probably would for you too if you hadn't called him names," he teased her.

Sirena smiled at him but looked at him, confused. "What do Xan and Theo have to do with me being in the right place?"

"If you weren't the right leader, I don't think those two would follow you willingly. Xan strikes me as a bit of a hothead," Neo winked at her.

"He can be sometimes," she nodded.

"And opinionated."

Sirena nodded in agreement again.

"Like I said, everyone is grateful they aren't in your position. But they all trust you and maybe not being trained and primed to be the next Queen of the merpeople is a good thing."

"How so?"

Neo looked thoughtful for a moment before he replied, "Things have not gone well these last hundred years. Maia plunged us into the depths of the ocean. And what was her plan? Do you know? I know what it was, she told Leander. She was going to leave us down here. The Midnight Zone is our new home. Was our new home."

"Leander told you that?" Sirena whispered.

"Oceans, no. I overheard them. I'm an excellent spy," he gave her another wink.

Sirena didn't speak. Trying to process what she had learned of Maia's plan. Finally, she said, "She told me she thought we could live a human lifespan in the Midnight Zone, until we were myths again."

"Eighty years? Ninety?"

Sirena nodded. That had been what Maia had told her.

"Those little humans would still grow up to tell their children what they had seen. We were looking at a few human lifespans to become a myth again."

Sighing, Sirena agreed. That had been her thought as well when Maia had told her she thought a human lifespan would be sufficient.

"But with you leading the charge, there's hope again," Neo's eyes glimmered.

Sirena swallowed her fear and guilt down again. The way her friends were looking at her, the way Neo was looking at her. She could see it in their eyes, hope. And it absolutely crushed her.

"I'll try not to let you all down," she whispered.

"Unless you leave us here to die in the Midnight Zone, you won't," he reassured her.

Sirena didn't speak. She didn't know what she could do to make the upper levels of the ocean safe for the merfolk.

Neo interrupted her thoughts. "We're not naïve, you know. We all know that some of us won't make it. That we'll have to fight for a better life for the rest. But we're all willing to do that under your leadership. I can't speak for everyone, but I know your pod is more willing to die for you than they ever would have been for your sister."

Sirena didn't respond again, but the silence between them became more comfortable and she felt better knowing that her pod was rooting for her. However, she could still feel sadness infiltrating Neo's warmer personality. He differed from the moody Sirens she was used to. Part of her knew that the reason she was so drawn to Cat and Nova was because they were lighter than the dark broodiness of the Sirens. Even though she didn't like to admit to her cold Siren heart that she appreciated the kindness and empathetic nature of the other mers.

"I shared my feelings, so it's your turn," she said playfully.

His face showed he didn't want to share, but then he took a deep breath in through his gills. Turning to face her, he said, "Leander sent me with you because he thinks I'm an idiot and I'm going to get us all killed."

Sirena couldn't hide the shock she felt.

Neo continued, "When you said that he didn't show emotion over Maia's death, I can promise you he thinks he's getting even with you by sending me with you. He sent us all to our death. When you called him a blowfish, well, there are worse things you should have called him."

"I knew I hated him. You might think he loved her, but I think he loved the idea of being partnered with a Siren," Sirena spat out.

"You may very well be right there. I don't know. He seemed to love her; I think."

"He could have handed off the Morgen territory and lived with her when they committed to each other, but he didn't. He stayed in his territory until he knew for sure she was Queen," Sirena argued.

"He always said he wanted to remain in our territory until it made sense to move. With us fighting humans daily, he didn't want to leave us vulnerable."

"You were the next of kin. He could have handed off the territory to you and been with Maia," Sirena stated pointedly.

Neo scoffed. "I'm never going to be the ruler of the Morgens. That wasn't the plan. Ajax was next in line."

"Ajax?!" Sirena almost screamed. "He's older than my parents were," she said with complete disbelief.

"I told you, Leander and I don't get along," Neo was brushing it off and chuckling.

Sirena stared ahead of her. The few meters in front of her face were all that she could see in the dark. Her body was shaking with anger. These leaders of the clans were ridiculous. Leander was going to hand off power to someone outside of a ruling family, Bia of the Mami Wata drove her people into the Abyss and left the rest of the clans to suffer and Orinn and Sophie were going about their lives as though everything was normal although the last hundred years had been an absolute failure. What in all of Coralis was going on?

There were two ways for power to transfer from a leader. The first and most common way was the death of the ruler in power, as what had happened with Malee, Maia and herself. The second was a peaceful handoff of power, where the ruler conceded to the next in line or to someone else. Leander was going to hand off power to a merperson outside of a ruling family when there was a living relative. That was unheard of. Sirena might not be well versed in council politics, but she was sure that a vote would have been necessary.

"Did the council vote on that? I don't think Maia knew," Sirena asked.

"They did, and she knew," Neo said softly.

This was part of the reason that she felt ill-prepared to be the Queen of the Mermaids. She did not know of the inner workings of the council, and she obviously didn't know what Maia had been doing.

"Maia's gone. I can see that you're next in line."

"Thank you, but no. With Maia gone, Leander won't be leaving, anyway. Not soon. Besides, I've never wanted to be a leader. That's not anywhere close to what I want for myself," Neo spoke thoughtfully.

"And what do you want for yourself?" Sirena asked.

"A home," Neo sighed. "I've been Leander's burden for a good portion of my life. I told myself after he left to join Maia, things would be different, that being Ajax's advisor would be better. But I don't think he intended to keep me around."

"Something you overheard in that conversation with Leander and Maia?" Sirena asked hesitantly.

Neo nodded. "Since he's staying, I don't think *I* want to stay. Ajax was going to send me to the Aicaya. I've been thinking I might go, anyway."

Sirena didn't know what to say. Her sister had been no different from the elder merleaders. Sophie and Orinn had voted to put Ajax in power over the Morgens. Their actions may not surprise her but Maia did.

"The Aicaya are great merpeople. Welcome and warm-hearted. I've visited them a few times, with my father. I loved them," Sirena said absently.

Neo didn't respond, and she realized what she had said.

"You don't need to go there, though. Unless you want to," she said hurriedly, trying to correct her blunder. "You're welcome to stay with us, unless Leander insists you need to stay on as his advisor."

"He won't," Neo said coldly.

"The offer stands then. You can remain with my pod and the Sirens. You don't have to decide today."

The ice in Neo's gaze melted, and he thanked her. He fell back into his own thoughts, and Sirena sank into hers. She may not have been close to Maia, but she had thought she still *knew* her. Why would Maia have agreed to go outside of bloodlines? Why would she plan to leave them in the darkest and coldest layers of the ocean without a plan? That seemed absolutely absurd to Sirena.

Maia, it seemed, had even less direction than she had and she had spent her whole life preparing to take over power. And Orinn, the human word for betta, came to mind. Orinn was a bitch. The human word seemed more powerful than betta. Bettas were beautiful in fact and she didn't know what a bitch was in human language, but it felt worse. Where did Sophie stand? She must have voted with Orinn and Maia, too. The other clan leaders must have as well.

Sirena was understanding why her friends were looking at her with hope in their eyes. She might very well be the last damn chance they had. A hundred years wasted. Lives wasted all because too old merpeople refused to admit they didn't know what the shell they were doing. Disgusting.

Before her rage could get carried away, Sirena felt a hand grab her by the throat. Her gills squeezed tight, and she felt the air rush from her lungs and leave through her mouth in strangled bubbles. Her hands flew to her throat, but there was nothing there. Next to her, she felt Neo struggling against the same invisible force.

They had reached the Mami Wata.

Chapter 15

Neo

Neo reached out in front of him, trying to shove the invisible force off of him. His hand pushed up against a wall, despite his eyes not actually seeing one in front of him. He shoved hard against the wall, pushing himself backwards and freeing himself from the invisible hand. Choking as water rushed into his gills, he looked to see Sirena struggling as well. He grabbed her by her shoulders and yanked her into him.

She spun around to face him, fear in her eyes.

“What was that?” she said.

“The wards, I think,” Neo was still trying to slow his breathing.

“Ugh,” Sirena said, rubbing her throat where the invisible wall had strangled her.

“We’ll have to wait for the others to catch up,” Neo said. “They shouldn’t be more than a few minutes behind us.”

Sirena agreed and turned her gaze to the invisible wall that was only a meter in front of them. She frowned as she stared ahead of her and Neo watched her, hoping she had an answer. He knew she was trying to calculate the amount of power required to break through the wall, but he doubted that defeating a Mami Wata ward would be easy.

“Save your resources, Sirena. Wait until the rest of the Sirens get here. We do not know what’s on the other end,” Neo warned.

“I know. I was thinking how unbelievable it is that the Mami Wata hid themselves and my parents let them with no way of contacting them. What if we all died, and it was sheer chaos up here? They’d be none the wiser.”

“I think that was the point,” Neo laughed softly.

“You’re probably right, unfortunately. I don’t understand what the council was doing. Why didn't my mother stand up to them when they disappeared? Every other clan fought to save *all* of us."

"I guess you're seeing what the rest of the merpeople have seen for so long, Alcie," Neo said tauntingly.

Sirena huffed, "Don't call me that, and my parents were good rulers. They must have had their reasons for letting this happen, even if I don't understand it. It's not like I can ask them, anyway."

"I never said they weren't good rulers," Neo said softly, speaking more empathetically this time.

"Didn't you?"

"No," he shrugged. "I only said that you're seeing what the rest of us saw."

"And what did the rest of you see?"

"Bending the rules for the favorites. Those that are well liked get what they want regardless of what's right."

"Were the Mami Wata well liked?"

Neo glanced at her for a moment and then said, "They cursed the Rusalka. The Sirens looked the other way when they buried themselves into the Abyss."

He watched as she processed what he had said. She pondered his situation with Leander and contemplated the Merrows' exile, even though it had been one Merrow that had caused trouble. He could see her mulling over the various decisions the Sirens had made over the years, and a pained look crossed her face.

Finally, she looked up at him and said, “I see how it looks like favoritism.”

“Looks like it?”

“Neither of us were there. We’re both making assumptions. My parents’ decision to permit the Mami Wata to hide away and save themselves, while every other clan stayed to fight, is something I can’t comprehend. I wasn’t there, and I can’t change what happened, but I can make sure that things are fair from now on, and I guess our current mess is for me to resolve.”

Her maturity amazed Neo. She was half his age, and he could not quickly assess and conclude like she had in a matter of seconds. When Orinn wasn’t around scoffing and huffing, Sirena seemed to think and decide for herself.

“Why did you stop? Are we there?” Kassia’s cheery voice broke into his thoughts.

“Yes,” Sirena confirmed. “And we can’t get through. There’s this wall that will choke the life out of you.”

Kassia squinted her eyes and leaned forward, not seeing a wall. She arched backwards and asked skeptically, “Are you sure? I see nothing.”

“It’s invisible,” Neo answered.

Orinn rolled her eyes and glanced behind her to see if Xan and Theo were approaching. Satisfied that they were, she turned to them. Before she could say anything and pass judgment on Sirena, Neo steered the conversation.

"Sirena was going to blast it, but I told her to save her strength until the rest of you got here. I think it's best if we wait until we have all the Sirens in our pod here," Neo waved his hands in front of him in an exaggeration of how she looked when she used her magic. Sirena rolled her eyes but let a small smile slip.

"Our pod?" Orinn asked and raised an eyebrow.

"Can we do that? Blast through the wards?" Kassia asked, ignoring Orinn. She mimicked Neo, waving her hands.

Orinn huffed a response that wasn't audible. Sirena reined in her smile.

Disregarding her, Neo responded, "It would be surprising if it was that easy."

Kassia shot a stream of energy a short distance in front of her toward the wall. Nothing happened. She frowned and looked at him.

Well, that was concerning, he thought to himself. He tried to keep his emotions from his face and gave her a slight head tilt and an eyebrow raise, indicating they needed to wait.

Xan and Theo were in sight's distance and Neo held his breath as they approached, remembering the tight grasp the invisible force had on his throat.

Kassia saved him the trouble and gave the rundown of where they had left off. "Sirena and Neo ran into an invisible wall that choked them but I blasted it and I see nothing," Kassia again mimicked him with her hands when she said blast.

Xan and Theo gave her an odd look and Xan patted her on the shoulder before approaching Neo and Sirena. Neo fought his laughter.

"If they said there's an invisible wall, then there's an invisible wall. Our finger beams aren't the solution to all of Coralis' problems," Xan laughed and Neo felt himself allowing a smile to break through. Despite the situation they had all found themselves in, he was appreciative that the Sirens weren't always as dark and serious and he had thought them to be.

Xan was next to Sirena now, and he waved to the water in front of her. She tilted her head in agreement and he stuck out an arm. He contacted the wall and Neo watched as he felt the solidness of the wall, but the invisible hand didn't seem to grab him.

"Definitely solid. Like a rock. A smooth rock anyway. I'm still breathing though," Xan confirmed.

At his announcement, Sirena floated towards the wall again and felt the wall, but the hand didn't make an appearance again. "That's an improvement, I guess," she looked at Neo.

"We were both strangled, I promise. I couldn't breathe, and I had to pull Sirena away." Neo looked almost offended that the wall had attacked no one else.

"Wards work differently for each merperson. One mer could see a wall, another could see coral. The Mami Wata are masters of illusion." Orinn's voice was flat and unamused.

"What do you propose we do, then?" Theo said, but was looking at Sirena.

"Maybe we should ask the wall nicely to let us in," Orinn cooed sarcastically.

"Helpful," Xan rolled his eyes.

Sirena turned to face the wall again. She shot a quick wink at Neo. "Oh, great wall," she said in a singsong voice. "Can you please let us in? We'd like to speak with the Mami Wata."

"Cute," Orinn said.

Sirena looked quite pleased with herself and Neo couldn't help but wonder if knowing more about the poor decisions the council had been making for centuries was giving her confidence. Or was she finding it more difficult to hide her hatred for Orinn? He decided it was probably the latter. He didn't like Orinn either.

She had her hand on the wall again, pushing against it. He squinted at her, trying to see what she was looking for. He glanced at the rest of the pod. Xan and Theo were watching her while Cat and Nova were murmuring to each other.

Leaning over so only she could hear him, he whispered, "What are you doing?"

"Looking for an opening," she shrugged. "Not as easy as asking it to open for us but, there should be an entrance, right?"

"I don't think there's an opening. You really think there's going to be a drawbridge that opens?" Neo teased her. Sirena ignored him and continued her search.

"Is it a wall or an enclosure?" Xan asked.

"I do not know. Why?" Neo responded.

"If we could come down into the territory from above the wall, then we wouldn't need to go through it."

"We descended into the Abyss a while ago," Neo confirmed. "That might be the case then, if we follow the wall upward." He looked upwards, guessing how far up the top of the wall might be.

Xan's gaze had drifted from Neo to Sirena, and Neo followed it. Sirena had a hand up to the wall, her hand flowing with Siren magic, but instead of shoving her power towards the wall, it looked as though she was drawing energy from it.

"What are you doing?" Xan whispered to her.

"Shh," Neo said, raising a hand to quiet him. He kept his attention on Sirena.

Neo watched Sirena as she focused on the space before her. Both of her hands were up, glowing and shaking as she drew energy from the wall. The invisible wall created lineation in the water and it looked like she was drawing the wall towards her, bending it. He looked at Xan and he tilted his head as if to ask, 'are you seeing what I'm seeing?'

Whispering to Xan, he asked, "Is she absorbing the wall?"

"I think so."

"Can you do that?" Neo asked him.

Xan, eyes wide, slowly moved his head side to side, showing he couldn't.

Sirena was glowing brighter and brighter as the wall bent and caved towards her. Theo had approached her and floated beside her, watching her as intently as Neo and Xan were. The rest of the pod had stopped talking and were turning their attention towards her. Neo took notice of the sour look on Orinn's face. She reminded him of a female version of Leander. His heart went out to Sirena for a moment. He knew what it felt like to live with constant disapproval.

The glow coming from the wall grew more intense as it fell away. The light coming from Sirena illuminated the darkness surrounding them and he gasped as he saw what looked like rocks and boulders crumble and fall into the darkness below them. He didn't hear them hit or see where they went. The depths below them were endless. His stomach fluttered at the thought of it.

Sirena gaped at them, her body absorbing the energy from the wall and the light dimming. She held her hands out in front of her, looking between her hands and the pod. Neo reached out and grabbed her by the wrist, pulling her towards himself and Xan.

Xan immediately grabbed her other arm, looking her up and down. "Are you ok?"

She hovered in place, looking between himself and Xan. Slowly, she said yes with a slight nod of her head. Theo let out a loud sigh, sending water waves towards them. Nova was on top of Sirena in an instant, hugging her.

"That was incredible! You powered through that wall like it was your job," Nova exclaimed.

"I didn't power through it," Sirena said slowly, her eyes wary. She gave Neo the same expression that Xan had given him earlier when she was devouring the energy from the wall.

Nova's face twisted with confusion, and she looked at the others before turning to Sirena.

"She ate that wall," Neo said with a gasp, answering for Sirena, who was still processing the energy she had taken.

"What?" Nova looked at him blankly.

Xan answered this time, "She sucked the energy from it. Inhaled it. I've seen nothing like it. That rock wall was bending to you."

"I do not know how I did that," Sirena looked down at her hands again as if they had the answer.

"It was brilliant, whatever you did," Neo gave her applause. The others appeared too shocked to join in, but Nova mustered a small clap.

Sirena shot Neo a small smile but still looked confused. "I hope this feeling goes away soon."

"What feeling?" Neo grabbed her wrist again and noted that Nova was doing the same. She didn't feel or look any different to him, but she had absorbed energy and was lighting up the darkness of the Abyss like they were on the surface at midday.

"I'm not sure how to explain it, but it's almost anxiety-like nervousness. A rattling in my chest and, well, like I'm full of energy."

"Who knows how much energy you absorbed? It looked like you took down the entire wall, not just this section in front of us. I'm sure it will wear off soon," Xan reassured her.

She nodded and bit on her bottom lip in contemplation. They all waited for her next move.

Sirena shrugged after a moment. "I guess we proceed." She gestured to the darkness in front of them. When no one moved, she led the way.

***

Neo found himself at Sirena's side again and while Xan and Theo had taken up their post to the rear of the pod again, they were no longer swimming meters apart from one another. In a close pod formation, they moved slowly and cautiously with Sirena holding her hands out, lighting their way.

As Neo looked at their surroundings, the scenery had grown darker and more condensed. The dark open water that they had seen when Sirena first dropped the wall had seemed almost serene. As they crept further into the lair of the Mami Wata, it felt claustrophobic. Plants grew plentiful in the Sunlight Zone and occasionally he had found kelp in the topmost parts of the Twilight Zone. The Midnight Zone, he had discovered, held nothing but deformed creatures that could live without light. However, there were plants growing from every rock and ledge for as far as he could see. The bright green foliage, vibrant in the dark black water, made him realize he had missed kelp and seaweed.

Sirena caught him looking between the rocks and met his gaze, confirming what he was thinking. The plants could only be sea witch magic. There was no other explanation. Neo felt his chest tighten as the rocks and plants grew more prevalent around them, their path narrowing until their wider pod formation became two-by-two lines. He didn't know if he felt warmer because the water had grown warmer, or if Sirena was heating a path for them. He probably didn't want to know the answer.

The space above and below them was open, he thought. It was so dark that the only way he could know for sure was to swim higher or sink lower, and he was not about to go exploring. He felt Sirena link her arm through his as she turned and gave orders to the rest of the pod to do the same. He squinted his eyes to see what had spurred the order from their new Queen. His blood went cold with fear and he came to a halt.

He tightened his grip on Sirena, forcing her to stop, too.

"Sirena, we have to turn around," Neo whispered.

She shook her head no. Crossing her free arm across her body, she hovered her glowing hand in the space between their shoulders and tilted her head, telling him he should look. The mermaids behind him had seen what he saw, and Xan and Theo had a sickly gray hue to their faces. A new wall had replaced the space behind them, resembling the one in front of them, convincing him to urge their retreat.

He had first thought that rough edges and stones covered the walls. Looking closer, he saw the black beady eyes of fish. Stonefish. The fish were lining the walls to their front and back. Their murky yellowish green colors looked bland against the bright green plants to their sides, but those eyes bore right through him. The venom of one stonefish could kill them all.

"There must be thousands," Sirena whispered in his ear.

All he could do was nod slightly to not make a large enough movement to wake the fish.

Sirena pointed down and looked at him, then looked at Xan and Theo and motioned downward again. The mermaids trapped in the middle looked pitiful, their dread highlighting every inch of their faces. He might have enjoyed the sickly white that Orinn had turned had he not been so terrified himself. Holding his breath, he forced his body to sink lower as Sirena had already descended and was lightly pulling on him to follow her.

Slowly they sank, inch by inch. He knew he was holding his breath and his lungs ached, but his gills felt plastered to his neck. Quick breaths were all that he could manage. Sirena had dimmed her light to a subtle glow. He didn't know if stonefish could see light, but he much preferred not being able to see them.

Something brushed up against the arm not linked with Sirena's and he pulled away and into Sirena. Her eyes wide, she aimed a glowing hand towards his side to see what had caused him to retract in fear. Neo kept his gaze on her and when she pulled him closer, he felt that ice cold fear run through him again.

He heard Catalina whisper "El canal de las pesadillas," to Sirena.

Nova translated for him.

The Channel of Nightmares.

Any space that they had between them was gone. The pod was tight to one another to avoid touching the rocks to their sides. Curiosity got the best of him and Neo looked to his right to see what had scraped his arm. Regret filled him as he saw isopods skittering up and down the rocks and ledges that were once covered in beautiful plants. He held his breath again as one, presumably the one that had touched him, stood on a pair of its hind-legs and wriggled its body in the air. Spiky, dark brown legs waved at him while its antennas angled toward his face. Neo was an average length merman, perhaps about three meters, and he estimated the isopod to be about half of his length. If it wanted them dead, there would be no way he could stop it. There wasn't enough space for them to move away, and they'd only move into more isopods.

The isopod's mouth opened and closed while its feelers reached out, looking for something to grab onto. He would prefer he not be that something. Sirena jerked his arm suddenly, pushing him behind her. She had pulled Kassia up towards her now.

Scanning the pod, he saw the Sirens were forming a circle around Nova, Catalina, and himself. He felt a bit of resentment for a moment. He may not be a Siren, but he had *some* magic.

The isopod let out a shrill shriek and reared further, preparing to launch.

Sirena shot magic into the isopod that had been reaching for his face and it disintegrated in front of them. Okay, he thought, I don't have that kind of magic. Looking pleased, she turned to look at the group with a stern look. The rest of the Sirens raised their hands and pushed the pod closer together.

Neo felt the rocks rumble around them as the isopods scurried and scampered around the ledges. He closed his eyes for a second, hoping that they were retreating. When he opened them, Sirena was sending frantic streams of magic at the quickly encroaching creatures. Within seconds, the Sirens in the pod were firing.

Chapter 16

Sirena

If she had to pick a creature that she hated more than the multiple headed squid she had found in the Midnight Zone her first week there, it would probably be isopods. The clicking of their feelers and the scratching of their legs sent shivers down her back and covered her arms in bumps. Between the stonefish and the isopods, she'd had enough creepy crawlies for a lifetime.

She had shoved Neo behind her when an isopod had lunged for him. Morgens had some magic, but she did not know what he was actually capable of. Leander could move objects without twitching one of his giant arms, but she did not know what the others could do.

Kassia was rapidly firing next to her. She could hear the squeals from the isopods as they crumbled and fell to whatever was waiting for them below. She risked a brief glance at Xan, to her right, and saw that he was also dropping isopods. As she blasted the creatures in front of her, nothing but dust remained. What the shell had been in that wall? She could still feel it coursing through her.

Nova and Neo were at her back and she instinctively opened her arms wider to shield Nova as an isopod came storming towards them. She felt bubbles hit her neck as Nova let out a relieved breath. Movement in her peripheral caught her eye, and she turned to see the wall of stonefish awakening and preparing an attack.

Left with no other options but to yell over the sounds of Siren magic, she shouted to Xan and Theo, "The fish, they're moving!"

Xan turned one hand to the wall and started shooting, but Theo was a second late. As she and Kassia fought off the wall in front of them, Sirena heard shouting from behind her.

"What's happening?" her voice was shrill and unrecognizable, even to herself.

When no one answered, she repeated herself.

With unusual calmness, Xan uttered, "Something struck Theo."

Sirena felt movement in the pod behind her and heard muffled voices.

"Orinn, help Theo," she commanded.

"Can't."

Kassia screamed, "Orinn, that was an order!"

Orinn didn't respond and remained focused on what was in front of her. Sirena felt anger swell in her chest. Orinn had only the isopods in front of her. The rest of the Sirens were managing a wall and rock ledges.

"We've got him," Neo reported, and Sirena felt Nova's body shift against her as she took some of Theo's weight in her arms.

"Theo?" she asked. A low grunt followed, and Sirena felt her heart lift. He was alive, at least.

"How long are we going to do this for?" Kassia asked, her voice tense.

"Not much longer," Xan said. He was holding the rear of the pod alone, and Sirena could feel anxiety emanating off of him.

"Kassia, cover the front wall. Xan, cover the far wall," Sirena ordered as she pulled Kassia in front of her. Lifting a hand to each side of her, she sprayed her beams over the side of each rock wall. Glaring at Orinn, she tail-flipped Orinn in front of her, directing her to move up front by Kassia. With Neo and Nova holding Theo between the two of them and Xan holding the back of the pod, she felt more confident in their position.

She closed her eyes and pushed her magic from her core through to the tips of her fingers, hands burning from the sudden rush of energy. "We're going to drop on my command," she said.

"Drop?" Orinn shouted at her.

"Yes, on my command. Drop as fast as you can."

"Are we doing this on a count or…?" Neo asked.

She inhaled sharply in frustration. "No, drop…. Drop *now*," Sirena screamed as the stonefish had closed in on Kassia.

Orinn had stopped firing for a moment, regaining energy, but Kassia, Xan and Sirena held strong as they dropped hundreds of meters in mere seconds. She could feel the water rushing over her and through her hair and fins as they fell deeper and deeper into the Abyss. Nova and Neo were dropping faster than she was with Theo's weight, pulling them down. Sirena pulled her fin up as tight as she could to her and pushed herself down as hard as she could to catch up. Kassia followed suit and Orinn was about a meter behind them.

The isopods and stonefish continued to swarm them and Sirena could see that Kassia and Orinn were tiring, their streams of magic growing lighter. She knew Xan could last longer. He had trained extensively and knew how to conserve his energy. But for how long? How long was this channel? She pushed harder downwards and tried to count the seconds.

They dropped for a minute.

Two minutes.

Kassia targeted her magic streams at the closest approaching stonefish and isopods, no longer sending out constant beams of deflection.

Nova let out a small yelp as her body came into contact with the ground. She felt Neo fumble with Theo's motionless frame. The channel was now above them, and there was a large opening in front of her. Their predators were crawling up the channel, waiting for their next target.

"Towards the opening," Sirena ordered, and the pod moved towards an enormous cavern off from the channel.

Neo and Nova were setting Theo down on the ground as Sirena turned around to face him. She took a deep breath through her gills, grateful for the open space away from the walls and creatures.

She shined her light over him, assessing the damage. A stonefish had slipped through and took a sizeable chunk out of his abdomen below his chest cavity. A quick look told her that his organs were there and intact, but the wound was a deep, long gash across his torso. Neo floated at her side and placed his hands over the wounds.

Sirena looked at him, but before she could ask what he was doing, he answered her thoughts. "I have limited magic, but I can heal. Save your energy and let me help."

Sirena nodded, fully capable of healing Theo herself but allowing Neo to take the lead. She sat on her fin and watched as Theo's chest and stomach mended together. Grabbing his hand and holding her other illuminated hand over him so Neo could see, she waited.

"You're going to be fine. Hang on. You're almost there," Xan was in his brother's face, reassuring him.

Theo's face was a pale gray, and the pain in his eyes was unbearable. Sirena watched as Neo closed up the last open stretch of the gash and paused a minute longer. Her heart broke as she watched the brothers talk in whispers to each other. Xan reassured Theo everything was going to be alright and Theo told his brother that he loved him. She broke her gaze from their conversation to check on Neo's progress.

"Something's not right, Sirena," Neo panicked.

"What do you mean?"

Theo was still shaking, and Sirena inspected his abdomen, seeing Neo's source of panic. Red swirling circles had formed where the wound had been. She moved her hand closer, illuminating Theo's abdomen. A gasp nearly strangled her as she identified the req squiggles that were crawling across his stomach.

Sirena had never seen this before. Bloodworms had infected him. The creatures were crawling under and through his skin, weaving themselves around his ribs and through his navel. No thicker than a blade of thin grass. No eyes, no ends. The red mess of worms was stretching across his stomach and chest, expanding towards his limbs.

Sirena threw her hands over him and tried to heal Theo, hoping her magic was stronger and could rid the worms. She could hear Xan's voice telling Theo they had healed him. If he looked down now, he'd see his brother's condition was much worse. The worms slowed their wiggling and swirling through Theo's skin, but they didn't stop completely. Nor did they disappear.

"Come on, come on…" Sirena whispered to herself in desperation. She continued to throw her energy towards the worms, only to watch them wave at her slowly, as if they were giving her the middle finger.

Out of desperation, she reached to grab one to pull it loose, and it recoiled from her grasp. She couldn't grab it; it was too quick. The second and third worms she chased did the same.

Sirena closed her eyes and took a deep breath, focusing her attention on the worms tormenting her friend. She tried to reverse her magic like she had done with the wall. If she couldn't heal them, maybe she could wrench them out of him.

After a moment, she opened her eyes and found the worms were still there but they had stopped moving and spreading. They laid quiet, some underneath the surface of his skin, others frozen in their movements above his skin. Sirena studied the creatures for a moment and determined it was one long worm. No end in sight.

She turned her attention to Theo's face to see if she had done anything to quiet his discomfort.

Theo met her gaze as she took a deep breath and prepared herself to give him the good and bad news. "The wound healed, Theo. You were infected with bloodworms, though. I can't get rid of them. I froze them but…" she trailed off.

Theo grabbed her arm and nodded. "I know. I felt the movement stop. It's better. Not great, but better."

"Can you sit up?" she asked.

He groaned as Xan helped him into a sitting position. Theo looked down at the red worm hanging out of his chest and abdomen. He raised a hand to touch them and hesitated.

"I don't think you want to do that." Xan did nothing to hide the look of horror and disgust that crossed his face.

Theo seemed to agree and dropped his hand. His voice halted in his throat for a minute as he tried to speak.

"Take your time. We seem to be safe for the moment." Sirena surveyed their surroundings.

Cat and Nova were on the other side of Theo, from where she and Neo sat. Kassia was next to Xan, helping support his sitting position. Orinn circled around, scrutinizing their location, which seemed to be a large room with several hallways stemming in different directions. Focusing her attention on Theo, Sirena squeezed his hand, trying to comfort him.

"I don't think I can swim," Theo said with defeat. "The pain is still there, but it doesn't feel like it's ripping me in half anymore."

His voice was labored, and while he wasn't that sickly gray any longer, he still looked quite unwell. His shoulder length hair floated behind him, exposing his neck, and Sirena could see his jaw was tight and his neck tensed. He tightened his grasp on her hand as he leaned into Kassia and Xan, unable to stay upright on his own.

"What are we going to do with him, Queen?" Orinn's voice came from behind her. Taunting her.

"What do you mean? What are we going to do with him?" Sirena snapped angrily. Orinn's tone of voice set her off.

"We can't take him with us like this," Orinn's voice had resumed its usual coldness.

"Yes, we fucking can." Xan's rage matched Sirena's.

"This is another mission. We don't leave anyone behind. Everyone comes home," Sirena stated, reciting the first rule Theo had ever told her. He squeezed her hand again as he recognized her, repeating his instructions.

"I can carry him," Neo joined the conversation again. "Nova and Cat, can you help?"

"Yes, of course," Nova was nodding her head emphatically. Catalina echoed Nova's words.

"Then it's settled. Nova, Cat and Neo can help Theo get through whatever this is." Sirena gestured to the hallways that lie before them.

"Kassia and Orinn, you bring up the rear of the pod this time. Xan, you're up front with me. We have to decide where we go from here."

Sirena scrunched her face a bit, trying to think through their next movements. She looked at the four hallways. The one that they had come from was to her right, leaving three more to choose from.

Orinn sighed and moved towards the closest hallway. She motioned to a spot on the wall. "The Channel of Nightmares," she said flatly.

"What? It really says that? No way…" Kassia floated over to the wall and looked down at the engraving. "Sure shell. It does!"

"I wasn't serious when I said that!" Cat paused for a moment, shock spreading across her face. "Then what was that?" Catalina pointed to the hallway that they had come out of.

"Uh, Tunnel of Terror?" Neo shrugged.

Xan let out a sharp laugh. Sirena fought a nervous laugh herself. She was still holding Theo's hand, and she felt him relax some.

"The Mami Wata weren't trying to keep out merfolk, I don't think. They made it difficult for anyone to get to them, so maybe that sign is a strange sort of peace offering to us? They heard us and know we're here?" Neo said, more to himself than to anyone else.

"What makes you think they weren't trying to keep us out? Because that all seems very 'stay out, we don't want you here' to me," Kassia said sarcastically.

"It's what my mom told me when she had talked to me about where we came from. I guess I never asked why. I was a pup. Sorry," Neo's sorry matched Kassia's sarcasm.

Sirena looked down at Theo. They had to keep moving if he had a chance of making it out of here. "It doesn't matter if they were trying to keep us out or not. We need to keep moving because they are trying to keep us out. Find the Mami Wata, find their leader, and get out."

She motioned for Neo to lift Theo, giving Theo's hand one last squeeze and resting the other on his shoulder. Their eyes met, and he tilted his head slightly and managed a small smile, telling her he would live.

Sirena could see Theo swallow sharply as Neo helped lift him off the ground, slinging an arm around Neo's shoulders and slinging the other around Nova's. She caught Nova staring down at the vile red worm hanging out of their friend. Nova looked up at Sirena and winced. Worry covered every inch of her face. Sirena tried to give her a reassuring look, but she was sure it looked more like a grimace than anything comforting.

"Are you going to make it?" Xan asked his brother.

Theo nodded a yes, but his face was that sickly gray again. Sirena felt Kassia bristle at her side when she looked at Theo. They were all realizing the gravity of his situation. How long were they expected to travel through this maze of terrors?

"Let's get moving," Sirena pointed towards the channel opening.

Sirena lit the way again, hands raised in front of her, lighting the path several meters in front of the group. The channel was wider than the tunnel had been, but where the tunnel had grass and plants; the channel was nothing but large, dark rocks. She looked at the ground underneath her and saw that it was thick, black clay. If she didn't know better, she'd say they were in the trenches, the absolute lowest layer of the oceans. They wouldn't be able to survive there for long though, so she brushed the thought from her head and kept moving.

The quiet calm of the channel was oddly peaceful. However, she felt her senses heightened as she waited for something to attack and or make their journey more difficult. As the seconds turned into minutes, Sirena felt her mind wandering.

Neo's comments about favoritism bounced around in her thoughts. Sirena had often felt that her parents played favorites, her mother more so, but sometimes even the loving Asterios had seemed to favor his older children over Sirena. She didn't doubt that her mother loved her. Malee always said so and had given Sirena no reason to think otherwise, but their relationship was not like the one Malee and Maia shared. When Sirena had been younger and fought for her mother's attention, she was told that Maia was the future Queen and Sirena needed to understand that her mother's focus was on preparing her sister. It was an explanation she had accepted.

Without Apollo and his friends, she would not have gone on rescue missions and when she thought about the training that Asterios had given her versus the time Theo and Xan spent preparing her, it was embarrassing. If her friends wouldn't have helped her, would Asterios let her get herself killed or, worse, put the others in danger?

Her parents didn't include her in the responsibilities of the royal family. She didn't know even half of the other council leaders; she hadn't even met Neo, and he was an advisor and council member. They left her wildly unprepared for the situation she found herself in. She was responsible for the merpeople and she didn't even know much about the council members or why the Mami Wata allowed to disappear. When the Ningyo had tried to remove themselves from rescue missions, Malee had refused. But the Mami Wata, who were actual sea witches with curses and the ability to protect the merpeople, could hide. She'd love to know what the Mami Wata were capable of and why they hadn't enchanted the oceans to protect the rest of the merpeople.

And Maia, voting to skip bloodlines and hand off the Morgen territory to a member of the council rather than the next relative. Why?

She felt alone and angry, yet desperate for her family at the same time. Anger with them and she rattled her and that feeling of despair set in again. No direction, no idea how to get her pod and her people out of the situation they were in, and yet, everyone wanted an answer. If they could stop looking at her like she had all the answers. If they could stop looking at her with *hope*.

Xan paused next to her, dragging her sluggishly from her thoughts.

Sirena looked around the small channel, not seeing anything out of the ordinary. Xan's face had gone white, and he froze in place.

"What do you see?" Sirena whispered.

His body shook, but he didn't move. Sirena stared at the space in front of them, trying to brighten her light to see what had stopped Xan. Still nothing. The rest of the pod had stopped behind them.

Theo, hanging off of Nova and Neo's shoulders, lifted his head slightly, but was growing more lethargic by the minute. Panic rose in her chest.

"We have to keep going. We need to get out of here for all of our sake, but especially for Theo's," she directed her gaze over her shoulder at Theo.

Xan didn't acknowledge her, but he started moving when she did. They crawled through the channel. Sirena was certain that sea snails moved faster than what they were. She tried to hide her impatience and kept moving, picking up her speed and hoping the rest of the pod would move quicker.

A gasp behind her halted the pod again, and Sirena whipped around to see what was happening behind them. This time, she found Kassia cowering on the floor of the trenches.

Hands over her eyes and curled into a ball, she was quivering. The channel wasn't big enough for Sirena to get past the three merfolk in the middle of the pod, so she took to looking over Nova's shoulder to see what had dropped Kassia to her fins.

Again, Sirena saw nothing. Raising her illuminated hands higher, she scoured the trench floors and the space behind Kassia and Orinn.

"What is it?" Sirena called out.

Orinn was simply floating in place, watching the shaking Kassia. Kassia muttered something through her hands, but Sirena couldn't understand her.

"She said 'they're everywhere'," Orinn said, unamused.

"What's everywhere?" Sirena asked.

Kassia looked up through her hands and said between sobs, "Humans."

"Humans?" Sirena couldn't help it but she let out a surprised laugh. "Kassia, they would never survive down here. We're in the Abyss and potentially even in the trenches, by the looks of it. I don't think there are humans down here."

Kassia continued to shake and cry until Orinn hauled her up by the arm. "Open your eyes and look around. There aren't humans down here."

Her eyes opened wide. Kassia appeared as though she had woken up. Her gills flapped open wide as she took in a large breath and blew it out of her mouth. The violent shaking had subsided, but Kassia was still shivering.

"What was it, Kassia?" Catalina asked softly.

"I…I was on the surface. One moment I was here with all of you and then the next I was on the surface and there were humans everywhere. I couldn't get underwater and…" Kassia stopped and took in another deep breath. "It's a nightmare that I have on and off. More regularly these days."

Catalina slung an arm around her friend and tried to comfort her.

Orinn had dropped the harsh look on her face, but her lack of emotion remained. "We're in the channel of nightmares. It appears you are all going to see your worst nightmares. They aren't real. They're illusions," Orinn said.

"That would have been helpful to know before we got here," Sirena said angrily. She was tired of Orinn withholding information, and even more tired of her judgmental behavior.

"I knew nothing about the channel, and know nothing about any of this. Based on what Kassia saw and Xan's ghost face, my best guess is that it's the Channel of Nightmares. The sign at the entrance of this channel seems to be a product of Catalina's doing. Neo might be right about the wards hearing us," Orinn said, sounding bored.

Neo shifted uncomfortably under Theo's weight, and Catalina looked down at the trenches. Feeling her anger rise again, Sirena swallowed and took a breath in. "Xan," she said, "did you see something too? A past nightmare of yours?"

"Yes," quiet and without further information, Xan replied.

"We know that whatever we're seeing isn't real, so unless you physically can't move, we have to keep going," Sirena left words unspoken, but they all knew. They needed to get out of this channel soon.

She surveyed the group and received acknowledgement they needed to keep moving. Xan linked his arm through hers. She looked down and felt her heart flutter quickly for a beat or two. Pushing aside the split-second moment of excitement, Sirena led the group forward again.

***

Sirena could feel herself growing impatient. They had been swimming for hours in the channel. Every member of her pod had paused briefly at one point, fear striking them. Despite her instructions, the pod members had to stop for several minutes each time nightmares struck them. She had thought Theo was dead when the affliction hit him, and she screamed and shook him until he snapped awake.

She thought she had lucked out and would not experience the same terrors as the rest when she felt Xan's arm disappear from hers. Sirena had looked to her side to see that Xan was missing, as well as the rest of the pod.

She was alone in the channel. Alone with her thoughts, fears and insecurities. The pressure of the water changed around her, and she felt like the channel was closing in on her. Her tail dragged in the black sludge of the trench and she reached her arms out. When she had reached out her arms to push the closing walls away from her, she had discovered that the walls were meters away.

Sirena had sunk down to the trench floor while the channel had disappeared, leaving her in the dark, empty, and cold waters. She was alone and small, out in the open. Panic hadn't hit her, though. Oddly enough, she had felt a moment of peace. Sirena had simply sat in the trench, her tail curled under her, staring into the dark water and waiting for the nightmare to pass. It hadn't felt like a nightmare and when she regained consciousness in the channel, her friends staring at her, she longed for the calm of that trench again.

With Xan's arm through hers, she focused on leading them through the channel and getting everyone out on the other side alive. Whatever the other side was, she hoped it was soon.

Traveling for hours in the dark with her friends and herself having waking nightmares was getting exhausting.

Xan stopped suddenly and pushed her behind him, causing her to stop projecting light through the channel. She found she didn't need light to see what was in front of them. They had made it to a large, beautiful room. In the room's front sat a stone throne and in it, the leader of the Mami Wata.

Chapter 17

Sirena

The vast space was larger than the throne room in the Siren's original territory. The Sirens had arranged sculptures and decorated their throne room, but it had never looked like this. Sirena took in the high stone walls and the ornate carvings of merfolk. Pillars lined the outer edge of the room, built into the walls. She looked up to see the pillars reached an extraordinarily high ceiling covered in bright colored coral. The throne room of the Mami Wata looked as though it belonged on the surface. Sirena had to remind herself that this was all an illusion, a product of the curses of sea witches.

She had stopped, paused completely to take in her surroundings, but the Mami Wata hadn't stopped their doings. Merfolk flitted around the room, talking and going about their days. Only their leader had taken notice of their arrival. She sat, unmoving, staring at them.

Xan bent down to whisper in her ear, "She saw us."

Before she could snap at him with a snarky comment, the leader merely waved them over. Quietly and subtly, she beckoned them. That cold fear ran through her again, and she could feel her stomach flip. Theo made a low rumbling noise behind her, and she instantly started moving. Her fear of this unknown sea witch was insignificant compared to the fear she had of losing her friend.

"Forget the Rusalka and the rest of the merfolk. I have everything I need right here," Kassia muttered in Sirena's ear. Sirena looked to see that Kassia had switched places with Nova and was helping Neo drag the injured Theo through the channel.

Sirena shot her a warning look and Kassia smirked and tucked herself in under Theo's arm, winking at Sirena. Brushing her off, Sirena slowly led her pod around the outer edge of the room and towards the throne. Mami Wata were taking notice of them, some stopping and staring at them while others looked horrified. If they had truly been down here since the start of the wars, she wondered if any of them had seen other merfolk since then. Surely no others had ventured down this far.

"You broke my wall," the voice was flat and disinterested.

Sirena blinked a few times before responding, "I'm sorry about that."

"You left us no other choice. We needed to speak with you." Orinn had floated her way up to Sirena's side.

"Orinn?" the leader of the Mami Wata asked.

"Bia."

"You look old," Bia replied.

"So do you."

"No, I don't. We don't age like the rest of you," Bia was giving a grin that left Sirena uneasy.

"With the spells and magic you cast around so freely; I'd hope not. I'd use it to keep my youth too," Orinn said, gesturing to the elaborate spells that had made the throne room quite the spectacle.

"Why are you here?" Bia asked.

Before Orinn could speak, Sirena interjected. "Your stonefish injured one of my pod members. I'd like you to undo whatever this is that has left a bloodworm invading his body." Sirena tried to speak with authority, but her voice came out high pitched and panicked. She took a deep breath.

Bia eyed Theo up and down and nodded, but didn't speak.

"Well?" Sirena asked.

"You're a Siren with loads of magic. Cure him."

Sirena paused and released a small huff; she was offended. Did she really think she hadn't tried that yet?
"I said, cure him." Bia's eyes bore a hole in Sirena.

Sirena stared at the leader of the Mami Wata, matching her intensity. Bia was a short and round mermaid with a dark gray tail. Her tail was as elaborate as the walls of her throne room. Black and silver glittering swirls accented the dark gray tail, covering nearly every inch of her. When Bia shifted on her throne, Sirena noted that her gray tail had a purple iridescence to it. Her arms had the same swirling decorations as her tail. Bia had beautifully accented her black hair and skin with jewelry in the vibrant colors of the plants and coral she had decorated her throne room with. If she hadn't been so afraid of her, Sirena would have been in awe of her beauty.

"I tried. I couldn't help him." Sirena felt guilt wash over her.

"Try… again…," Bia spoke slowly.

When Sirena hesitated again, Bia shouted at her, catching her off guard. "Child! You don't have all day."

Neo and Kassia had laid Theo on the floor. Neo had resumed his place in the pod, but Kassia had sat on the ground and placed Theo's head in her lap. Sirena, lost in her own thoughts, hadn't checked in on Theo for a few hours and noticed he had taken a turn for the worse. The worm was moving again, and this time it had spread. Thin red lines covered his arms.

Sirena hovered over him; her hands outstretched. She let her magic tingle at her fingertips, unsure of what she should do. Did she try to power them out of him, try to draw them out, or was there another option? Theo groaned, and she decided that anything was better than nothing. Her power trickled out of her in soft gold strings, wrapping themselves around the tangles of the worm hanging out of Theo's abdomen. She watched in shock at her own power, slowly pulling on the worm and dissolving it piece by piece.

Sirena was certain she had no control over this and let her magic take care of the rest of the bloodworm. Theo coughed as the worm in his chest and presumably his lungs disintegrated. His gills moved more freely and his color returned to normal. The worm was no longer visible, but Sirena let her power drip longer, ensuring every bit of that bloodworm was gone. Theo sat up, and Kassia threw her arms around him. The rest of the pod watched as Sirena backed away, once again finding herself staring at her own hands.

"Was that so hard, child?" Bia asked her.

"I couldn't do that before. I could only stop it from spreading. What did you do?"

"I did nothing," Bia said. The side of her mouth, upturned with the hint of a smile.

Sirena pushed her frustration aside. Theo was fine, and she was quickly adding new magic skills. She'd figure out how to use them all later. The Rusalka had been so far from her mind the last day or so as they fought through the wards but they moved to front and center in her thoughts.

"The Rusalka are free. They've left their territory. They killed my sister and took my brother."

"Ah, is that why we have the tiniest Siren here?"

"Until we find Apollo, I'm the last of the royal Sirens."

Sirena found herself pleased at the shock that flashed across Bia's face. She didn't know that Malee was gone.

"Malee?" Bia exhaled the word.

"Gone. About a month. Humans killed her during a rescue mission. Maia was the Queen for three weeks before the Rusalka broke loose and killed her," Sirena felt herself squinting ever so slightly at Bia. The look Bia gave her when Sirena had said that Malee was gone was confusing.

"And you are?"

"Sirena, the youngest of Malee and Asterios' children."

"No."

Sirena squinted her eyes at her. "No?"

"Sirena isn't your name. Malee did not call her daughter Siren."

Neo snorted with stifled laughter, and she felt Xan fight his own laugh. She rolled her eyes.

"Alcina. Alcie, if you must call me by my real name."

"Ah," Bia nodded knowingly. "If you knew what your name meant, you wouldn't be calling yourself Sirena."

"It means strong-willed."

"Yes, it does, but you're missing half of it. Alcina means strong-willed sorceress and a master ruler of magic."

Sirena stared at the leader of the Mami Wata, unsure of what she had heard.

"Ooohhh, this explains the wall…" Kassia sang.

"I got that," Sirena said to her friend without turning around.

"I'm calling you Alcie from now on," Neo chimed in.

"No one is calling me anything but Sirena," Sirena felt annoyance rising within her.

"What are you here for?" Bia interrupted the pod's banter.

"I told you, the Rusalka are free from their territory." Sirena did nothing to hide her impatience.

"And that has what to do with me? You tore down my wall and riled up my pets because the ghosts are loose?"

If Sirena didn't know better, she would interpret Bia's expression as impressed, or maybe amused? She couldn't read the sea witch's expressions.

"My mother was a Mami Wata, and she told me you helped the Sirens with the curse that kept the Rusalka in their territory," Neo said.

"We had to drop into the Midnight Zone when Maia became the Queen. The humans are still after us and we have the Rusalka chasing us. We need your help to reinstate the curse," Sirena added.

"No."

Sirena sighed and asked, "No?"

"No. I'm not leaving here to go up to the Twilight Zone, where there are still humans hunting merfolk, to put a curse on the Rusalka."

For a moment, Sirena thought she might cry. She had not dragged her pod through stonefish and isopods and their worst nightmares to be told no. Not by the leader that had abandoned the merpeople when they had needed spells and curses the most. This throne room only proved how absolutely absurd it was that they could hide down here while their enemies bought and traded the rest of the merpeople.

"No? No? I am your Queen and that will not work with me. I don't know what arrangements you had with my parents, but they're both dead and so are those arrangements. The number of enchantments down here is insane. You mean to tell me you couldn't have saved the merfolk with a few enchantments? Instead, you hid and left us all to die so it's time for you to do your part and get your fin up to the rest of the world and put the Rusalka where they belong," Sirena's words spilled out of her and she could feel the rage percolating in her fingertips. She clenched her fists. She couldn't shoot daggers at Bia and leave alive.

"Go get her!" Kassia squealed.

Catalina thumped her hard on the shoulder, cheering.

"My child, you know not who you speak to."

"Oh, I know very well who I'm speaking to. The coward of the Mami Wata."

Sirena heard a few gasps behind her, but she didn't back down. Bia would not best her, not after the trip they'd survived.

Bia readjusted her position on her elaborate throne and held Sirena's fiery gaze. She could feel her friends twitching and shifting, uncomfortable with the tension between the two leaders. The other Mami Wata in the room stopped their movements a while ago and were all frozen in place, holding their breaths as their leader spoke with the new Queen.

After several moments, Bia softened her gaze.

"I won't go with you, but I can tell you what you need to do. You might have the magic to enact a curse. I'm not sure." Bia waved her hand dismissively.

"No," Sirena held firm.

"Unless you're going to physically carry me out of here, this is your only option."

Sirena raised her hands, prepared to see whatever new magic might come out of her this time.

"Put your hands down, child. You will do nothing to me with that Siren magic. The only reason the Sirens are the rulers of the wide, great seas is because you were here first, not because you're the strongest."

Sirena's heart filled with rage again. They could have prevented the wars. All the needless deaths because of the Mami Wata.

"Seems you did alright down here. Not being the ruler seems to have worked out for all of you. Down here, living in splendor while we fight to live every day," Sirena's anger was burning through her again.

"How presumptuous of you. You think we choose to stay here?" Bia's words hung in the water.

Sirena let the words linger for a moment before she asked, "What do you mean?"

"I'll give you the curse. Recite it in the Rusalka territory and hope for the best. Maybe have the crossbreed try it. Maybe his mother's side is stronger." Bia motioned to Neo.

Neo growled at being called a crossbreed, but said nothing.

"You didn't answer my question," Sirena stated.

"You should position yourself in the center of the Rusalka territory. The curse binds their souls to a radius around you. If you go to the edge of their territory, I can't promise that it won't extend the territory. I don't know, honestly. It might re-bind them to the current territory or it may extend it or move it to wherever you cast the curse."

"Why do you think it's possible that I might use the curse?" Sirena asked.

"Where do you think Mami Wata got their magic from? Where does our power of spells and curses come from? Orinn, have you not told her anything?" Bia turned to Orinn.

Orinn shrugged, but the look on her face gave Sirena the feeling that Orinn might not know this story.

Sighing, Bia explained, "The first Siren was the most powerful there ever was. She was a goddess. The powers that you see in the different clans come from her. As our species grew, we distributed our powers. You Sirens took her song and energy. We got her spells and enchantments."

"Did you know Atargatis?" Sirena asked.

"Ha! How old do you think I am, child? I may be old, but I'm not that old," Bia laughed at her.

"That still doesn't answer my question, Bia," Sirena used her name for the first time.

Bia gave her a menacing smile and leaned forward on her throne. "Child, your name means strong-willed sorceress. You are the ruler of all magic. I can see it in your eyes. No one, Siren or not, should have made it through my enchantments."

Kassia let out a whistle, breaking through the tension between the two mermaids.

"You really wanted to keep out the merfolk?" Neo asked.

"I set up the wards specifically to keep out the merfolk," Bia snapped at Neo.

Sirena didn't want to spend another second here. They were getting nowhere with Bia, and she had more questions than answers.

"Give me the curse. Tell me how to use it."

Bia flipped a coin at her fin. Sirena didn't bend down to pick it up. She hadn't seen where it had come from.

"The curse is on that coin. Recite it in the center of the Rusalka territory and leave me and my mers alone."

"Why did you say that I was being presumptuous?" Sirena asked for the third time.

"You got your curse, and that's all that you'll get out of me. Go."

Xan picked up the coin and handed it to Sirena. She tucked it into her top and stared at Bia for a moment longer.

"I expect a clear path with no wards on our way out," Sirena said coolly.

Bia waved her hand again and pointed to an opening in the rock room to the right.

Sirena turned around before leaving the room to look at Bia one last time. She might have been mistaken, but she was certain Bia was looking at her with admiration. Or was it hope?

Chapter 18

Alanna

Alanna looked over at her sister as they swam towards the Siren's territory. They had sunk to the bottom of the Twilight Zone and she was cold. When she thought about the situation that they had found themselves in, she grew more frustrated with Orla and the rest of the Merrows that still insisted on chasing after humans.

She remembered the last words Malee had said to her when she exiled the Merrows all those years ago.

"Keep your merpeople away from the rest of us, Alanna. We are done with your clan."

Alanna would have given anything at that moment to turn on the Merrows and join the Sirens. The words had been on the tip of her tongue. She had held back, though, unable to verbalize her thoughts.

Regret filled her every day. Not for what the Merrows had done. She didn't feel responsible for any of that. Regret for not being able to vocalize her disgust at her people. Alanna regretted her failure to disown the Merrows that day and refused Malee's order to rule.

Anger flooded through her as she looked over at her sister, swimming peacefully next to her. Alanna let her tail turn black and felt her hair itching to turn its natural dark color. After a moment, she gave in, her black locks flowing behind her.

Chapter 19

Sirena

Bia's words were still ringing in her ears. *How presumptuous of you to think that we stayed willingly.* Was that not the story? That the Mami Wata had fled at the first sign of a human attack, warded themselves and refused to contribute to the rescue efforts?

She had tried to ask Orinn shortly after leaving the Mami Wata territory, but she had brushed Sirena off, mumbling something about never believing the words of a sea witch. Part of her had to agree with Orinn. It had seemed odd to her that her parents would have let the Mami Wata abandon the rest of the merpeople when they needed magic and enchantments the most, but…the thought of them forcing the Mami Wata into exile. That seemed even more unbelievable.

Ruler of all magic. Her. Sirena. Alcina. She had thought little of her birth name ever, really. She had received an 'A' name like her father. Like Apollo. Maia received her name after their mother because she was the next in line. She had never thought much of it and had never asked what her name meant. Her parents must have known, though. They must have known about her magic.

Sirena felt a mix of hurt, anger, confusion, and offense because her parents never helped her with her power. Here she was in the middle of a war, with Rusalka roaming free, ruler of all magic without a damned clue about how to heal her friend or take down enchantments. If she had known how to use her power, she could have prevented Theo's injury. Images of the large, ugly gashes across the front of her friend's body replayed in her head. The bloodworm protruding from his skin, winding itself through his flesh and organs. She gagged at the thought of it.

Most of the pod was resting, huddled together in a cave outside of the Mami Wata territory. Although Theo healed, the ordeal had exhausted him. When they had finally made their way out of tunnels and trenches and out to the open water, half of her pod had collapsed onto a ledge. Judging by the hunger pangs she felt and her own fatigue, she had guessed that they had spent two days in the Mami Wata territory. Mers could go days without sleep or food, but they still experienced weakness when they didn't rest or eat. It was going to be at least a full day before Theo was ready to continue.

Sirena stared at the edge of the Mami Wata territory. They had risen to the bottom of the Midnight Zone and were looking down onto where the ocean transitioned into the Abyss. The water rippled differently around the sea witches' territory. Bia had wasted no time putting her wall back up. What she had missed when they first approached the wall was blatantly obvious to her.

The wall had been invisible, of course, but the scenery of dark water and ripples were the same scenes playing on repeat on the wall. A mere illusion so that it looked as though it was open water space. Where the strongest ripples were, that's where the hands reached out, looking for predators. The hands roamed around the territory, never resting.

How many days since she had actually rested? Since she had laughed and had talked with her pod about something other than the dark and cold, or about her mother's death? She tried to think back to Maia's death. They had left a few hours after Maia had floated by her cave, lifeless, and transferred the Siren power to her. It couldn't have been more than a week.

Xan floated in next to her, where she perched outside the cave.

"Theo's healthy, like nothing happened, but…" Xan trailed off.

Sirena didn't look up, but took a deep breath in. "I know. He's weak. We all are. I think we were down there for a few days. Time moves differently down there."

"I think it was four days," Xan replied.

Sirena's head snapped at him. "*Four*?"

"I'm guessing, of course," he shrugged.

"I thought two?"

"Maybe, but based on how weak we are…" Xan trailed off. She couldn't deny how tired he looked. He looked as though he had aged while they were in the Abyss. His normal, chiseled features look diminished. He had lost weight, she thought.

She sighed. "We spent a lot of energy in that tunnel. It took everything we had to keep the creatures at bay."

Xan tilted his head. He seemed to understand her point. He turned to her and quietly said, "What's happening with you? With your magic? I ran low towards the end, but you didn't show any signs of letting up."

"I don't know. I think it's the energy from the wall that I absorbed, maybe?" Sirena asked, but didn't expect him to have the answer. There wasn't anyone to help her understand what happened to her.

"But how did you absorb the wall in the first place?" he asked her.

"I don't know. I don't know if I could even do it again." Sirena looked down at her hands.

Xan nodded and then, "Do you feel any different? You said before you hoped that the feeling went away. Back when we were at the wall…"

Sirena had said that but, she wasn't sure if she had felt differently or if this anxious feeling would be her new normal. "I felt different, I think. Not sure. I felt energized, excited, maybe, when I pulled the energy out of the wall. Not like when the Siren power transferred to me, but I had a ton of energy. I don't know if it was adrenaline from taking down the wall and not knowing what was ahead of us."

"Hmm," Xan gave a thoughtful murmur, but didn't speak.

"I feel normal, I think. After that initial burst of Siren power, I felt normal again before the Rusalka attacked. I guess both were initial rushes of energy and then I felt fine shortly afterwards. I wish I knew how to turn on these new powers, but I don't. They both kind of happened. It's different from when we focus on our energy or when we heal. I don't know how to explain it. I feel anxious, though. Constantly."

Xan sighed. "This is all a mess. This whole situation."

Sirena's heart dropped. Xan knew this wouldn't end well, her being the Queen. She looked down at her hands as if they held the answers to this new power she wielded. "I'm so sorry," she muttered, tears forming in her eyes.

"No, that's not what I meant, Sirena. You know that," Xan spoke quickly, grabbing her arm and pulling her to face him. He leaned into her as he said, "This is not your fault. They have given you a colossal mess, a disaster. The council will not be of any help. Orinn is outright insubordinate to you and Leander. Well, he should be out here with us. He's a senior member of the council."

It took everything in Sirena not to swim away from him, from everyone. Xan's words fell on closed ears as her focus remained on him calling this a mess. Calling her a mess.

"Sirena, listen to me." He pulled on her chin, lifting her eyes to meet his. "I will keep saying it until you hear me. This is not your fault. But it is your problem. You have all the power in the oceans now. It's not fair, and it's not right, but this is your problem to fix. You need to remember, we're all here to help you," he waved towards the sleeping merfolk.

She shot him a look, and he backtracked a bit.

"Almost all of us are here to help you. Orinn is part of the problem." He looked at her intently, his voice firm.

Sirena maintained his intense eye contact, his dark eyes burning into her. For a moment, she hoped for more and leaned into his grasp. Xan didn't move.

"Thank you," she said finally.

Xan gave her a quick smile and dropped his hand from her face, his expression returning to one of thought. The sudden drop of his touch left her cold. He sat next to her for a few moments longer before moving to leave. Sirena's arm shot out from under her, grabbing his wrist and holding him in place for a moment longer. Xan made eye contact with her and then dropped his gaze to her hand, pulling him towards her.

"It's going to work out, Sirena. Get some rest." Xan pulled his arm free of her grasp and patted her on the shoulder before leaving her to her thoughts again.

She watched as he swam away from her. She tried not to see the sag in his shoulders as he left. The disappointment of the situation they had all found themselves in displayed itself in his body language as he swam away from her. Weeks ago, she took directions from Xan and Theo, still a novice on their rescue missions, and now they were taking orders from her. Her stomach twisted into knots as the reality of her rulership fluttered through her.

Movement in her peripheral caught her attention, and her head flipped to her right. Off in the distance, she could see a

Rusalka hovering. Or could it be swimming towards them? She felt the tingling starting in her fingertips as she went on the defensive. Squinting her eyes, she tried to see the direction it moved in.

Her gills flattened to her neck as she held her breath, frozen in place. Waiting. It took her a minute to see the Rusalka's figure getting smaller. It moved away from them and her gills relaxed. She drew in a long breath. Shaking, she surveyed the immediate area around them. There wasn't a sign of more, only cold, dark water.

Slowly, she made her way to where her pod had made themselves at home. Xan still awake and settling in next to Theo, kept a watchful eye over his brother. Orinn and Neo flanked the back sides of the ledge and Nova, Catalina, and Kassia were curled up next to each other. Sirena sank in between Nova and Catalina, curling up tightly between the two of them, careful not to wake them. She caught Xan watching her and thought about telling him about the Rusalka. Changing her mind as sleep weighed heavily on her, she laid her head on her arm and closed her eyes.

Chapter 20

Apollo

Flitting in and out of consciousness, Apollo tried to listen to the surrounding sounds during the moments that he was awake, but he found he couldn't concentrate. The ringing in his ears made his head pound. He finally gave into the darkness and let himself drift off to sleep.

Apollo's dreams ran wild, and he relived experiences he didn't want to remember.

The scenes from memories ran through his mind, projecting their images against the blackness of his eyelids. Asterios' death haunted him and Apollo tried to redirect his thoughts. He felt helpless against his unconsciousness.

He watched as the humans caught and speared his father through the heart. Apollo felt the spear pierce Asterios' heart as if it were his own and he felt the rage that had coursed through him that day. The rescue pod helplessly watched and eventually fled before anyone could catch them, but Apollo stayed long after the rest had left. Hidden and off in the distance, he had watched his father's captors and plotted his revenge. He didn't want to return to his mother without his father, but with limited options, revenge became his second-best outcome.

Apollo had followed them for miles, staying out of their sight until Theo had found him and forced him to return home. Wracked with guilt, Apollo struggled to control himself for the entire journey home. Unable to look at his mother, he had retreated to his room in their underwater Siren castle. Malee found him eventually and had assured him he wasn't to blame, but he had known then that his father's death and his inability to prevent it would forever haunt him.

Malee's death was distant in his memory despite only happening weeks ago. He hadn't been there. Maia and Sirena had been on that mission. His mother and sister rarely went on rescue and recovery missions. The Queen and future Queen, stayed behind and ruled over the council, working with the other clan leaders. However, frustrated at multiple failed missions and the Ningyo trying to remove themselves from the missions, Malee had decided they would take part. It had been an attempt to show Aiko why the Ningyo must stay within the mercouncil and it had dire consequences.

Maia had told him she had heard their mother sing a few notes, temporarily distracting the humans. When he had asked Sirena, she had confirmed that she did as well. Apollo felt a wave of jealousy that both of his sisters had heard their mother, the most powerful Siren in existence, use her song. Sirens hadn't sung since before the war started and he had never heard another Siren, let alone his own mother.

He didn't have a memory of how his mother had died, but his mind had improvised and he tried to push the thoughts away. Apollo attempted to calm his mind, but his thoughts wandered back to a few days earlier, when someone had forced him from their territory.

He heard Sirena's scream and saw the flash of lightning rip through the ocean. The cave where he dwelled wasn't far from Sirena's and he could see her shocked face and the Siren's power take hold of her.

Then the blackness had surrounded him.

He returned to those few moments before Sirena's scream. As he had laid there awake, there had been the feeling that he wasn't alone. The hair on his neck had stood up. His mind fully entrenched in the memory; he could feel himself in the cave. A cold sweat had broken out on his skin and he had looked around his small dwelling. He *had* been alone. But he hadn't felt alone.

Apollo looked to his left and right again in his cave. He turned and looked behind him, running his hands against the walls. When he turned to face the opening of the cave again, a shadowy figure floated in front of him. The figure's hair floated around them. Her. A mermaid.

He reached out to touch the mermaid, to push her through the opening. His mind went blank, and Apollo felt his body convulse with frustration. Trying to return to the memory, Apollo let himself drift off further into his subconscious.

His mind remained blank.

Apollo felt his heart sink. He hadn't seen his assailant, but it had been a mermaid. Giving up on the memory that wasn't there, he let himself drift further into the quiet and tried to forget the memories that were haunting him.

Chapter 21

Sirena

Sirena woke suddenly, gasping for air, her gills working overtime to keep up with her rapid breathing. She looked around and saw that half of her pod remained asleep while a few were moving a bit. Someone was missing. She couldn't find Orinn. She looked again to make sure everyone else remained.

"Have a nightmare?" a voice behind her whispered.

She looked to see that the whisper belonged to Neo. She conveyed her thoughts with her eyes but didn't speak yet, still trying to shake the thoughts from her head.

"Want to talk about it?"

Sirena whispered, "No." Nova stirred next to her.

"Morning," Nova said sleepily, stretching her arms over her head.

"Morning? Do we know that, or do we assume it's morning simply because we woke up?" Kassia chimed in.

"Good evening then," Nova frowned.

"Good? Do we lie to ourselves? There's nothing good about being…"

"Okay, I get it. Congratulations on waking up alive," Nova interrupted her.

Both mermaids were grinning at each other. Sirena didn't know how long it had been since she'd heard her friends bantering like this. Despite the constant struggles on the surface, they had always found time to be normal, to pretend they weren't being hunted. The last few weeks, however, since they'd been in the Midnight Zone, everyone had been so bitter, so short with one another. Even in their dire circumstances and the unknown of what lay ahead of them, Sirena was grateful for the momentary reprieve from the gloom that had hung over them. Sirena smirked as Nova continued her fake huffing and grumbling. Catalina rolled over and looked up at her. "Do we have to move? Can we lie here for another day?"

Sirena felt herself grinning. Cat, as an Encantado, tired easier than the Sirens. Nova did too, but as a Merrow, she had more strength than Cat. Sirena often told Cat to shift into her dolphin form to swim. It would preserve her energy, but since she didn't like her dolphin form, she refused to shift. Maybe she didn't remember how? Shifting into her dolphin form put Cat at risk from human hunters, and so Sirena had never pushed the issue.

"We can rest longer, until Theo feels strong enough to continue, but we don't have endless time to waste."

Xan and Theo were awake, Theo sitting up against the overhang on the ledge they had all curled up on.

"We haven't stopped in a week," Catalina grumbled.

"We can't stay here for too long. The Rusalka are still out there," Sirena said quietly but firmly.

Catalina rolled her eyes. "We know, but they will not get anymore dead. They can wait a day."

"No, I saw one last night or yesterday? Today? Before I went to sleep, I've lost track of time down here. It doesn't matter if it's day or night, I guess, but I saw another one," Sirena said.

Xan's face twisted with concern. "When? Before we talked?"

"No, after. You had gone to the pod," Sirena answered.

"Why didn't you tell me?" Xan scolded her.

"It moved away from us. It didn't know we were here."

"And you went to sleep and left us all vulnerable?" Orinn showed up out of nowhere.

"I…It wasn't close. It swam in the opposite direction. I waited until I couldn't see it any longer." Sirena instantly realized she had made a momentary lapse of judgment. Aware that Orinn was looking for an excuse to reprimand her, she felt her defensiveness rise through her.

"We're fortunate it didn't return, or another one didn't find us," Orinn's voice was bitter.

"I made a mistake. It won't happen again." Sirena didn't feel the need to defend herself further. She wouldn't have been able to stay awake any longer and neither could anyone else. Also, she was the damn Queen and had more power in her fingertips than the rest of them. She shot an irritated look at Orinn.

"We'll take turns watching the next time we stop," Theo spoke up, looking at Sirena.

"Yes, from now on we take watches when we stop. No one could have stayed awake yesterday, though. No excuses, my mistake," Sirena looked at Orinn only to see the mermaid staring at her icily.

Kassia cleared her throat and spoke to Theo. "How are you feeling?"

"Better. Almost brand new," Theo smiled at her, trying to reassure her he had healed.

"Good, because you looked *terrible* yesterday. So gray and gross."

"Thanks?" Theo asked warily.

Kassia laughed and blew him an air kiss full of mermaid bubbles. "Love you, Theo."

Theo rolled his eyes at her, but his dark eyes glowed as he gazed at her affectionately. Sirena felt warmth spread through her as she watched her friends. Kassia had slept close to Theo while allowing Xan his space to watch over his brother. Had Xan not been there, Sirena knew Kassia wouldn't have left his side for a moment. The two were insufferable. They thought they were discrete when they absolutely were not.

Catalina made kissing noises at Kassia, and Xan stifled his laughter.

"What am I missing?" Neo asked, a look of confusion on his face.

Laughing, Cat stopped her obnoxiousness and answered him, "They think we're all dumb, but Kassia and Theo are a *thing*."

"Oh, I assumed," Neo shrugged, causing Catalina to launch into a laughing fit. Nova joined in.

Sirena laughed, too. Theo and Kassia were bright shades of red while Xan tried to hide his amusement at their uncomfortableness.

"It's not funny!" Kassia insisted, which only caused the group to laugh harder.

Theo finally floated over to her and tossed an arm around her waist, and pulled her close to him. "If you all knew, why didn't you say anything?" he asked them.

"It was more fun to see how long you thought you could hide it for," Xan responded.

Kassia rested her head on Theo's chest. She looked up at him. "I didn't think you were going to make it," she breathed.

The laughter halted, bringing the group back to the gravity of the situation that they had found themselves in.

"I'm not going anywhere. I promise," Theo kissed her forehead, and Kassia curled herself into him.

Sirena smiled at her friends, happy with the moment of peace and happiness between the two of them.

Xan cleared his throat. "How much longer do we wait here?"

Reality hit her again, and Sirena thought for a moment. Taking in a few breaths and gathering herself before she asked, "How many days do we have before we hit the Rusalka's territory? Three maybe?"

Xan looked upwards for a few moments, calculating. "Three, if we really move. Four if we take breaks and rest. Which we should probably do."

Sirena nodded and pulled the coin from her top. "And I need to figure this out, too. I don't understand these symbols or words."

Neo pulled himself across the ledge and leaned over her shoulder to look at the coin. He frowned for a moment, and then his eyes lit up. "It's Spanish," he said.

Sirena looked at it closer. She saw it, but she didn't speak the language. Tossing it to Cat, she said, "Tell me what this says."

Catalina studied the coin, reading it once to herself before translating.

"*Souls that wander*
Souls that are lost
Though your time was short
Here you shall remain
In your grave
Until the end"

Sirena waited a moment and when Catalina looked up, confirming she had read all that the coin offered, Sirena burst out, "That's it? That's not anything!"

No one responded for a moment. Catalina flipped the coin around a few times and finally handed it to Sirena. Sirena looked down in disbelief.

"It doesn't even rhyme. Is that really a curse or enchantment?" Sirena glanced between her friends, landing on Neo.

Neo winced when he realized she wanted an answer from him. He gave her a wistful look.

"What do I do with this? Hold this coin and say this stupid phrase?"

"Cat read it out loud and nothing happened," Kassia said.

Sirena shot her a look. "I know. That's what I meant."

"Oh, got it… sorry," Kassia grimaced.

Sirena shot her a look of apology. "I thought there would be instructions or something. I don't know."

"I told you the Mami Wata were a waste of our time," Orinn leaned against the ledge with her arms crossed and not even attempting to hide her gloat.

"Then what's your suggestion?" Xan shot at her.

Orinn simply brushed off his question.

Sirena watched as Xan shot her a look of disgust. Xan turned to Neo. "Do you know anything about curses? Like actually performing them?"

"Some," Neo admitted. "But I don't think I could cast one. You saw the extent of my powers when I closed his wounds," Neo gestured towards Theo.

Xan nodded at him, but his frustration was obvious. "Can you tell Sirena what she needs to do?"

"Maybe? I think so? The curse is odd, though. Sirena is right, it doesn't seem like she gave us the whole thing. It doesn't call for us to do anything. Normally, with a curse, you need something to go along with the words."

Xan closed his eyes and slumped to the floor. He rubbed his temples and took a few breaths. "Is this a lost cause? What else did she say to us?"

"That I'm the ruler of all magic," Sirena said dryly.

Xan looked up. "She said that. Maybe it will be different when you read the curse." He sounded hopeful.

"Too bad I can't practice. We can't tie the Rusalka somewhere else or we encroach on other territories," Sirena said distantly, lost in thought.

Kassia made a noise, and Sirena turned to look at her. She was still curled up under Theo's arm, obviously happy that their secret was out. "Does it matter where we tie them to? I say tie them here, right by the Mami Wata."

"Agreed," Nova said. Catalina nodded her agreement as well.

"Like, drop a curse and swim away? Hope for the best?" Sirena hid her nervous laughter.

Xan looked at them. "What would stop them from breaking it again? I'd love to follow this plan, but I think we need to talk with Desdemona herself."

Sirena didn't want to agree with him. The idea of trying the curse and then getting the fin out of there sounded a lot better, but he was right. She also didn't want to admit what she actually thought. Bia tricked them. She didn't have any intention of helping them and this coin and this curse was simply a trick to get them out of her territory.

"Xan is right. We have to go to their territory and find out how this even happened. Bia said I needed to be in the middle of the territory," Sirena said.

"She said she didn't know if the territory would extend out if you weren't in the middle," Catalina corrected.

Theo shook his head. "Xan and Sirena are right. We have to go there. They most likely have Apollo as well. Enacting a curse here doesn't help find Apollo," Kassia looked at him lovingly but also like she wanted to be anywhere but in the Rusalka territory. Sirena understood the feeling.

Sirena sighed and positioned herself closer to Xan. "We rest for longer and then we start out again." To Xan and Theo, she said, "Can we talk through this? What's our plan?"

Xan smiled at her. "It's another mission. We're going to plan this like any other mission."

A wave of comfort ran through her. Another mission with her friends. But there was one last thing she needed. "We need a backup plan if this curse doesn't work," she held up the useless coin.

"Our backup plan is simple," Theo said. "If it doesn't work, we get the shell out of there as fast as possible."

Chapter 22
Sirena

Sirena knew they were approaching the Ningyo territory. They had passed the Merrows but hadn't seen them. The Merrows wouldn't be in the Midnight Zone because they didn't know any better. She felt a twinge of guilt when she thought about it. The Merrows were still in the Sunlight and Twilight zones, being picked off one by one, with no hope of rescue or reprieve. Their exile was something she would need to reconsider once she returned home.

The information surrounding their situation seemed to show her that her predecessors, her mother and sister included, weren't making decisions with the merpeople's interests in mind. She knew she needed to call a council meeting and meet the other leaders of the clans as soon as she had this mess under control. If there wasn't a Rusalka attack minutes after she took the rulership, that would have been the first thing she would have done.

Passing the Aicaya had proved uneventful. There had been a few mermaids out and she had simply acknowledged them and kept her pod moving. The Aicaya mermaids had returned the wave and went about their business. If they knew she was their Queen, they didn't show it. She didn't know how fast the ocean nymphs had spread the word. Maybe the other clans knew and maybe no one knew. A constant unsettling feeling lingered in her, and Sirena couldn't help but feel that this was a fool's mission.

The more that she contemplated their situation and her current journey to the Rusalka territory, the more she felt that she should have stayed in her own territory and sent for the other leaders of the clans. They should have met and discussed the threat the Rusalka imposed and made a plan together. Instead, she had let Sophie and Orinn send her out to a territory she had never been to before to confront a leader that may very well be killing off the royal Sirens one-by-one. In the middle of a war on merpeople.

She had taken the two strongest warriors the merpeople had ever seen with Xan and Theo and, as grateful as she was to have them with her, if something happened to them, she had taken both of their best protectors. Sirena had left the Sirens and the rest of the merpeople without protection. Yes, they all had their own magic, but Xan and Theo had experience in fighting off humans. Another wave of guilt swept through Sirena, and she felt her frustration rising again.

Xan was right. This wasn't fair, but this, all of this, was her problem. A problem she felt increasingly unqualified to solve. If she was honest with herself, she doubted her capabilities less. It wasn't so much that she didn't have the capability or skills to be the Queen. Maia had spent her whole life training for it, and Sirena knew she had been guessing when she'd made her orders. No, it wasn't her lack of capabilities that frustrated her anymore. The fact she did not know of the things happening around her hindered her more than her lack of training ever would. The elders, and her sister and maybe even her mother, were playing a game that she didn't know the rules to.

Squinting against the darkness, straining to see further than her light allowed, Sirena suspected the Ningyo was ahead of them. She thought she could see a group of merpeople ahead of her. Xan led the pod with her now that they had passed the Mami Wata territory. She reached out to tap him on the arm to get his attention, afraid to make too much noise that would scare the merfolk ahead of them. Sirena didn't know the Ningyo well, but she knew they had tried to leave the rescue missions before Maia had taken control. With the missions canceled, maybe they would be more willing to help. She doubted that, but she felt herself clinging to hope like the rest of her pod.

Xan whispered to her he saw the group ahead of them as well and that they should approach them more cautiously. The Aicaya had been apathetic to their passing, but tensions were high with the Ningyo. Sirena made her light brighter and showed to Xan that he should do the same.

Sirena turned to look at the rest of the pod. Neo wasn't leading with her, but he remained close behind her, as did Kassia and Nova. Catalina, Orinn, and Theo were at the back of the group. The pod had moved closer together, mostly arm's distances away from each other.

Kassia gave her a side-eyed look and when Sirena followed her gaze, she saw Kassia looking at Neo. When she looked at Kassia, she winked at Sirena. Sirena shot her a questioning look and Kassia suppressed a laugh. Shaking off her confusion, Sirena focused her gaze in front of her again.

Xan caught her eye and gave her an inquisitive look. Sirena shook his gaze off and muttered, *don't worry about it.*

Xan whispered to her, suggesting she should inform the group of their arrival soon. Sirena took in a deep breath and sent her voice through the water to the group of merfolk in front of her. It surprised her they hadn't seen their lights.

The merfolk looked up and turned in their direction. The Siren's lights caused the merfolk to shrink back. Sirena sent another message through the water; *we mean you no harm.*

This time, she saw a mermaid in the pod ahead, lifting her gaze upwards. Sirena followed her gaze and saw what the mermaid was looking at. They were no longer swimming through open water but were now making their way under rocks, caverns, and cliffs. A cliff spanned the rest of the distance between their current location and the merpeople in the distance. The mermaid lifted a hand and the rock cliff shook.

Sirena grabbed Xan's arm in shock. Eyes wide, she looked at him with fear. They couldn't get out from under this cliff quickly enough if that mermaid dropped it on them.

"Make her stop, Sirena," Xan said to her. No longer trying to be quiet, he shouted loud enough that the rest of their pod heard his command.

Nova gasped when she saw what the mermaid's plan unfold and Sirena felt the rest of the pod pull up and slow down. Waiting to see what their next move would be.

Sirena sent another message to the merfolk; *I am your Queen.*

The rocks above them rumbled harder.

Sirena held her breath while she extended both hands ahead of her, turning off her glowing lights for lighter Siren beams of energy. They were close enough that she could send her beams through the water to wrap around the mermaid threatening them. She wrapped invisible chains around the mermaid, holding her arms down, and keeping her in place.

The mermaid struggled and cursed at her while the others flailed around her, escaping and leaving their friend behind. Sirena looked at the mermaid while she screamed.

"Calm down. We're not here to hurt you." Sirena felt annoyed at the mermaid's continued aggression.

Still, the mermaid thrashed and struggled against Sirena's invisible restraints. They were face to face with her now, and Sirena couldn't help but let her emotions get the best of her.

"Stop it! I'm your Queen. We're passing through on the way to the Rusalka territory. Calm down, please." Sirena raised her hands to show that she meant no harm to her.

Before the mermaid could respond, Sirena saw a flash of red light in her peripheral vision. She turned her head to see Aiko swimming towards them quickly.

"Let my mermaid go," Aiko screamed through the water, her face twisted with rage.

"I had to restrain her. She tried to kill us all," Sirena said exasperated but calmly.

Aiko sped towards them in a rage, as if she hadn't heard Sirena. She sent spirals of energy towards Sirena's pod and Xan caught a small blast to his arm. He reeled backwards slightly and looked down at his arm in shock. A gash across his biceps bled profusely. He started healing slowly and Neo reached up and tapped Xan's arm to quicken the healing.

Sirena's annoyance turned to anger when she saw Xan's arm torn open. She let her invisible restraints on the mermaid in front of her go and tossed the mermaid through the water and out of her sight. The mermaid's screams dissipated throughout the water as she disappeared into the darkness. Turning her attention to Aiko, she sent her own energy towards Aiko. Spears and daggers of light ripped through the water and towards Aiko.

Aiko shrieked and rolled to her left in the water, dodging one of Sirena's beams. Not giving her a moment to recover, Sirena sent stream after stream of energy towards the Ningyo leader.

"Get back," she spoke fiercely to her pod.

She felt Xan float up next to her, defying her orders.

"I said get back," Sirena ordered him.

Xan faltered, but he fell behind her, remaining within arm's distance of Sirena. The rest of the pod fell further still, and Theo and Kassia positioned themselves in front of Orinn and the other non-Siren members of the pod.

Satisfied that her pod was far away enough to not be Aiko's next target, Sirena attempted to throw restraints on Aiko. To her dismay, Aiko shrugged them off as if they were only kelp floating against her shoulders.

"We're not here to harm you," Sirena said again. "I am your Queen. Hold your attack."

Aiko held her ground and continued to throw her own energy towards Sirena. Sirena had ceased her fire and put up a large shield of magic around herself and her pod, blocking Aiko's attacks. Aiko grew angrier as her attacks fizzled in the water, unable to harm Sirena and the other merpeople.

"Stop your attack. I am your Queen. I am Sirena, ruler of the merpeople." Sirena held her voice firm despite her growing panic.

Aiko held her hands up in mid-strike and stared at Sirena for a moment. Unsure of what this meant, Sirena kept talking before Aiko could resume her attack.

"Aiko, it's me. Sirena. I'm not here to cause problems."

"Why are you out here tying up my merpeople?" Aiko cried angrily.

"She tried to drop that cliff and crush us. I restrained her, only to stop her from killing us. I didn't hurt her." Sirena remained calm, but her annoyance at the situation ate away at her. The Ningyo were overreacting to their arrival and insubordinate to their ruler.

"What are you doing here?" Aiko demanded, her hands still raised and ready to attack.

"If you don't know by now, then consider yourselves fortunate. The Rusalka are loose and we're on our way to their territory."

Aiko made a huffing noise but didn't speak.

Sirena gave her a confused look. "Have you seen the Rusalka in your territory?"

"No."

"Then, like I said, consider yourselves fortunate."

Aiko stared at her. Neither mermaid moved nor spoke for a few moments. Sirena realized she should ask the clan leader for help with their situation, but hesitated. Aiko reacted aggressively to their arrival, and she didn't think the threat had been mitigated. She felt confused about Aiko's behavior and this confrontation.

"What do you know about the curse on the Rusalka?" Sirena asked, trying to sound as though she were simply asking a friend their opinion and not like she was completely clueless about the history of the curse.

"Nothing. You'd have to ask Bia about it." Aiko's hands lowered, but the icy glare and tone remained.

"We did, and she gave me a coin with what I supposed is a curse of some sort."

"Then why are you asking me?" Aiko said, annoyed.

Sirena thought for a few seconds. How did she tell Aiko she didn't know what to do with the coin or curse without sounding completely useless?

"Sirens don't enact curses. I've never done it before," Sirena decided honesty was her best chance for help. "I have the curse, but I wasn't around when they created it so I'm asking what you know."

Aiko laughed at her. "Silly little Siren. This isn't my problem. This is yours."

Xan interrupted. "It is actually all of our problem if the Rusalkas continue to roam free."

Aiko laughed crossly and tossed her hands in the air. "I'm so glad to see you do not differ from your mother. Ruler of all, and yet you make the rest of us do your work. No desire for a Siren to do the hard work or lose their own. No. The rest of us suffer while you hide in your castles."

"Do I look like I'm hiding?" Sirena asked her, holding her ground.

Aiko opened her mouth to speak, and then quickly closed it. A small smile escaped her. She was out here with her pod, not hiding in their territory. Sirena had battled through the wards of the Mami Wata, fought a Rusalka and was on her way to the Rusalka territory. She didn't hide from conflict.

"I'll also remind you that prior to being the Queen of the merpeople, I'm a member of the Siren rescue missions and I've saved many of your merpeople over the years," Sirena's voice grew cold and firm. She stood her ground and would not allow herself to be bullied.

Aiko still said nothing, but the fire in her eyes remained.

"I am asking you one more time. What do you know about the Rusalka and their curse?" Sirena spoke slowly and with intent.

"Nothing!" Aiko spat out instantly. "I know nothing about the Rusalka or the curse. I haven't seen them and I don't know what you're talking about. Maia told me that the rescue missions were done and we were free to exist on our own as long as we moved down here." Aiko gestured to the Midnight Zone around her.

Sirena took a deep breath in and calmed her rage once more. "Maia ended the rescue missions, but you are still the leader of the Ningyo and still a member of the mercouncil. I am your Queen and I am asking for your help. You have a responsibility as a leader of the mercouncil."

"I have nothing to tell you," Aiko spoke angrily, but Sirena sensed panic hidden in her rage.

"Fine. I assume you will refuse to travel to the Rusalka territory with us to resolve this then."

Aiko made a huffing noise that sounded like no.

"Noted. As soon as I return to my territory, I will call a council meeting. You will be required to attend. There will be no exceptions and you have advanced notice. I expect your attitude to be different when you show up in my territory versus what I have seen from you today." Sirena waved a hand in front of her, referring to the attack that had occurred.

Sirena turned to her pod and motioned for Theo to lead the pod out of the Ningyo territory.

She looked at Aiko and contemplated her thoughts for a moment. Straightening her posture and holding Aiko's gaze, she asked the question that had been plaguing her for days.

"Where is Apollo?"

Aiko recoiled as though Sirena had slapped her.

"He's missing and I suspect you know something about it."

Aiko seemed to regain her composure. "What makes you think I know what you're talking about?"

"Call it a hunch," Sirena said coldly and authoritatively. She could feel Xan off to the side, holding his ground alongside her.

"What you're talking about. I didn't even know you were our Queen. Are you going to tell me what happened to Maia?"

"I think you already know."

"I don't."

Sirena didn't speak but continued to glare at Aiko, holding her stance and searching for answers in Aiko's mannerisms. She could feel Aiko squirm under her gaze and allowed herself a smug smile.

Aiko lashed out at Sirena, "I don't know what you're talking about. I don't. Maia was my *friend.* I did nothing to her, and I certainly did nothing to Apollo. I haven't seen him in years, and I have no desire to see him ever again. You certainly know that. Maia let the Ningyo leave the mercouncil and I'm done. I'm done with the rest of the clans and the council and the Sirens. My priority is my merpeople. They are my responsibility and that's where it ends. You can take your rag tag pod of merpeople out of my territory and don't you ever come back or the next time I will end you."

No longer able to hold her temper, Sirena let out a blast of her energy, catching Aiko off guard. She slashed Aiko's arm open like she had done to Xan.

"Maia did not excuse you from the mercouncil. Even if she did, I'm the Queen and we're done with that. No more clans going off on their own and leaving the rest of us to our own defenses. We are stronger together and we will learn to get along. You want someone to commiserate with, you can cry on Bia's shoulder because both of you are leaders on the mercouncil and both of you are required to fulfill your responsibilities. If you don't want to be members of the council, I will remove you as leaders of your clans and we will find merpeople who want to be a part of the solution, not part of the problem. The next time you injure or attack one of my pod members, I will end you. I will remember what happened here today," Sirena said her piece and turned away from Aiko, motioning to Xan to follow her.

She caught Xan glaring down Aiko for a few moments longer before he turned to follow her. When he caught up to her seconds later, he had an ear-to-ear smile.

"I'm proud of you," he said to her.

"That's great, but we probably shouldn't have turned our backs to her," Sirena tried not to glance over her shoulder and show her fear.

"No, that was perfect. She knows you will not give into her tantrums like Maia or your mother did," Xan spoke excitedly.

"She might kill us all. Her magic, she matched with me. I know the Ningyos have magic, but not like ours yet. Her energy matched mine."

Xan gave her a perplexed look. "Like your magic now? Or your magic before you became the Queen?"

"Now," Sirena said quietly.

Xan pulled away in surprise. "How is that possible?"

"I don't know, but she was defensive. She knows where Apollo is and what happened to Maia. I can feel it. She overreacted to our arrival. She's involved, somehow."

"Normally I would say we don't have enough proof but, I think you're right. I noticed her defensiveness. She wasn't only mad that you restrained her mermaid, she's hiding something."

Sirena nodded her head in agreement. Then a chill ran through her and she looked at Xan, wide-eyed, as reality hit her. "Apollo and Aiko were a couple. Decades ago."

Xan gave her silent agreement that he knew what her next question would be.

"Is she an angry, jilted mermaid?" Sirena asked him.

"She might be."

"Did we leave Apollo there?"

Xan gave her a grim look. "We might have."

Chapter 23

Sirena

Sirena and Xan caught up with the rest of the pod and, when they were a safe distance away from Aiko, she pulled the group to a stop. She and Xan had taken up the rear of the pod, keeping a shield between the group and Aiko until they were far enough away.

Kassia grabbed her arm sharply as soon as they stopped. "What the shell happened? Her power matched yours?"

"Her energy sure did, yes."

"How?" Sirena could feel Nova's question burning through her. She wondered the same thing.

"I don't know. Of course, the Ningyo have powers and Aiko is an older and powerful mermaid but I'm not sure how she's matching Siren power." Sirena looked at the group but felt herself drifting her gaze towards Orinn. Orinn floated motionless off to the side of the group.

Xan mentioned the highlights from the discussion that they had had while catching up to the group. "Apollo has to be there. You saw how she reacted when Sirena asked about him. The overreaction. If she was clueless, she wouldn't have been so defensive. Why wasn't she concerned?"

"Why would she be concerned?" Neo asked.

Catalina interjected this time. "They were a couple for a long time."

"Not that long," Sirena shuddered. "A few years. A while ago."

"He ghosted her," Catalina added.

Neo winced a bit at Catalina's last statement. "That could make someone angry."

"Seems it has. Furious," Xan said.

Sirena followed the conversation, feeling her head ping to each merperson as they interjected their thoughts. Thoughts about her brother and his past relationship. She took a deep breath in and tried to calm her fears slightly.

"Regardless of their past relationship, I think it's obvious that she has Apollo. Or at the very least, she knows where he is. If he's not with the Rusalka, I will go to Aiko and find him, but for now, I need to know how she has that kind of power. That kind of magic. I thought the Ningyo could only mimic another mer's magic. I didn't know they could be on the same tier as Sirens. Orinn, what do you know about Aiko?"

Orinn shrugged and didn't uncross her arms. She simply stared at Sirena and didn't speak.

"You know her. You've been on the council with her for years," Xan spoke directly to Orinn.

Orinn dismissed them again. This time she showed some actual concern, but it fleeted as fast as it had appeared.

Sirena closed her eyes for a moment and tried to calm her rage. After a few moments, she realized she had failed. She let her Siren form take hold of her.

Jet black circles filled the space where her eyes should have been. White hot energy shot through her arms and into her fingertips. She looked down at her glowing hands to see her talons out in full force. Her razor-sharp Siren teeth pierced her gums, hiding her normal teeth. She gave Orinn a wicked grin, displaying her new terrifying look. Orinn didn't flinch.

Sirena looked down at her glowing fingertips and her dagger-like nails and charged at Orinn. She dug her nails into Orinn's throat with one hand and her other hovered in the air, ready to reach into Orinn's chest and pull out her heart. Sirena could feel her gills working overtime, drawing water and filtering the air rapidly to keep up with her frantic breathing.

Orinn continued to look bored, as if Sirena merely told her a story that she didn't like.

Sirena could feel one of her pod members gently lay a hand on her shoulder to calm her. She shook it off and continued to stare down at Orinn. If Orinn wouldn't talk on her own, Sirena would make her.

"Tell me what you know. Now. I'll slit your throat right here. I don't care if you're an advisor or one of my mother's best friends. My mother is dead. Merpeople are dying. We have Rusalka on the loose and the leader of the Ningyo is oozing power that she shouldn't have. Talk!" Sirena hissed at Orinn, increasing her grip on Orinn's throat.

"The only merpeople dying seem to be the royal Sirens, so explain to me again why I should help you?" Orinn struggled to speak against Sirena's hold, but somehow her tone matched Sirena's intensity as she spit out her words.

Gasping, Sirena dug her claws in further and brought her teeth within inches of Orinn's neck. She whispered in her ear, quietly so the others couldn't hear, "You are dragging us out here to die. I will kill you for insubordination."

Orinn laughed, "Insubordination? Such a big word for you, Sirena. You are nothing but an aimless mermaid who followed the merboys around. You would have never gone on those rescue missions if you hadn't been a mermaid in love." Orinn rolled her eyes, still unmoved by Sirena's Siren form.

"She is a great warrior. Sirena fought the humans right alongside us and held her own. She's saved hundreds of merfolk. That's more than you have done," Theo spoke up so quietly that Sirena had to flip her head around to confirm he had actually spoken.

Xan chimed in with his agreement. "It's true. Sirena has saved as many merfolk as Theo and I have."

"You clueless fool. You do not know," Orinn laughed again, this time at Xan.

"Don't," Sirena whispered her threat in Orinn's face. Much to her surprise, Orinn gave her a slight nod and stopped.

"I can't tell you anything about Aiko because I don't know. What do you think happened at council meetings? We didn't sit around and talk about our powers and feelings. I do not know what Aiko is capable of," Orinn spoke defiantly in Sirena's face, not breaking her eye contact.

"Let her go." Nova pulled on Sirena's arm, pulling her away from Orinn. Sirena let Nova guide her away. She let her teeth retract, but kept her claws out and her eyes black. She briefly glimpsed Neo and if her true form had scared or disgusted him, he wasn't showing it, at least. His face and demeanor were stoic as he watched the scene play out in front of him.

"She's not worth it." Kassia moved to Sirena's other side. Sirena noticed that Kassia's eyes were also jet black and her claws out. She smiled. Her friend supported her and had been ready to join in if necessary.

Xan pushed his way between Orinn and Sirena and looked intensely at Sirena with his own black eyes. Sirena felt her stomach flip-flop. Theo and Xan had also readied themselves for a fight. She peered at her friends and felt her rage subside. They may be in an awful mess at the moment. Her brother was missing, the mercouncil was corrupt and Coralis was falling apart around her, but her friends were standing by her and ready to fight with her. Her heart felt full and overwhelmed.

Catalina looped an arm around Sirena's waist and gave her a tight squeeze. "Since the old maid won't talk, I think we have to let the Aiko situation go for the present and talk about what we're going to do with the Rusalka."

Sirena nodded and sighed. She could feel the coin that Bia had given her pressing against her ribcage from where she had tucked it into her top.

"I'm not really sure what our best option is," she admitted.

"If they're free, who's saying they'll even be in their territory?" Neo asked.

Sirena contemplated his statement for a moment. "You could very well be right. They might not even be there. Not all of them, anyway."

"Desdemona will be there," Xan added.

"Right. I would guess that she wouldn't leave," Sirena said.

Neo gave her an inquisitive look.

"Desde might be the leader of the Rusalka and her past is well, it's tragic, but she wouldn't leave her territory. I've not met her, but I know she has helped the Sirens in the past. Apollo has told me how we've used the Rusalka as a sort of prison prior to the wars. For merfolk that committed heinous crimes." Sirena said, "Desde always ensured the Rusalka never physically harmed merfolk during their sentence, but they paid for their crimes."

"It's true. I've delivered a few prisoners to her personally over the years," Xan added.

"The leader of the Rusalka is loyal to the Sirens?" Neo asked.

“I don’t know that loyal is the word I’d use but, we’ve had an agreement,” Xan said. Neo seemed to accept this and turned to Sirena, waiting for her direction.

Sirena quickly surveyed her pod and noticed that they were all waiting for her. Again. She had run through the options since they had set off for the Rusalka territory. Should they secretly infiltrate the territory and get to Desdemona without the other Rusalka seeing them? Would they be safe to enter and could they float into the territory like they belonged there?

Were there other options?

Sirena turned to Xan and Theo, her leaders, for the missions. “Xan, Theo, what are your thoughts?”

The looks on their faces told her they both had ideas about what they would do. They had likely discussed it, but they were giving her the opportunity to share her thoughts. She shot both of them a look, not hiding her frustration.

“Right, well, I think… and I might be completely wrong, but…what if we went into their territory and spoke to Desde? She knows Xan and I think Theo, you too?” Sirena looked at him for confirmation. Theo nodded. She was correct. “She knows both of you and she worked with my parents when they needed her to. I don’t think she will harm us.”

“You know of the times we’ve dropped prisoners off or retrieved them,” Theo said.

"We never fully went into the territory. She met us on the edge and for handoffs," Xan added.

Sirena knew they had been to the territory and that the interactions were brief, but she had hoped they knew more. Had interacted with Desdemona more.

"I think there are two situations," Sirena said to the group. "One, Desdemona knows about the boundaries dropping and she's as frustrated as we are. Or two, she's behind it."

Xan gave her a look that told her he thought the same before he added, "I only hope that if she is behind it, we would have heard from her already. She would have made her intentions known."

Sirena had thought about that as well. "Yes, that's my thought, too. I don't think that the Rusalka made their own great escape. I think they're a distraction. Let loose to keep us busy chasing them around the oceans. A distraction from what, that I don't know and probably don't want to know."

"How many Rusalka are there?" Neo asked.

Sirena looked at Orinn, who expressed she didn't know. Xan muttered something under his breath. Sirena didn't catch it, but suspected he was questioning why Orinn was here.

"It seems we don't know, so we don't know what we're swimming into, but I think it's better to enter like we know what we're doing rather than trying to sneak in."

She looked at Xan and Theo for confirmation, and they both shot her a look of approval.

Xan added, "If Desde is who I think she is, she'll want this under control as much as we do."

"Agreed. She may have been bitter and cursed tragic souls to an eternity with her but she had an agreement with the Sirens and she worked with your mother," Theo added.

"Perhaps she even knows something about the Mami Wata curse and she can help return things to normal?" Sirena asked them.

"No ruler wants their territory in chaos, and she was there when the curse was placed," Theo said in agreement. You might be right and she might know how it worked. I think it's probable that she agreed to it," Theo hypothesized, looking at Orinn with frustration.

"Alright, unless anyone has any other thoughts, then we go in as a pod and ask to see Desdemona." Sirena looked around the group for confirmation.

"No," Orinn said flatly.

"She finally has something to say," Xan snapped.

Sirena had the same thought as Xan, but fought her sarcasm. "What did you have in mind, Orinn?"

"We split up. You think a large pod of merfolk floating in the entrance of the Rusalka territory is going to work? Some elite warriors you two are." She shot a disapproving look at the brothers.

Sirena watched Xan's eyes turn to Siren black as he stared at her in dismay. "What have you done for the last hundred years? Before the wars? What have you ever done, Orinn? What made you qualified to be an advisor to the Sirens?"

"I don't owe you an explanation."

"Of course you don't. You don't owe us an explanation. You don't need to tell us what you know about the council or the other leaders. Or the curse on the Rusalka. You interject your useless opinion whenever you see fit and judge us for our decisions. Orinn, you don't know the first thing about being a leader or an advisor. If you did, we wouldn't be hiding out in the Midnight Zone trying to escape humans and cursed merfolk ghosts," Xan unleashed his rage. As Xan shifted to his full Siren form, Sirena felt her eyes blacken, this time to match his.

"Xan," Theo said warily.

"No, I've had enough. This is what I've been telling you, Theo. The leaders of these clans, come on! The rules don't apply to them and they've spent the last century making it up as they go along. Now here we are, fighting against ourselves. The Rusalka are loose and we all know a merperson is responsible. Curses don't expire. The Ceasgs, Kelpies, Selkies — who knows if any of them will be left by the time we fix this mess. Not to mention, how many merpeople are still stuck on the surface? How many of our kind are up there praying every day that one of us pulls them from some zoo or worse, someone's bathtub?"

Sirena winced. There had been several missions where they found merfolk trapped in a bathtub in some human's house. Forced to bring their captor good luck and fortune while being trapped in the smallest space imaginable. Xan's anger was justified.

"Either you talk and tell us what you know or we move on without you," Xan finished.

"Are you going to let him talk to me like this?" Orinn looked at Sirena.

Sirena gave her a confused look and shrugged. "I don't see why I would stop him. It's all true."

"Siding with your crush. Not a good look for a leader," Orinn smirked. How she even knew was beyond Sirena. She certainly hadn't told her.

"Her what? Orinn, stop," Xan continued to stare down Orinn.

Sirena didn't know if she should feel relieved that Xan didn't believe Orinn or hurt that he was still clueless after all these years. Regardless, this wasn't the time to contemplate Xan's feelings or lack thereof.

"I think it's more dangerous to split up and sneak into their territory. If I were Desde, I'd come out swinging if someone hid and crept through the Siren's territory," Theo added.

"Can someone fill me in on exactly what powers the Rusalka have again?" Nova asked.

Sirena sometimes forgot that Nova's memory loss included general knowledge of the merfolk and their surroundings.

"Incredible speed and strength. They can kill us before we even see them coming," Xan explained.

"Hmm, that's what I thought." Nova looked at Sirena as if she was trying to make a point to the group. Sirena was unsure if her comment supported Sirena's plan or Orinn's so she stared at Nova for a moment, waiting for clarification.

When no one responded, Nova tossed her hands in the air. "Really? They can kill us before we know they are there and we're going to separate and try to sneak up on them? I agree with the rest. We go in and make ourselves known. Sirena is their Queen. They wouldn't risk killing her off."

"Yes, they would. Especially if they're behind Maia's death and Apollo's disappearance," Orinn argued. "Separating everyone is the only way to make sure that Sirena isn't the primary target. With us spread out, they'd have to find us all and they most likely won't think that she would come herself. We can create distractions and Sirena can find Desde undetected."

Sirena knew that there was a possibility that the Rusalka were behind it all. That perhaps even Desde herself had been behind Maia's death and Apollo's disappearance, but she still found it unlikely. In her heart, she knew Aiko was involved. Maybe she was working with the Rusalka but she was sure that Aiko caused the recent events. She hated to admit that there was some merit to Orinn's thinking.

"If what you think is true, and the Rusalka are behind all of this, then I would be a target. Is separating us really the best idea then?" Sirena asked.

"You're a sitting duck in the middle of us if we go in as one big happy pod," Orinn retorted.

Sirena looked at Xan and then at Theo. They both looked at her with blank stares, and she knew they were thinking the same thing. Orinn had a point but the thought of splitting up made her anxious. If something happened to a member of her pod, especially the non-Sirens, she didn't know how she would live with herself. Orinn intentionally ignored the growth in Sirena's power when she designed her plan.

Xan and Theo didn't move still, and Sirena felt all eyes on her. "Fine, we'll split up. But into two groups," Sirena said. She could feel Xan's gaze on her.

"No, into four," Orinn countered.

Sirena went rigid and felt her frustration rising. No matter what she conceded to Orinn, it would never be enough for the betta.

"Kassia and Neo will enter the Rusalka territory first on the northeast side and cause a distraction. Nova and I will enter minutes behind them, causing a second distraction. Xan and Theo, you'll be our backup and help us hold off any attacking Rusalka. While the Rusalka are busy with us, Sirena and Catalina will enter through the southernmost entrance of the territory and seek Desde," Orinn leaned away from them. She had clearly been planning this out for a while.

"We're sending Sirena in with an Encantado?" Xan's tone was flat and emotionless.

"Yes, we need all the Sirens we can get defending us when we're setting ourselves up for an attack," Orinn explained.

"We're leaving Sirena alone in the territory, then," Xan explained.

"I'll be with her," Catalina looked offended.

"Great," Neo interjected this time, his voice not hiding his frustration. "At least I could speed up her healing. Send me with her."

"At least do that. At least send Neo with her," Xan agreed.

"No. This is the plan. Anyone that doesn't like it can go home." Orinn glared at Xan.

Sirena looked at Xan and Theo, and they simply looked at her. She gestured to Orinn that they should continue with her plan.

"What the shell, Sirena?" Xan grabbed her arm as she swam by him.

Sirena gave him a hurt look and wiggled free of his grasp, swimming ahead to leave with Catalina.

Chapter 24

Aiko

Aiko could feel the power of her magic fogging her thoughts as the adrenaline still pumped through her. Sakura had curled herself up in the bottom of Aiko's den and watched her partner pace and shake out the aftereffects of too much magic. If her heart could slow down, maybe her head could catch up.

"If you don't stop moving, you're going to give yourself a heart attack and you would not make an attractive Rusalka," Sakura said, trying to make a joke.

"Can you be quiet? I'm trying to think," Aiko didn't raise her voice, but her tone might as well have yelled across the room.

Sighing, Sakura rolled over and kicked her tail up into the water above her, stretching her arms overhead before curling up. This time, facing the wall rather than Aiko. Aiko noted her change in position and ignored the theatrics.

Before she could resume her pacing, she felt waves behind, causing the hair on her neck to rise. She didn't need to turn around to know who spoke behind her.

"Seems the Sirens might be onto you," the voice said, emotionless.

Turning, Aiko found herself face to face with Eevie, the leader of the Finfolk. Eevie's face looked taut despite her being a rather fleshy mermaid. The slimy green skin that the Finfolk possessed looked darker and more grotesque in the darkness of the Midnight Zone. Aiko shuddered when she recalled the one time that Eevie had brushed up against her, leaving a sticky residue on her shoulder.

"They're not," Sakura responded, not bothering to turn around.

"Mmm, is that so?" Eevie replied, still looking at Aiko. "Then why did they show up in your territory, magic blazing?"

"Sirena is the new leader of the Sirens; you must be aware. It seems our plan went a bit too well, and the Rusalka killed Maia.

How did you let this happen? This is *your* fault." Aiko pointed her finger into Eevie's face.

"My fault? Dear, that's not even possible. It is you who holds the magic," Eevie's smile darkened, and she gestured to the large pearl that Aiko had taken to looping around her waist rather than carrying around her neck.

Aiko blinked at her and clenched her fists. The adrenaline pounded in her temples and she could feel it bursting behind her eyes. It may be dark in this zone of the ocean, but she could almost see her anger radiate off of her. "My magic? Mine? Magic has nothing to do with this. You were the one that wanted to let the Rusalka free. *You!*"

Eevie noted Aiko's rising anger and brought her smile down to a smirk before she responded. "You were quick to accept my help. I've fed you Merrows for years. I helped you gain that power that you wield. If the Sirens find out, it is you that will be responsible. Not me. I'm merely a simple-minded Finfolk. I could have never done this on my own."

Aiko's mouth hung open in disbelief. How could she have been so ignorant? When this was over, Eevie would escape blame. Aiko looked down at the pearl on her hip, overflowing with the souls of Merrows, the source of her stronger than normal magic.

"Who's going to think I had anything to do with this? Surely you wouldn't need me to prey on Merrows and harvest their souls for your own gain?" Eevie's voice raised a few octaves higher as she feigned innocence.

"By that time, it won't even matter, Aiko. You'll be more powerful than all the Sirens combined. Wipe them out of existence and move on," Sakura lazily rolled over to look at them.

A daring grin spread across Eevie's face and she looked at Aiko threateningly.

Anticipating what Eevie was going to say, Aiko shouted, "No!"

"Sakura, do you know why Aiko was so quick to break the curse on the Rusalka? Do you even know why she helped me?" Eevie's face, positively gleeful. Aiko's stomach rolled.

"We're all angry with the Sirens. These last hundred years have been even more ridiculous than the hundred years prior to the war." Sakura looked bored.

"Mmm. Yes."

"Stop Eevie," Aiko's voice was barely above a whisper. She touched a hand to the pearl, readying herself to engage her newfound magic.

"Drop that hand, Aiko. Think twice before you use what I've given you against me."

Reluctantly, Aiko removed her hand from the pearl but hovered it close by.

"What she doesn't want you to know is that she is responsible for Malee's death and her history with Apollo won't help her much with the rest of the Sirens if they ever find out," Eevie's words floated in the water and Aiko felt her gills constrict, refusing to work for a moment.

"She wasn't even on that mission with Malee," Sakura's voice sounded cross.

"Hmm," Eevie purred.

"She wasn't," Sakura repeated, sounding less sure of herself.

"Is that so, Aiko?" Eevie grinned at her.

Aiko took a deep breath in, feeling her gills stretch to their capacity as she struggled to get oxygen into her constricted lungs. "I was there."

Sakura tilted her head slightly and twisted her mouth slightly as she looked at Aiko. She shrugged and shook it off. "It's not like you were the human that stabbed her, so I don't see how it's your fault."

"A human stabbed her, did they?" Eevie winked at Aiko.

Aiko felt like she was drowning. She looked with pleading eyes at Sakura. "I'm sorry."

"What did you do?" Sakura sat up; eyes wide.

"Yes, what *did you do*?" Eevie's arms were in front of her with her hands clasped at her pronounced midsection. She peered at Aiko with wide eyes brimming with sarcasm and glee.

"I..." Aiko couldn't bring herself to tell Sakura what she had done and hesitated. Guilt she hadn't confessed her part in Malee's death to her partner overwhelmed her.

"I...I... I..." Eevie mocked her.

Rage swelled again and Aiko rested her hand on the pearl, making eye contact with Eevie before she continued.

"I had tried to remove myself and the rest of the Ningyo from the rescue missions. We were dying up there. Malee wouldn't even hear me out. She forced us to the surface to rescue the animals." She cringed as though the thought of the shapeshifting mermaids disgusted her. "I had been siphoning souls off of Merrows for years. It started off with a few here and there and then Eevie started sending them to me regularly. I gave them legs for their souls and good fortune."

Sakura shrugged. She knew about the Merrows and where the power had come from.

"Almost a month ago, on the last mission that I went on, things had gone poorly. Malee had hidden in the Sunlight Zone, waiting for our return. Theo led the group and Maia, Sirena and I, were teaming with him." She paused for a moment before composing herself again, rage visible on her face. "They used me as bait. Bait. Draw out the humans from their hovel while Theo and Sirena rescued a Selkie. Maia was supposed to be my support and Malee hid in the shadows to take the Selkie to safety while the rest of us fled for our lives. A standard mission. The bait and the rescuers fleeing for their lives while the merperson, stupid enough to get caught, whisked away to safety."

Sakura still seemed unphased. "Sure, a standard mission."

"But was it a standard mission, Aiko?" Eevie gloated.

"Maia lost sight of me for a moment and I took it as an opportunity. I wanted out of these missions. I had been absorbing Merrow souls to protect us, our people. The Sirens weren't doing anything. Nothing. Rescue mission after rescue mission, but they didn't fight humans. They could have used their magic, but yet they tried to take the high waters and they let the humans attack again and again without consequences."

"Well, yes, but… don't think I'm defending the Sirens because I most certainly am not…didn't they try to blast humans into oblivion but they couldn't above the surface? Isn't that how Asterios died? He tried to use his powers but other than growing legs, he couldn't? Their songs have been gone for almost a century," Sakura looked confused again.

"So, they say," Eevie said, hinting that hadn't been the case.

"That's what we were told, yes. But I don't believe it. I saw Sirena use her powers on that mission. Saw her blast a door open and walk right into a human's house. They'd been lying to us. Maia wasn't where she should have been. They left me on my own as bait. I had my pearl with me and I shifted into a human."

Sakura's gills flared as she put the pieces together.

"I waited until Maia found me and then I charged at her. She set off her warning signal and Malee came out of nowhere. Theo and Sirena were there in an instant, and I knew if I had to battle with both of them, I'd never win. I couldn't shift to my mermaid form. What would I say? I went after Malee instead and she instantly attacked, eager to get Maia and Sirena out of there."

"A mother's instincts," Sakura whispered.

Aiko nodded. "She even let out that Siren song of hers. Albeit slightly garbled and raspy. I didn't mean to kill her, but it was the first time I used my full power and she would not let up. It made me so mad when I heard her sing. They can still sing. At least Malee could."

Aiko slumped to the floor and stole a quick glance at Eevie, who glowed with excitement. Disgust rolled through her as she continued.

"When Malee was…gone. I waited a few moments and then shifted. I found Maia first."

"She shimmered like a damn beacon of light. Couldn't miss her. I played innocent and acted surprised. I let Maia know that I had become separated from her and heard Malee's scream.

"She believed you?"

"I think so. There was no reason for her not to think so. Her mother had died, and she was still absorbing the Queen's powers after all." Aiko looked uncertain.

"Why does Eevie know this and I don't?" Sakura demanded.

Eevie's grin widened as she answered before Aiko could explain. "Because I was there, and I saw it all happen."

"Blackmail?" Sakura looked horrified as she glared at the Finfolk leader.

"Oh, I wouldn't say that. I'd say I called in a favor." Eevie raised an eyebrow, that hint of a smile still lingering.

"Eevie saw it happen and decided that it was time I use my power to help her or she'd tell Maia."

"Evil. Pure evil," Sakura seemed to contemplate for a moment before continuing. "I'm not disappointed, though. I never liked Malee."

"Ah, but see how this looks for your partner. It's not good. She's responsible for the death of two Siren rulers and her falling out with Apollo. Mmm, not good at all," Eevie said.

"Apollo is in the past."

"Is he? Then why are you hiding him?" Eevie chimed in.

"I'm not upset about that. Apollo broke her heart, and he never spoke to her again. No explanation, no closure. If she wants to mess with him. So be it. I don't care," Sakura said defensively, showing Aiko that maybe she cared a bit.

"I felt a little braver after Malee, I guess. With the lifting of the curse on the Rusalka, I thought I'd get even a bit."

"Oh, is that so? You weren't keeping him safe from the Rusalka attack on the Sirens?" Eevie gloated.

Aiko once again felt shock rolling through her body. She turned to look at Sakura and to deny the accusation, but the damage had been done. Sakura seethed.

"And is it true that the first time you used your new power was the day you killed Malee?" Eevie almost hummed the words, taking great pleasure in the position that Aiko now found herself in.

Sighing, Aiko lowered her eyes. "No, it was not the first time."

Sakura floated motionless. What she thought had simply been rebellion against the Sirens had resulted in two murders and the exposure of her partner's still warm feelings for her ex-partner. Aiko watched Sakura process her thoughts and could already feel the distance growing between them. Sakura may hate the Sirens, but treason and the murder of the Queen, two Queens? Aiko knew her partner wouldn't want to live with the consequences of her crimes.

Chapter 25

Sirena & Catalina

Sirena and Cat swam kilometers ahead of the rest of the group. Right or wrong, Orinn's decision to stagger into the territory seemed better than any battle plans Sirena had. Sirena had planned to talk to Desdemona. If the Rusalka attacked them on the way in, she guessed her plan would have been to use her power.

"Which Rusalka are we going after first?" Cat broke into Sirena's thoughts.

"We're not going after anyone."

"You know what I mean. What are we doing when we get there? What's your plan? Everyone else is distracting them and we're going straight for Desde, or do we look around first?"

"I didn't ask for any of this. You know that, right?" Sirena looked at her friend for confirmation.

"I know you didn't. This is your luck. Should have snagged yourself a Ceasg and got out of Siren territory when you had the chance," Cat winked at Sirena.

It was hard not to return the smirk. "They were only friends, nothing more."

"Right, I forgot. It's Xan you really want."

Sirena pretended to look offended, but they'd had this conversation more times than she cared to admit.

"I'm sorry Sirena Oscura," Cat said, using her full nickname, "He doesn't love you. At least not how you want him to. He's too preoccupied with being the best Siren warrior there ever was. Like I said, you should have grabbed one of those Selkies."

"You said Ceasgs and I know he doesn't." She knew that she and Xan were only ever going to be friends. Catalina was right, a handsome Scottish merman was much more likely to be in her future than Xan ever would be.

"Ceasgs, Selkies. Either of them would do," Cat said playfully.

The Ceasgs, Selkies and Kelpies were all located close to the Sirens, and Sirena had grown up playing with them. The wars had taken quite a few of her friends and, with the clans fighting each other, Sirena was sure she had lost more. She struggled with the aftermath of the wars, not because of the loss of her family, but because so many of her friends were fighting with each other.

They had forgotten their childhoods, and that they had once been friends. Everyone was angry with each other because when survival instincts kicked in, they turned on their friends and defended themselves. Sirena did not know about the number of her childhood mermaid and merman friends from the Scottish clans that remained.

She made a silent promise to herself that she would end the fighting between the clans as soon as she found Apollo and figured out what was going on with the Rusalka. She'd make a decree if she had to. They had to listen to her, right? She really didn't think that would work or Maia or, their mother for that matter, would have done it. Or maybe they wouldn't have. The information that she gathered showed that her sister and mother had motives she didn't understand.

Sirena, lost in her thoughts, continued to head north and Cat followed without question. The scenery in the Eastern region was beautiful and different from what she had grown accustomed to in the Sirens territory. They were in the Twilight Zone right now since that's where the Rusalka territory existed. The surrounding beauty made her temporarily forget that she was out of the safety of the Midnight Zone and the Abyss.

Below her she watched as fish floated about their business, oblivious to the struggles of the merpeople. Yellow fins and tuna were plentiful, and she felt herself longing for home, for their own schools of halibut or cod. When they passed a family of Orcas, she felt her heart twist at the realization she had lost almost her entire family. Maybe she had lost them all.

The whales spoke to one another, and she listened closely. Family chatter and nothing of use to her. They watched the mermaids pass by and one calf bobbed their head in a hello to them. Sirena had thoughts of asking the family if they had seen or heard but the realization that if they were seeing whales, they had gravitated into the Sunlight Zone, quickly replaced anything.

She looked at the cliffs and ledges that they passed. As she looked at the cliffs and ledges that they passed, she noticed her surroundings and how stunning they were, realizing she wasn't terribly familiar with where she was. She had spent most of her time in the Western region. In the Eastern region, she only knew her way based on instinct and her magic. She had no choice but to let her magic guide her.

"Where are we going?" Cat hesitated a bit, as though she might know where they were.

"We're in the Sunlight Zone."

"Right, yes. But why?" Cat kept moving as she side-eyed Sirena.

"I don't know. We must have been swimming higher."

"Damn it. I knew it. Can we turn around?" Cat tried to not beg.

"You're welcome to if you want, but I'm going to sink lower," Sirena led with the crown of her head deeper into the ocean.

"I meant to get closer to the rest of the pod."

"They're in the Twilight Zone still. We need to descend lower. I don't know why we floated higher." Sirena knew she sounded desperate. They had floated higher because she got lost in her thoughts and didn't pay attention. She focused her attention on getting them lower into the ocean, leading her friend to safety.

Cat stayed quiet for a while and they swam straight downwards until Sirena could almost see the Midnight Zone. The change in layers was only truly noticeable by surveying one's surroundings, and she was unfamiliar with this region. Her panic subsided as she noted she could no longer see more than a meter or two in front of her face.

Not one to stay silent for long, Cat started up with her usual chatter.

"I think everyone is still reeling from war. It's only been a few weeks. A lot of misplaced anger and distrust. Clans were tossing other clan's merpeople on shore out of pure survival. I think we all lost sight of what is important. We started fighting individually instead of together. We have magic and we can sink to the depths of the oceans to get away from humans. Instead, we took it as a chance to take advantage of anyone that ever wronged us. Why didn't we escape right away?" Cat looked downcast and didn't respond.

"Deep thoughts from Catalina," Sirena smirked.

"I know. But really, I think we all looked out for ourselves out of instinct. Survival instincts maybe. No one wanted to leave their homes, so we stayed and fought the hunters. I'm not really sure when but, things changed so quickly. We were all friends and now, the Scottish are killing each other off, and I'm sure the Encantados would hang me to dry if they ever saw me again."

"I don't think that's true," Sirena said softly.

"I know it's true. There aren't many left and they'd use their last breaths to kill me," Cat said coldly.

"We were pups, and were born into these wars. There was a danger we didn't understand then. Sometimes bad things happen," Sirena said for what felt like the hundredth time. They had had this conversation so many times before.

Cat was out exploring when humans captured her parents. She longed to see the surface. The Encantados were in the Western hemisphere, off the coast, and she had heard that it was beautiful. An innocent child's curiosity.

Sirena had been in the Encantado territory with her father. Asterios had been traveling from clan to clan, meeting with advisors and leaders of each to discuss the most recent attacks and the future rescue missions they were planning. Sirena had begged to go with and he had let her. This one time only, he had said. Sirena smiled fondly at the memory of traveling with her father. She had admired how he interacted with the other leaders. All had loved him and her mother. They may have been under attack, but they were all united during those times.

Sirena and Cat had become fast friends, as they were about the same age. Since Cat's parents weren't leaders or even part of the advisors for the Encantados, they were hesitant to let Cat tagalong with Sirena, not knowing what Sirena's responsibilities were but Asterios had assured them it was acceptable for the pups to go off and play. Sirena, while a royal, wasn't in line for leadership and was young enough that she didn't have responsibilities. She was a pup so she could play with the other pups.

Cat had begged to see the surface, and while Sirena had refused to go, she agreed to cover for her. A decision that Sirena knew she would regret for the rest of her life.

Cat had been gone too long, and when Sirena told Asterios and Cat's parents, they had taken off in search of her. Asterios in one direction and Cat's parents in the other. Asterios returned with

Cat, but Cat's parents hadn't returned. When Asterios and the advisors had gone to look for them later on, they returned with a look of defeat written across their faces.

It was then that Sirena had insisted that Cat return with them to the Siren's territory. Asterios had wanted to leave her with her clan or take her to the Aicaya but Sirena had begged and pleaded and eventually Asterios had given in.

Apollo had shared the details of the rescue mission only a few years ago, after years of Sirena pleading with him. He made her swear never to share the details with Cat.

Sirena knew that Cat still blamed herself for her parent's death and while they didn't talk about it much anymore, it had been a regular discussion as they were growing up. Cat's heart still ached from the loss, and Sirena knew she often pondered how her life would have turned out if her parents had survived. Cat had assured Sirena repeatedly over the years that she was grateful to the Sirens for taking her in because she knew what the other option might have been. The Encantados were more ruthless than other clans and often handed their strays to the Aicaya. Not that the Aicaya were terrible merpeople. They were a group of mers that knew their clans did not want them and, therefore, merpeople tried to find a pod that wanted them before joining the Aicaya. Aicaya territory had become the most welcoming of all the territories.

Regardless of their background or origin, every merperson without a home found acceptance in the Aicaya territory.

"I know, only pups," Catalina repeated Sirena's words, interrupting the painful memory.

"I don't think your clan would have turned on you. From what I remember, no one seemed to even mention anything of the sort," Sirena assured her friend.

"It wasn't what they said. It's how they looked at me, but it doesn't matter anymore. That was so long ago and we have bigger problems."

"I know I should know this but, do we even know what the Encantados are doing? Are they keeping to themselves or… are any of them left?" Sirena trailed off. She should know what the statuses of the other clans were.

"I don't have a clue. I'm sorry. You know everyone that I talk to. We're together all the time," Cat poked Sirena in the arm and laughed.

Cat's playfulness turned to horror as she stared past Sirena's head.

Alarmed, Sirena turned to see what Cat saw.

A Rusalka mermaid floated on the edge of a cliff to their right. Sirena could reach the mermaid in a few strokes of her tail. They were nearing Rusalka territory, but they weren't close enough to see the ghostly mermaids yet so this Rusalka had most certainly escaped.

Sirena called out to the mermaid, the Rusalka. "How are you out?"

She greeted them with a haughty glare and silence. The Rusalka weren't only in the Siren's territory. They had broken their borders.

Sirena swallowed her fear and spoke to the ghost. "I'm Sirena, Queen of the Sirens and leader of the merpeople. Answer me!"

Again, silence accompanied a stone-cold stare.

"She's speaking to you," Cat broke the terrifying silence.

The Rusalka's ghostly face contorted, exposing rows upon rows of jagged, sharp teeth. Indicative of a past Siren. Siren's natural states were not the beautiful appearance they normally portrayed. This Rusalka was no different, and they put on a display of sharp claws, jagged teeth and a hideous face. The Siren ghost before them looked much like Sirena had looked only hours ago. Sirena couldn't deny this ghost had once been a Siren.

Sirena let her magic tingle at her fingers as she raised a hand, prepared to defend herself and Cat if she needed to. The Rusalka stared at them, chest heaving, teeth out. Sirena could feel her body vibrating as her magic ran through her and as her anxiety rose into her throat.

She could feel Cat shaking next to her as the Rusalka approached them.

"Stop right there! I command you to stop. I am your ruler," Sirena's voice choked, barely above a whisper. She let her magic release from her fingertips; it dripped in long strands, waiting to be released. Would a blast even work on this one? It looked different from the one that had been in their territory.

She threw sparks at the encroaching mermaid, only to have her fear confirmed. Her magic didn't do a thing to this Rusalka. The sparks fizzled out behind the ghost, having no effect.

"You didn't expect that to work, did you?" Cat whispered angrily at her.

"It did on the one in our territory," Sirena retorted.

"There were three of you then."

Sirena shrugged but, before she could respond, the Rusalka had reached them. It hadn't swum or moved towards them. The figure had blinked and then reappeared in front of them.

The Rusalka wrapped her cold, ghost fingers around Sirena's neck and brought her face to meet Sirena's. Coldness surged through Sirena's body and down to the very tips of her fins. Heart racing and her arms shaking, she struggled to bring her own hands up to where the Rusalka's were, holding her head up to the undead face. She got a few fingers under the thumb of the ghost to allow herself to speak.

"You know not what you do. You will fail. You have failed," the Rusalka whispered in Sirena's face. Sirena shook in the mermaid's grasp, struggling to break free.

"Let her go!" Cat screamed and swam around behind the Rusalka, trying to grab at her hands.

"You must leave."

As the Rusalka spoke, her teeth receded into her mouth and her face returned to normal. Sirena gasped and felt weak, her heart feeling as though it might give out.

Maia.

"Maia," she squeaked out while still flailing in her dead sister's gasp.

Maia spoke in short sentences that had a sickly staccato feel to them. It was not the Maia that she knew. "You failed all of us. You failed me. You will lose. Get out,"

"You're a Rusalka? How? How are you out this far?" Sirena barely mustered up the courage to speak after the sheer shock of seeing her dead sister as a ghost.

"You have failed."

"What happened to you?"

And then Sirena realized she could ask what she had wanted to know since her sister died. "Who murdered you? Who was it? Tell me!" Sirena screamed, freeing herself from Maia's grasp. They were staring eye to eye, rather than Maia hovering over her.

Maia said nothing at first, but did not break eye contact with her. She spoke, only repeating her previous words.

“Leave. Now. You have failed us all.”

With her last words, Maia’s ghostly image vanished right in front of Sirena. Sirena remained motionless. Her throat, still throbbing from Maia’s grip.

When it had felt like hours had passed, Catalina finally spoke. “What happened here? And why is she a Rusalka?”

“She met a tragic end. Of course she’s a Rusalka,” Sirena replied sadly. She continued to stare at the space her sister had been in.

The two sat a while longer, without speaking, before eventually continuing their journey north.

“You’re right. We knew someone murdered her. Of course she’s a Rusalka,” Cat said softly, touching Sirena’s arm lightly to console her.

“You heard her. I failed them. I failed everyone.”

Sirena shook off her friend’s touch and resumed her journey.

Chapter 26

Xan

Xan was still bitter about splitting up. He knew that his anger emanated off of him and he didn't care. Orinn should have stayed behind. She had no business here. How could an ancient mermaid who had never once been on a rescue declare that she knew what was best for them?

He had seen the look on Sirena's face. She didn't agree either. He hated to admit it to himself, but he felt frustrated with Sirena, too. She should have pushed harder; she was their new ruler and she could have overruled Orinn.

"You need to let it go," Theo interrupted his thoughts.

He glared at Theo and sped up.

"Get control of yourself."

He spun around to look at Theo. "We're in the same position as we were before. You know it. Sophie and Orinn run the world. Coralis. All of it. They did it with Malee. Maia would not be any different and they're doing it with Sirena. You saw the look on Sirena's face. She doesn't like this either."

Theo nodded at him. He agreed, but didn't say a word.

"Why separate us? Why? Even on rescues, what's our number one rule? Everyone stays within earshot of each other. Can you hear Sirena if she needs us? Or how about Nova? No, you can't."

"If we were going to separate, she should have separated the two of us. Put one of us with Kassia and Neo and the other with Sirena. Sirena should be with one of us," Theo agreed.

"And why is she doing this to Sirena? She left her with Cat. Cat!" Xan's anger bordered on terrifying, but Theo had seen him worse.

"Sirena can handle herself. You saw her with the wards and with Aiko. Whatever the shell that was," Theo's face contorted as he considered the consequences of what they had witnessed of Aiko's power.

"Of course she can. That is not the point and you know it. Why separate the new Queen of the Mermaids from us? Send her on her own with the last of the Encantados? What's Cat going to do? Screech at the Rusalka? Turn into a dolphin and swim away?"

Theo gave a slight grunt of acknowledgement and kept swimming.

"You know damn well that it should be you, me, and Sirena. That's it."

"And Neo," Theo looked pointedly at Xan.

"Sure, for the Mami Wata wards, Neo. But what about now? He's never been on a rescue. He's smart as shell, I'll give him that, but we do not know if he can fight and this will be a fight."

"He held his own with the wards and his brains balanced out your brute strength," Theo grinned at him.

Xan tried to laugh but made strangled grunts more than anything. "You're right. Neo has been helpful. He heals faster than any Siren I've ever seen. Faster than even Sirena, maybe."

"With the addition of Neo, I agree with you. You, me, and Sirena should be out here. The rest are liabilities," Theo agreed.

"I don't understand why we have to keep Orinn and Sophie around. What have they done for the last hundred years? Swim around and complain. That's it," Xan fired himself up again.

"Maybe it will be different with Sirena. We agreed to support her, encourage her. Orinn's decisions influenced her because we failed to intervene."

"Nothing? I think I fought hard enough. I thought she would stand up to her. After the wards and what Bia said, I thought," he trailed off, shaking his head.

"Because a sea witch that she doesn't know told her that her name means strong willed and that her magic is something that she's never seen before? Think about it, Xan."

Xan stared angrily in front of him, but didn't speak.

"If you were in her position, how would you feel?"

"I'd have gotten rid of Orinn immediately. Probably Sophie too."

"That's not what I mean, and you know it. Her family is gone. She's Queen of all the merpeople when that's something she's never wanted and she has Rusalka roaming around the oceans. The merpeople are fighting with each other. Then there is Aiko and, well, that's an additional problem."

"I know." Xan's rage started to quiet but guilt replaced it.

"If something happened to you, I can't imagine having to move on as if nothing happened minutes later. She lost Maia and Apollo weeks after her mother. We've lost them all too, you know."

A long pause followed as Theo's words hung in the water between them.

"Do you think he's alive?" Xan asked.

"I don't know, but I can only hope."

"Sirena's power. Do you think it's heightened because the rest of the royal family is gone? Maybe all of it is living in her?"

Theo appeared nervous as he said, "I can't think about that."

"I think Sirena feels it too. That Apollo's gone; I mean. The channel of nightmares, her face. Did you see it? She saw her family. I'm sure of it."

"I don't think that at all," Theo disagreed.

"You don't?" Xan asked, surprised.

"No, what did you see?"

Xan hesitated. He didn't want to share what he saw.

Theo didn't wait for him. "It shows you your nightmares, right? My biggest nightmare is crabs."

"Crabs?" Xan's voice squeaked in disbelief.

"Yes, giant ones coming up from the Abyss and picking us off one by one."

"That's the dumbest thing I've ever heard."

"It's a nightmare. They are dumb. It shows you your nightmares. Not your fears. They're not the same thing," Theo chuckled at his own dumb dreams.

Xan pondered this for a minute. After pondering for a minute, Xan hesitantly offered, “I saw that rescue mission where the humans almost caught us. You remember the one. One of our first. That little cottage where the little human screamed and screamed when we were trying to get that Kelpie out. Humans are scary enough, but the little ones,” Xan shuddered.

Theo laughed, “I remember the one.”

“Not our fears, but our nightmares, then. What do you imagine Sirena has nightmares about?” Xan asked.

Theo shrugged, “Guess you’ll have to ask her. But I know it wasn’t about her family. She hasn’t had enough time to sleep since losing Maia and Apollo to have nightmares about them.”

Xan gave a grim smile at Theo’s attempt at humor and nodded.

“Instead of being angry with her and arguing with her, have some empathy,” Theo said directly.

“I haven’t argued with her,” Xan protested.

“Is that so?”

“Yes, I guess I did,” Xan sighed. “It feels like years ago since we last saw her and I know it’s only been hours. These last few days. These last few years…”

“Want things to change? You want to fight the humans and get back to rescue missions? Or do you want Sirena to change the ancient rules that we live by? Then help her. Get your anger in check and speak up. But speak up the right way. Not screaming at Orinn. Not sitting there waiting for her to come up with answers. We're both guilty of standing there these last few days while she looked at us for help. Nova and Cat are her friends but they aren't Sirens. They didn't do rescues with her; they don't know what she's capable of. We do. She needs to talk through things with someone. Sirena can handle this. All of it. But she needs her friends."

"You're right," Xan said calmly, his anger completely transformed into guilt.

"I'll be more supportive, too. I only deferred to you because you're closer to her. We trained her but once she had experience, she teamed up with you and I paired up with Apollo."

Xan took a deep breath through his gills before speaking again. His heart hurt at what he was about to confess to his brother. "Do you know what's really terrible?" He continued before Theo could answer and he lost his nerve. "I don't feel bad about Maia. I haven't, not once in these last few days. When I saw the power transfer to Sirena, the only thought in my head was, thank the oceans. I had hope again. And then Sophie and Orinn started up again with their orders and Sirena followed them."

Theo paused for a minute before replying, "I had the same feelings. Maia was a good mermaid, but nothing would have changed. We would have spent the rest of our lives in the Midnight Zone if she stayed the Queen."

"I have hope again," Xan said quietly.

"I do as well, so let's be her support so she can make the tough decisions." Theo took in a deep breath through his gills before speaking again. "We have to support her because if Sirena fails, we all lose. She is the last royal, and she's always been the most defiant which I think might be what we need. But she won't defy the older generations without the right support from the rest of us."

Xan nodded. "I'll do better."

"She loves you; you know that right?" Theo looked at Xan cautiously.

Xan didn't return the look, but nodded. "I know."

Neither brother said anything for the rest of the journey. It was right before they approached the Rusalka territory before Theo spoke. "Are you going to tell her?"

"Tell her what?"

"That you don't feel the same?"

Xan didn't respond and swam ahead of his brother.

Chapter 27

Orla & Alanna

They had been swimming for hours and Alanna felt exhausted. It wasn't the swimming so much that was wearing her out, but her thoughts. Her thoughts might kill her. Orla often harbored bitterness towards the Sirens and their exile, portraying herself as the victim and refusing to acknowledge her own role in the wars. Alanna, on the other fin, often felt insurmountable guilt for the wars. She often thought about the day when Malee had forced Orla to pass leadership to Alanna during their exile.

Orla had been a poor leader. Under her reign, the Merrows had fled the oceans to marry humans. Alanna knew she shouldn't fault them too much; it was Merrow nature to chase after humans. Their history was littered with stories about Merrows that fell in love with humans. She had never quite seen the appeal. However, when Orla passed off rule, the depletion of their numbers was so significant that Alanna wasn't even sure how many Merrows she actually ruled over. Maybe a few hundred?

Alanna rolled around at the idea that Malee was gone in her head. Perhaps they could get into the council and help end the wars. She didn't much care what happened to the rest of the Merrows most days but, she'd be lying to herself if she didn't admit that the thought of her merpeople completely devastated and captured by humans upset her in ways she couldn't fully understand.

She looked around at her surroundings. They had traveled between the Twilight and Sunlight Zone. Alanna knew the rest of the merfolk had plunged down to the Midnight Zone, which gave her hope that they could get through the Scottish territories without getting caught up in any of their internal battles. It was bad enough she had to worry about humans but other merpeople that already hated them and each other, that seemed worse.

The Sunlight Zone was beautiful, and Alanna took a moment to appreciate the surrounding beauty. The schools of fish, the whales and the plants seemed more vibrant today. She realized it must have been a very long time since she had left her cave if this was how happy she was to see life going on around them.

Orla interrupted her thoughts. "Before you get upset, hear me out."

"The quickest way to make anyone mad is to tell them not to get mad," Alanna said.

"Hmm. Well, I was thinking, we're along the westside of Eurasia and…"

"And…"

Orla froze in place for a moment. Alanna stopped swimming, closing her eyes for a second to regain her composure. She turned towards her sister.

"What? We're on the westside of Eurasia and what?"

"I thought that maybe if you met him, you'd understand where I'm coming from," Orla spoke cautiously.

Alanna stared at her sister in disbelief. She knew Orla was a terrible ruler, but apparently, she was stupid, too.

"You don't think we're in enough danger? The merfolk population hates Merrows. Humans are hunting all of our kind and you want to introduce me to your lover? Are you daft?"

"I know you're not happy about all of this, but I thought that if you could see my side, if you met him, then maybe you'd be more accepting of me going to the surface and leaving you," Orla said sadly.

"You think I care about you going to the surface? I really don't. Go. Anytime you want. You are the reason they exiled us. You depleted our kind. Want to run off with a human? Go. If I could give you legs myself, I would."

Alanna watched as Orla cringed at her words, obvious hurt spreading across her sister's face. Yet, she felt nothing. No pity, no regret. Her heart hardened at Orla. It had to be to accept the current state that the Merrows were in without killing her own sister. She had grown her indifference to her sister over the last few years, keeping her close only because they were blood.

"I'm not going to the surface to meet your human. If you want to do that, you're going on your own," Alanna resumed her journey, leaving Orla sputtering and flailing behind her in surprise.

"I'm sorry, I thought…"

"Do what you want. The only thing I'm going to do is get my fins to the Siren's territory in one piece and hope to the gods that the Sirens don't filet me the minute they see me."

Orla swam silently slightly behind Alanna, not engaging in further conversation. Alanna hoped she had made it clear enough that the discussion was over and she had no interest in humans.

She was past trying to convince Orla to leave her human behind. There was no point.

While wrapped up in her own thoughts, Alanna noticed other merfolk off in the distance. She slowed but didn't stop, trying to get a better look. They were in a well-lit area and if the other merfolk were in the Midnight Zone; she wasn't sure what species was in front of her. She pushed Orla further behind her and focused her attention on the merperson in front of her.

As the light glinted off the top of the merperson's head, Alanna gasped. The figure in front of them was an Undine. The light reflected off the top of its white head and she could clearly see the jagged black tufts of hair that rimmed the head of the Undines. Their melted white skin was slimy and disfiguring and Alanna felt fear rising in her. Undines had fed so many Merrows to humans in search of a soul. She despised the soulless merpeople and felt hatred mix with her fear.

She would argue that they were barely merpeople. While other merfolk were beautiful and had their own powers, the Undines were grotesque and the only thing they shared with merpeople was that they possessed a fin. They were cold, calculating and brutes.

Orla could see the Undine in front of them, and she had come to a stop behind Alanna, grasping her sister's shoulder in fear.

"We need to take cover," Alanna whispered to Orla.

Orla nodded but didn't speak.

Alanna scanned her surroundings for a cave or ledge to hide them but realized that despite being surrounded by foliage and rocks, there was nothing that would truly conceal them from the Undines. Their bright and colorful fins stood out amongst the green plants and dark rocks that flanked the edges of the passageway they were in.

She pushed them backward a few meters and pulled Orla with her as they swam left, opposite of the direction that the Undine was swimming in. If she looked closely enough, she could almost swear there were two of them crossing their path. She didn't wait around long enough to see if she was correct.

They were hugging the edge of what she assumed was Africa to their left. They were so close to the surface, and she felt her stomach tighten at the thought of what was before them. Barely out of their own territory and they had seen Undines. If they swam into humans, what would she do then?

As they waited a few moments, allowing the Undines to put distance between them, Alanna looked up and saw that she could see the surface of the water above them. It had been years since she swam on the surface. She wasn't even sure she remembered the last time. An uneasiness spread through her as she realized the Undines were below them and humans were above them. She felt slightly claustrophobic as she realized the Undines and humans had them trapped.

Orla pushed herself up to the surface, and Alanna hovered in place for a moment in shock. She dodged Orla's flapping fin as she treaded water above the surface. Given the choice of fighting the Undines or humans, she would have chosen the Undines but her damn sister was up at the surface already. Alanna moved out of the way of her sister's fin and looked up at the water's surface again. Regret already filled her as she let herself float upward and break through the water line.

Alanna brushed water from her eyelashes and squinted her eyes against the bright sunlight. The water offered considerable sun protection when you were several layers below. She had forgotten how bright it was above the surface. The water drained from her ears and she felt her gills sputter and then flatten to her neck, no longer needed above the water. She gasped as her lungs stuttered with their first solid air breath in years.

As her ears cleared, she heard Orla chattering away and after a few moments; she realized the chatter was not at her. They were not alone.

Blinking and regaining her eyesight, Alanna saw water nymphs surrounding them. The water nymphs comprised ocean, sea, and river nymphs. Ocean nymphs; Ozara, Yara and Cara spoke in rhymes and rarely associated with the other nymphs. The sea and river nymphs were more pleasant and traveled together. Alanna found it hard not to give them a small smile. Since she didn't travel to the surface any longer, she hadn't seen them in years.

The nymphs were small and spritely, no bigger than the size of a herring. Their bright colors reflected the sunlight, creating multi-colored shimmers on the water. Alanna looked from Nerissa, a sea nymph; to Rian, a river nymph. She had considered them close friends at one point, when the Merrows were still part of the council and she traveled to other territories.

Nerissa squealed with excitement and threw her tiny body around Alanna's neck. Alanna fought the urge to laugh and gave the nymph a quick hug before setting her in the water.

"It's been years!" Rian chimed.

Alanna gave a small smile, acknowledging the truth in her statement. Nervous about being at the surface, she took a quick look around, feeling that they weren't alone.

"Tell me, ladies, how have you avoided humans for so long?" Alanna asked.

Rian cast her eyes downward and paused for a moment. Alanna looked at the nymphs and took a quick roll call.

Nerissa, Nori, Naiya for the sea nymphs. Rain, Rian, and… she didn't recognize the third river nymph.

"Where's Rina?" Alanna asked.

"We didn't all escape the humans. They caught one of us once," Rian spoke quietly.

Alanna's heart fell into her stomach. She looked at the newest nymph, whose name she didn't know. The nymph didn't make eye contact and stared at her hands, floating in front of her in the water.

"This is Ripley," Rain introduced her to the newest nymph.

Ripley smiled a small, but warm, smile. "I'm pleased to meet you, although I'm sorry it's under these circumstances that we've met."

Alanna replied, "Likewise."

"Orla says you're on your way to the Siren territory?" Nerissa chimed in.

"Yes, we're on our way to meet with Maia. With Malee gone, it seems like it might be the right time to ask for admittance into the council," Alanna said cautiously.

Confusion whipped across the nymph's faces as they looked at one another.

"Do you mean you're on your way to speak with Sirena?" Nerissa asked.

"Sirena? Why would we seek her out? Is she in a position to admit us into the council?" Alanna asked.

"I should think so. She's our Queen," Rian said.

Alanna looked at the nymphs in disbelief. Sirena? “Can someone fill me in on what happened?”

“We’re not really supposed to be talking to you even,” Nerissa looked ashamed.

“I know, but this seems kind of important. Ozara told us about Malee. What happened to Maia?” Alanna’s slight excitement over seeing the nymphs turned to frustration.

They looked at one another again before Nori finally spoke up. “We don’t really know. The Sirens don’t know either. When they killed Maia, the Siren power transferred to Sirena. There was a Rusalka attack in their territory shortly afterwards. Sirena and her pod are traveling to the Rusalka territory.”

“They’re probably there already,” Nerissa added.

“Yes, most likely,” Rian said.

Alanna was motionless. They had lost two Queens in a matter of what, weeks? Days? Sirena, the new leader? What had happened all these years while they were in exile?

“There’s one more thing you should know,” Nerissa said. She hesitated for a moment longer before continuing. Her guilty conscience was obvious as she wrestled with sharing information with exiled mermaids. “Apollo is missing as well.”

“What?” Alanna felt numb. They were down to their last royal?

Nerissa scrunched her face up as if she were in pain, her already pixie-like voice rising a few octaves as she said, "I know what you're thinking and yes, Sirena is the last royal we have. As far as we know."

"I don't even know what to think," Alanna felt frozen, despite the warmth of the sun.

Nerissa's guilt seemed to be gone or at least hidden at the moment as she rushed out her next words without taking a breath, "The Rusalka are free. The territory's borders have broken. Sirena and her pod went to the Mami Wata for help and they're on their way to the Rusalka territory. Maia had ordered all clans to the Midnight Zone and then the Rusalka showed up. It's an absolute mess, Alanna."

Alanna felt empathy for Sirena. This was a mess indeed, and the Merrows were at fault. "I can't imagine how Sirena is feeling. Her entire family is gone, and she's on her own. What can I do to help?"

The nymphs seemed to think this over for a few seconds before Rian said, "I think going and offering your help is probably what she needs right now. You have a longer journey to her territory than she does to get home. If you stay on your path, you'll arrive around the time that they return home."

"If everything turns out with the Rusalka," Alanna stated.

"Well, yes," Nerissa confirmed.

Orla remained silent as she floated next to Alanna. Orla's lack of surprise, and her unawareness of Sirena, were clear as she floated next to Alanna. She seemed preoccupied.

"Did you know?" Alanna turned to Orla.

"No. How could I? I'm hearing this the same as you," Orla responded.

The nymphs continued to shift, and Alanna made a point of holding Nerissa's eye for a few seconds. The nymph squirmed under her gaze. Alanna turned to Orla again to accuse her of withholding information when a shadow passed over them.

Shifting her gaze upwards, Alanna saw a man standing over them from the shore. She felt her muscles tighten, and she found herself unable to speak. Orla moved next to her and swam towards the figure. Horror filled Alanna as she found herself unable to speak or reach out to stop her sister.

Alanna noticed the nymphs didn't reciprocate her fear. They turned, and Nori waved at the figure. She drew a rough breath in and forced her throat to open enough for her to speak. However, she found she didn't need to say a word.

"Alanna, this is Edward," Orla threw her arms around the man kneeling on shore.

Alanna felt anger filling her. She knew her red hair was turning black and blue and she didn't care. Her sister deliberately put her in harm's way.

"Did you all know about her affair?" Alanna looked at the nymphs.

Nerissa nodded. "We thought you were here to see him. We didn't know you were traveling to the Sirens."

"Why would you think I'd be here to meet him? Unless…"

Orla bit her lip as she looked at Alanna apologetically. "Those Undines pass through around the same time every day."

"You knew we'd have to go up towards the surface. You lied to me."

"I'm sorry Alanna. I knew if you met Edward, you'd see why I love him." Orla looked up at the man.

Alanna looked at the nymphs, understanding how her sister had remained safe all this time while visiting the surface. They had watched over her. She pulled away from them in disgust.

Rian grabbed her arm, "Please Alanna, don't be mad. We kept her safe. It's alright and now you know. She can be with him and be human with no danger befalling her or the merfolk."

"I've learned a lesson today. Trust no one," Alanna glared at them. The nymphs, her sister, the strange man on the shore and when she could no longer quell her dark hair and fin from surfacing, she dove underwater and away from them.

Chapter 28

Leander

Swimming quietly through the Siren's territory, Leander searched for Sophie trying not to wake the pods of sleeping Sirens. It had only been a day since Sirena had told him about Maia and he had tried to wait a few hours before setting out to speak with Sophie, but found that his nervousness had gotten the best of him. He had told Ajax what happened with Maia and left his territory maybe an hour after Sirena's pod had left.

"I wondered when you'd show up," Sophie's voice came from behind him.

Leander turned around, surprised to see that Sophie had come from the caves that he had passed. "I came right away. What happened to Maia?"

"We don't know. Honestly, I don't have a clue," Sophie said helplessly. Leander noted how her age showed. How long had it been since he'd seen her? Not long enough for her to have aged this drastically.

"Maia was one of us. She believed in order, in our traditions," Leander trailed off, leaving the rest unsaid, but it hung between them.

"She followed the rules. She was going to keep things as they have always been. The senior leaders in control, the hierarchy is in place," Sophie whispered.

"And Sirena?" Leander asked.

"I don't know Leander. She's young, she's rebellious. Malee and Asterios didn't bring her up in the council. Sirena did whatever she wanted, gallivanting on rescue missions with those merboys."

Leander nodded. "What about Apollo?"

Sophie's expression was unreadable, replaced with a hardness that Leander couldn't decipher.

"We don't know where he is."

"Sirena told me that. I meant; will he follow the rules? Will he keep Sirena in control? Keep the natural order?"

Sophie waved her hand dismissively at him. "I know very little about him, if I'm being honest. He's not much older than Sirena and Apollo and Sirena share the same pod. Even if we could get Sirena to pass Siren rulership over to him, I'm afraid it would be much the same."

"Then what do we do?"

"Orinn went with them. They went to the Rusalka, you know that."

"I sent Neo with them. He'll be a hindrance to them and hopefully that eliminates any threat to my reign."

Sophie gave him a confused look. "Is he actually a threat to you?"

Leander sighed, "Probably not, but why take the chance? I saw an opportunity to eliminate a threat, so I took it."

"Sirena may be a Siren warrior, but she lacks confidence. If you saw her face when she realized she was the Queen…she's lost and clueless. There's absolutely no way that they'll survive the Rusalka territory. Xan and Theo, they might, but what will they do? They have no claims to the Siren throne. As long as Sirena doesn't make it out alive, Orinn will assume rulership."

"And Apollo?"

"If he's still alive, then Siren power will pass to him as the only Siren royal left, but we don't know where he is. Orinn will take over as our ruler."

Leander nodded in agreement. "Those issues aside, the problem remains that someone killed Maia. Another clan? Who would want her gone? The council would remain in power and order with her still here so a member of the council eliminating her seems unlikely."

"Agreed. That's a topic of discussion for when Orinn returns. There's a bigger threat than Sirena, I'm sure of it, but for now, I'd like to get the council back under elder control."

"So, we wait?"

"We do. It won't be long. Ozara told me that Sirena's pod will reach the Rusalka territory today."

"Send for me when Orinn returns," Leander said quietly and departed for his territory.

Chapter 29

Sirena

Sirena and Cat had finished the rest of their journey in silence, Sirena contemplating Maia's words. She may have had self-doubt when she received the Siren's power, but to say she had failed, failed how? There was no way she would have known what would happen to Maia and Apollo.

Maia's words haunted her. *You failed us all.* Apollo was gone, too.

Could he be a Rusalka as well?

She shoved the thought away; she couldn't think about that. There would be time later, but she couldn't think about that now, as she needed to contain the Rusalka.

She waited. In the dark of the rocks and shadows of the Rusalka territory, she and Cat waited until they saw the flashes of light from the other Sirens.

Xan and Theo were to create flashes of light and draw Rusalka towards them, and Kassia and Neo were to create another distraction. Moments apart from each other, Orinn gave her assurance that the commotion would draw Rusalka towards them and she would have a clear path to find Desdemona and cast the curse. Though she still didn't know what to do with the curse that Bia had given her. The coin felt as though it would burn a hole in her ribcage. She reached across her body and felt its form through her top.

Sirena couldn't help but feel as though she were playing a game. A game where she was Queen and when her parents told her it was time to come home, she would transform into a child again. Yet, here she was, floating in the dark in the Rusalka territory, waiting for her friends to go to battle with the ghosts of mermaids past so she could talk to the ruler of the undead. She could almost laugh if she wasn't so scared.

"How long do we wait for?" Catalina whispered to her.

"We wait for the flashes of light," Sirena whispered, holding her frustration back. This must have been the third time that Catalina had asked her this.

"It's been forever, though. What if we missed them?"

"We didn't. They had longer to travel than we did. We talked about this. We wait."

"They left ahead of us; they should have been in place before we even got here."

"They were going north of the rock formations. We are at the eastern entrance."

Catalina said nothing, but looked uncomfortable. Sirena understood how she felt, but she was in no hurry to roam the Rusalka territory.

They hid in the rocks that lined the shore of Eurasia and the jagged black rock formations that jutted above the surface in the Rusalka territory. Sirena had heard stories of the souls that wandered, trapped, in those formations, and she felt her body chill to the bone. She could see the sharp edges of the rocks, packed so closely together that nothing could grow or live. The Rusalka couldn't die, they were already dead, so scraping and cutting themselves on those rocks did nothing more than create temporary discomfort.

Catalina finally spoke, "We don't even know if the Rusalka are here. How many of them are there? They could all be out wandering the oceans for all we know. Who's saying Desde is even here?"

"She is. A leader doesn't leave her territory at a time like this."

"You did," Catalina pointed out.

Sirena shot her friend a look and Cat cowered slightly, raising her hands to show she would back off.

"Desde is a tragic soul. She wasn't vicious. She agreed to the curse, to oversee the tragic souls of the merfolk. I don't think she would let them loose. The Rusalka may be bitter, angry and evil merfolk, some of them anyway, but not all of them."

"Desde cursed the souls of merpeople that met tragic ends. She might be cruel," Cat pointed out the hole in Sirena's logic.

Sirena took in a deep breath and closed her eyes for a moment. "I know. But I think she was giving those souls another chance. She thought it was important to give them another chance at life, especially lives cut short. Even if it wasn't a life we would choose for ourselves."

Cat paused for a moment. "Maia was angry," she said cautiously.

Sirena agreed, "She was."

"What did she mean, you failed?"

Shaking her head, Sirena looked at the jagged rocks that waited before them. “I don't know. I’ve been trying to figure that out.”

“For what it’s worth, I don’t think you failed anyone or anything. The Rusalka are souls at unrest. I don’t think she even knew it was you.”

“Oh, she knew it was me.”

Cat followed Sirena’s gaze to the rock border of the Rusalka territory. Wide-eyed, she quickly turned to Sirena. Sirena nodded. There were Rusalka patrolling their border, and this was the third one she had seen twist in and out of the rocks.

“Yes, they’re here. Some of them, anyway.”

“Do you think the others…?”

“I think they’re fine. If there was an attack, we would see Siren energy.”

Catalina nodded and retreated to her thoughts. Sirena resumed her own as well, still tossing Maia’s words around her mind. They sat in silence for some time, watching Rusalka weave in and out of the rocks, lost in their patrol of eternity.

Sirena had a startling thought as she saw a Rusalka who looked eerily like Maia from a distance.

“What if Maia was telling me I’d failed them by coming here? She kept telling me I had failed and to leave. What if the threat isn’t here but at home? In our territory?” Sirena felt her heart sink as she thought about leaving her people on their own with only Sophie for protection.

"Like a distraction?"

Sirena didn't reply, but quietly lifted a shoulder to say yes. Fear surged through her body as she thought about the possibility of what this meant.

Catalina thought for a moment before saying, "You don't think Apollo is involved, do you?"

Shock spread through Sirena's face as she looked at Cat. "Like he's behind this? Maia's death? No!"

"I mean, he's missing and Maia's dead and this," she gestured at the Rusalka territory.

"No! He'd never. Don't even think that. Don't say that." Anger had replaced shock and Sirena stared at her friend.

"Maia's death… someone inside had to have done that. There was no one else in the territory."

"The Rusalka was there."

"The Rusalka in our territory was different. It wasn't like when we swam into Maia. Did Apollo ever want to be in control? Did he want to rule over the Sirens?"

Sirena contemplated the question for a moment. "Never. Apollo and I, we enjoyed our missions, our minor roles in the Siren affairs. He often said he'd never want to be responsible for the council like Maia was. He didn't even like half of the council.

Especially after he ended things with Aiko all those years ago. He said things were awkward."

"Aiko…" Cat trailed off.

"She's the one responsible. You know she is. You saw how defensive and angry she was."

Cat agreed, "She was." She looked at Sirena, unconvinced.

"What is it?" Sirena demanded.

Cat paused, hesitating for a moment. "I think you should keep your mind open to all possibilities. You're the Queen, like it or not. The lives of all merkind are on you. You alone are responsible for thousands of lives. You know I love Apollo and I don't think he's responsible for all of this but, where is he?"

Cat's words washed over her as she considered the possibility that Apollo was involved. There wasn't a single outcome or scenario that she could come up with that would put Apollo behind all of this.

She didn't have long to think, however, as twin flashes of light came from the north.

Chapter 30

Neo

Neo felt his gills shudder as he tried to pull in breaths. His heart jumped into his throat as he watched Kassia shoot flares from her fingertips. He hovered a few meters behind her, his eyes darting around them, watching and waiting for the Rusalka to appear.

He may not have Siren energy, but he was decent enough with hand-to-hand combat and if Kassia could hold them off long enough, he could pick out any stragglers that made it through her blasts. They had discussed their plan for most of their journey to this dreaded territory. Kassia had been a well enough companion, filling in the quiet moments with endless chatter about her life, Theo, stories from when they were pups. He had discovered that Kassia, Cat and Sirena had grown up with each other and were within a few years of each other. Kassia had told him how her brightly colored tail and hair differed from the typical Siren colors because she changed her appearance. When he had asked what her Siren form looked like, she had laughed and said; *you saw Sirena's? I look like the rest of them, dark and moody*. She was charming and bubbly, unlike the rest of the dark and brooding Sirens. Her endless stream of nonsense had quieted the nervousness of what lay ahead for them. However, his anxiety threatened to strangle him. The waiting for Rusalka seemed endless.

Kassia flashed her light again in another flare. Xan and Theo were now within eyesight, and he saw both of them letting out streams of energy as well. Theo looked at him, giving him a helpless look as they both waited in confusion.

Neo spun around in all directions, looking for Orinn and Nova. When he didn't see them, he turned to Kassia. "Again?" he asked.

She responded with another blast of light, Xan and Theo following her lead.

Xan held up a hand to them. "Wait," he mouthed to them. Kassia nodded and searched the darkness in front of her.

Neo put his back to Kassia and watched in the opposite direction, as Theo had done to Xan. Where were they? Had they really all left their territory? If that were the case, wouldn't they have seen more Rusalka on their travels?

A flash of light cut through the darkness, and Neo whipped around to see who it came from. The Sirens near him looked as confused as he felt. Judging from the direction of the light, he knew it had to have been Sirena. Had they found her?

"We need to go to her," Neo said frantically to the group.

Xan held his hand up, halting them. "Wait."

"For how long? Until she's dead? Until the last of our leaders is gone?" Neo snapped angrily at Xan.

Theo looked hesitant, as though he agreed with Neo, but didn't speak. Kassia turned around to face Neo, all four of them looking at each other, their backs turned to the Rusalka territory.

"Xan, we have to go to her. The plan didn't work. You and Sirena were right. We should have come in together," Kassia panicked.

Neo felt her emotions echo his own. He hadn't liked Orinn's plan either.

Xan paused for a moment, the look on his face showing he knew something had gone wrong. The Rusalka borders may have dropped, but they hadn't encountered enough of them on their travels. They had swum from one end of Coralis to the other and only encountered one. Where were they?

Before Xan responded, Neo saw movement out of the corner of his eye and turned around to look over Kassia's shoulder. A Rusalka lurked behind them, meters away. He reached out to pull Kassia closer to them and further away from the ghost mermaid.

As Neo grabbed Kassia's wrist to pull her away from the Rusalka, he made eye contact with her. Her eyes were black beads, the light extinguished from them. Blood swirled in the water between them as an ugly, red wound appeared on her chest.

A spear pierced through Kassia's chest and her body went limp. Neo held her wrist as her body sank towards the bottom of the ocean. He scrambled to grab her and keep her afloat.

Theo's screams tore through Neo as he felt Kassia's weight torn from him. Theo cradled Kassia as her body disintegrated. Sirens decomposed so quickly and Neo watched in horror as Theo desperately tried to hold on to what remind of Kassia. He flailed until there was nothing left of her. Her head and torso melting into the water.

Xan jumped into action and blasted the Rusalka away from them. Blast after blast, he pushed the Rusalka further until the ghost hovered in place and didn't move. Neo watched Xan and Theo in their separate battles and felt helpless.

"Where's Orinn?" Xan screamed at no one in particular.

Neo searched in all directions, coming up empty.

"Go find her Neo."

Looking around him, Neo saw a herd of Rusalka closing in on them. He watched as Theo choked on his emotions, letting the minimal remains of Kassia sink, joining his brother. Neo swam in the opposite direction, looking for Orinn and hoping to find Sirena.

Chapter 31

Sirena

They had moved at those first flashes of light, swimming right into a few Rusalka. Sirena had sent them off to wherever Rusalka temporarily went when they disappeared. Still confused why some disappeared while others were like Maia, Sirena continued to push through the territory in search of Desde. Cat trailed slightly behind her, keeping an eye out for any movement behind them.

Sirena had been careful to weave them in and around the large rocks unharmed. She didn't know where Desde spent her time, but, if she had to guess, it was at the center of those rocks.

Her family had always lived in the center of their territory, leaving the surrounding areas open for the other Sirens to inhabit. They believed their merpeople would protect the royal family before danger could find them. She hoped Desde felt the same. Although, what could really happen to the Queen of the Undead?

As they approached the center of the rocks, Sirena felt her body shake with fear. She saw that she had been right, as there was a large cave in the center of the rocks. The undead merpeople swarmed the opening. A quick count told her that there were at least a dozen Rusalka floating around outside of Desde's hidden home.

A gasp from Cat caught her attention and Sirena turned to see a Rusalka an arm's reach from them. A blast would catch the attention of the dozen ghosts in front of her. She held her breath, her gills refusing to work.

The Rusalka reached out and grabbed her arm, gently. She lowered her gaze down to the hand on her arm and then up to the face of the Rusalka. Her fear dissipated as she saw she was staring up at the ghost version of Asterios.

Tears burned her eyes. Her father's face was warm and gentle, a stark contrast to what Maia had been.

"Alcie," he whispered.

Unable to speak, her voice caught in her throat, and Sirena let out only a slight sound.

"So much has happened to you in a short amount of time. I'm sorry I wasn't there."

Sirena continued to stare up at her father, still too shocked to speak.

"This is not where you belong. There are greater dangers for our kind, Alcie. You are strong, you always have been."

"I have to… have to speak to Desdemona. The Rusalka borders have dropped and they're wandering the oceans," Sirena spoke, her voice sounding strange in her ears.

"They have," Asterios agreed. "Some have left, others remain. Speak to Desde and then leave. It's not safe here."

Sirena looked from Asterios to the cave where the other Rusalka guarded Desde. Asterios took her hand and led her out into the opening. He placed an arm around her shoulders and led her towards the cave, the other Rusalka retreating from them.

"Cat," Sirena whispered.

"I'll watch her. I'll wait for you here," Asterios said as they crossed the short distance of the opening and hovered at the entrance to the cave.

Sirena had so many questions for her father but knew she couldn't leave her friends out in the open battling angry Rusalka for long. She looked at the undead version of her father, covered in chalky white and age spots speckling his skin. He motioned to the cave again, and she finally entered, leaving her father and the answers that she wanted behind.

Chapter 32

Xan

"Theo," Xan called to his brother.

Theo grunted at Xan's voice, but he didn't stop or slow down. Rage fueled him as he held the swarms of Rusalka. They were diminishing in numbers, but too slowly. There was still no sign of Neo or Orinn. How long had it been since Neo left? A few minutes? An hour? Xan didn't know, but he would have appreciated the extra help.

They were facing opposite directions, sending their energy streams rippling through the water at the Rusalka that charged at them tirelessly. Xan grew tired, but he could feel Theo's rage circling around them and he continued to fight for his brother, for Kassia, for Sirena. His thoughts drifted to Sirena. The light flashes that they saw were hers. There was no mistaking her gold energy.

Theo had been wrong when he said that Xan didn't love her. He did. However, there were complications. Sirena was the younger sister of his closest friend and a royal. They spent a great deal of time together on missions and his feelings for her grew. However, they had grown up together. He couldn't quite figure out his feelings towards her. He knew he loved her but he wasn't sure it was the romantic, lifelong mate love that he felt for her.

He had promised himself that if they survived the Rusalka, he would talk to her. They could decide together how they approached any type of relationship. He had watched his brother lose his mate and the thought of losing Sirena without her knowing how he felt weighed heavily on him.

"Xan," Theo said, interrupting his thoughts, "Neo and Nova." Theo nodded towards his right, Xan's left.

Xan looked to see Neo and Nova making their way through the Rusalka towards them. Despite lacking any real magic or power, their combat skills impressed him. He had known Nova was scrappy, but to see her in action was another thing. Nova dodged the swings of the Rusalka in front of her while tail whipping the ghosts approaching her from behind. Xan felt pride when he saw her fist contact the face of a Rusalka that was hovering over her.

Neo proved to be as dangerous, holding a large group of Rusalka himself. A brief swirl of red circled from Neo's face as he sustained a blow from a Rusalka. His quick healing took over, and the gash disappeared within seconds. Neo, unfazed, continued fighting the Rusalka. He pushed himself and Nova closer to where Xan and Theo held their space.

"Why are some of them disappearing and others aren't?" Neo called out to them.

"We saw that too. I think the older they are, the easier they disappear," Xan called to him.

Neo acknowledged that he heard Xan but didn't respond, focusing on the Rusalka in front of him. Nova and Neo were closer to Xan and Theo, only a few meters away. Xan broke his focus briefly to push away a group of the undead in between them, clearing a path. Neo took advantage of the opening and grabbed Nova by the arm, pulling her towards the Sirens.

"Did you find Orinn?" Theo asked.

Nova sounded almost frantic as she responded, "I don't know where she went. When the commotion started, she told me to stay put, and she took off. Neo found me and brought me here."

"I didn't see her anywhere and once I found Nova, I thought it was more important we got to you," Neo said.

"Where the fuck is she? This was her *plan*," Xan yelled to no one in particular.

Theo and Neo grunted in agreement. Nova looked at each of them cautiously. She took out a Rusalka that had approached them and then turned to the merboys in front of her.

"Where's Kassia?"

Xan felt his stomach turn to ice. He gave her a sad look and then paused briefly when she started screaming. The herd of Rusalka took his brief break as an invitation to advance, and he quickly resumed his defenses. He watched helplessly as Nova collapsed in Neo's arms, sobbing. Theo shook and Xan didn't know if it was from grief or exhaustion.

The Rusalka numbers were dropping. What had started out as hundreds, maybe even thousands, were down to maybe fifty. He didn't know where they went or for how long when they disappeared, but he didn't want to wait around to find out. Summoning strength from the depths of his soul, he let out as much energy as he could. His fingertips burned red, and he felt his arms go limp. The last of the Rusalka dropped.

Theo ceased his energy beams and collected Nova from Neo. Xan gave them a few moments before quietly nudging them to move in the direction Sirena's light had come from.

Chapter 33

Sirena

"I've been waiting for you."

A voice came from the darkness of the rock cave. Sirena lit her fingertips with her golden light, illuminating the cave. Desde sat perched on a bench in the cave.

Sirena looked over at the Queen of the Undead. Despite being long since deceased, Desde was a beautiful mermaid. The same chalky white decay, characteristic of the Rusalka, covered her dark features, but her black tail still glimmered in various places, giving it an almost iridescent sheen. While Desde's dark skin remained unblemished, white streaks adorned her long, black hair. Sirena found her to be quite stunning and not at all what she expected.

"Your borders fell," Sirena stated the obvious, unsure what she should say now that she was face to face with Desde.

Desde smirked, "So it seems."

Sirena, realizing how ridiculous she sounded, swallowed her fear. She tucked her shoulders behind her and floated herself upright slightly. "What do you know about it?"

"We're going to get right to it then. No introductions?" Desde said, her smile growing. "I'm afraid I know very little about it. They fell a few days ago. Some of my undead have remained, not wanting to leave our beautiful home. Others have fled and roam free," Desde made a grand gesture with her hands.

Sirena flinched at Desde's beautiful home comment. This place was anything but beautiful. She may very well be called the dark mermaid herself, but even she had to admit, this place was dark and depressing.

"Why do some of your Rusalka disappear, like an apparition? Others are like living mermaids?"

"Tragic souls are sentenced here for eternity, but just because they're here forever doesn't mean they keep their full energy force forever," explained Desde, smiling at her again and clearly enjoying Sirena's lack of knowledge.

Sirena understood. More recently, deceased souls had higher energy than those that were here longer. Maia had only been gone for days.

"My family is here."

"Indeed, they are."

"Where's Apollo?"

At this, Desde looked confused. "Apollo? He's not here."

"So, he's alive?"

"I didn't say that. He's not here. I don't receive all the deceased souls, only those that have met tragic ends. You know that."

Sirena took a deep breath in, realizing she hadn't been breathing at all as she waited for Desde's answer. Apollo's absence indicated that he was not murdered. Cat's words lingered in her mind once again but she refused to believe he was involved.

"Sweet, young mermaid. There is a traitor in your pod. You must be careful."

"Who?" Sirena demanded.

"Hmm, that I can't say, but you must watch out for yourself. You are our Queen."

Sirena felt Siren rage within her again. She knew something, and she wasn't talking. Closing her eyes for a moment, she willed herself to calm and return her eyes to their normal color. She heard a whisper and snapped her eyes open.

"What did you say?" Sirena asked.

"I said nothing." Desde focused her gaze on Sirena cautiously.

"*Sirena, Sirena….*" the whisper said again.

Sirena paused, listening, but the voice had gone silent.

"I need to re-enact the curse. Put your borders up again. We're hiding from humans in the Midnight Zone and the Scottish merfolk are picking each other off one-by-one. Not to mention most of my family is here with you and I don't know where Apollo is. I don't need your undead loose," Sirena felt the words spilling from her. She felt she had sounded quite Queen-like there and she pushed her shoulders behind her and lifted her chin at Desde.

"You'll get no argument from me, little mermaid. But, how do you propose to do such a thing? You are a Siren and while you have great power, you are not a sea witch."

"*Sirena…*" the whisper vibrated in her head. This time, she recognized the voice.

"*Bia?*" she thought to the voice in her mind.

"*It is me.*"

"*How are you in my head?*"

A laugh shook her thoughts. "*The coin.*"

Sirena felt the coin burning on her side. She reached up and pulled it from her top, holding it in front of her and flipping it over in her hands. Desde watched her but didn't speak.

"*Silly child, you thought you could place a curse with a coin? I won't leave my home, but I will help you.*"

Sirena looked from the coin to Desde. "Bia will place the curse for us," she told the undead queen.

"You're going to put the borders where they were and lock all of those souls in here again?" Sirena caught a hint of sadness in Desde's voice.

"What else would I do?" Sirena asked, confused.

Desde rose from her bench and moved towards Sirena. Sirena fought the urge to swim away from the beautiful yet wildly intimidating mermaid. Desde stared intently into Sirena's eyes.

"Your parents, along with Bia, cursed the souls that met tragic ends here. Souls that are bitter and angry."

"No, you cursed the souls that met tragic ends," Sirena argued with her, all too aware of how close the Rusalka was to her.

"I gave souls cut short a chance to live another life. I gave them another chance. Your parents and Bia trapped them here. Forced them to remain in one place. They put limits on their second chance," Desde said, carefully choosing her words.

"Semantics. Fine. What do you want from me?" Sirena demanded.

"Release the souls."

"You want me to release souls? Am I even able to do that?" Sirena questioned Desde, but also the voice in her head: Bia.

"I can give you the same option I gave your parents…"

Before Sirena could ask Bia what she meant, Desde spoke. "You can see that some undead remained. Like I said, they want to be here. This is their home. Others left when the borders dropped. They don't want to be here, nor should they have to be sentenced to this fate. They met tragic ends. Murdered, tormented and killed by humans, accidental deaths, illness. Why should we sentence them to an eternity here if they don't want to be?" again, Desde gestured to the great Rusalka territory around her.

"What are you asking of me?"

"*Give the souls a choice*," Bia whispered.

Desde nodded as though she had heard the voice inside Sirena's head. "Bia will explain it to you. It's her curse after all."

"*No borders. You give souls the choice to decide if they want to move on or remain. Upon death, the soul gets to choose their afterlife*."

Sirena looked blankly at Desde for a moment. "What about the existing souls?" she asked.

"Give them a choice, too."

"I'm undoing the curse that you put on them? The one that sentences tragic souls to an eternity here?"

"No!" Desde shouted at her.

Sirena could feel Bia flinch despite not being able to see the sea witch.

"I gave them a choice. I gave souls the option to remain in this form," Desde gestured towards herself. "Or they could move on. The choice your parents made bound them here. They made the change. *All souls that meet tragic ends have no choice but to be bound to this territory for all eternity.*"

Sirena looked at Desde and while she couldn't see Bia, she could feel her presence fill her mind. She could feel the power of the two mermaids crushing her, waiting for a decision.

"How do I know your undead souls won't leave? That they won't get bored or angry or seek revenge someday?" Sirena questioned Desde.

"You don't."

Indecision shrouded her. Do what her parents had done and curse any soul that met a tragic end to the Rusalka for all eternity. Or, allow souls to choose their fate and drop the borders to the most dangerous territory in Coralis. She wished that any member of her pod was here to talk this through with her.

"Why would I change the agreement my parents made after all these years?"

"Why do you think it was an agreement?" Desde asked.

Sirena leaned away from Desde. This was the second time that another clan's leader had said this to her. Bia's words, not Bia this time, were in her head. *Why do you think this was a choice?* She had always assumed her parents had been fair rulers.

"My parents were hundreds of years old but the Rusalka are thousands of years old. You, I assume, are the oldest of all of us," Sirena said to Desde, waiting for confirmation. Receiving it, she continued, "What did your clan do before the curse?"

Desde smiled at this. "The Rusalka didn't venture out of our territory much, but when we did, we lived in peace with the other merpeople."

Sirena didn't hide her surprise. "They didn't attack other merpeople?"

"It happened occasionally, I guess. Mostly the undead harming those that had caused their demise. Rightfully so, if you ask me. It was a rare occurrence that a Rusalka endangered a living mermaid."

Sirena contemplated Desde's comments for a few moments, trying to understand the consequences of whatever decision she made.

"What changed?" Sirena asked.

"What do you mean?"

"Why did my parents have Bia place the curse? Something must have happened that they no longer felt safe with the Rusalka having free rein of the oceans," Sirena spoke pointedly at Desde, accusing.

A soft laugh came from inside her head. Bia was laughing at her.

Desde's face was full of empathy as she said, "Malee wasn't perfect."

Sirena fell into quiet contemplation when Bia screamed in her head, "*Think about it, girl*!"

"My mother killed another merperson?" Sirena's voice became barely audible.

"She was afraid for her safety. For her child's," Desde answered her.

"Who?"

There was another question on the tip of her tongue, but Desde silenced her, "It doesn't matter who. It's long since over."

Sirena said, somewhat frantically letting the question spill from her, "I want to know if my mother is here with the soul of the merperson that she killed."

"Ah, well, I suppose she is. I have yet to see Malee but I know she's here. I'd guess she doesn't want to see me or the other mermaid, so she's staying hidden."

"Were you my mother's friend?"

"What do you think?"

Sirena sighed. An answer from Desde seemed impossible.

"One last question."

Desde gestured for her to ask her question.

"I thought the curse had been around longer than it seems to have been?"

"Your timelines are off. The curse is only about as old as Maia, slightly less. Your advisors could give you the history," Desde said somewhat dismissively.

Sirena gave her a frustrated look. The oldest mermaid she had around her was Neo, aside from Sophie and Orinn. He couldn't remember when the curse was placed, and Orinn and Sophie weren't telling her anything.

Desde's face displayed what Sirena thought might have been empathy. "The curse was placed shortly after Maia was born. Bia put it into place at your mother's orders."

"Then, when the wars started, the Mami Wata called in their favor and could sink to the depths of the oceans to avoid the humans," Sirena added.

"No, that's not how it happened," Desde said. "You'll need to ask Bia, though. That's not my story to tell you."

"*Some other time, child. What will it be*?" Bia's voice sounded impatient.

Desde stared at her intently, also waiting for Sirena's decision.

"Why give me this choice at all? Why not kill me or force me out of here and let your merpeople roam free?" Sirena asked.

Desde looked shocked for a moment. After a long pause, she said slowly, "Despite what your mother did and the ruling that she cast down, I didn't deny that something needed to be done.

Tragic souls can be dangerous. I compromised with her. It's what you do. You compromise and work with other leaders and territories. Also, you've asked many questions since you said you had one last question left. What will it be, little one?"

"Why didn't my mother want souls to have a choice where they spent eternity?" Sirena ignored Desde's comments.

"That's complicated. Your mother made a ruling for me to follow."

The voice in her head added, "*You should ask your mother....*"

"Did my mother want an undead army? Was she building the numbers of Rusalka?" Sirena said out loud.

Desde stared blankly, and while Sirena thought Desde could also hear Bia, her reaction showed that she couldn't. "Maybe."

Full of questions but also sure she had reached the limit of what Desde would answer, Sirena found herself presented with a decision that she didn't know how to answer. She sat with her thoughts for a moment. Her pod, her friends, were looking at her to change their future. They wanted things to change and she couldn't very well change anything if she made the same decisions as her parents. Or as her mother, at least.

Looking at Desde, Sirena decided. "I will have Bia give souls the choice to choose their eternity. No borders. No curses tying their souls here; how you had originally intended, Desde. But if this becomes a problem, souls will be tied here. And Bia, I'm assuming souls can choose at any time to move on?" Sirena closed her eyes as she asked Bia.

"*Yes, they can choose at any time to move on or remain.*"

Relaying the information to Desde, Sirena spoke firmly. "Bia says that souls can decide to move on whenever they want. My offer stands then. For as long as your undead merpeople remain non-violent, they will choose their fate. Without the borders, it means that they can travel the oceans but if they so much as harm another mer, even one, it's over. We will replace the borders."

"Understood," Desde regarded her gratefully, not acknowledging the fact that Sirena seemed to talk to a mermaid that wasn't in the cave with them.

"And you?" Sirena asked.

"Me?"

"Will you stay or move on?"

Desde thought for a moment, clearly shocked she was being given a choice, before saying, "I'll stay. For now."

Sirena accepted this and pushed Bia into action. "Bia, you have my decision. Make it so."

Sirena felt her body grow warm and her vision went black. Bia immobilized her body as she entwined her soul with Sirena's and placed a new curse. A positive curse allowing souls the chance to choose their fate and where they spent eternity. Sirena pushed her self-doubt away and allowed Bia to reinstate the original curse that Desde had enacted so many years ago.

***

Xan found Cat crouching in the rocks, staring at the entrance to the cave.

"She's with Desde?" he whispered to her.

"Yes," she returned his whisper.

Neo, Theo and Nova filed in behind Xan. The pod waited impatiently for their leader as a flash of light came from the cave.

"Whatever she did, I think it worked," Neo said softly as the water threw several of the Rusalka upwards, causing them to disappear.

***

Her body still shook from Bia's power. Sirena looked at Desde fiercely.

"Do not make me regret this," Sirena threatened.

"I wouldn't dream of it."

Sirena turned to leave the cave when Desde called out to her.

"Remember, there's a traitor in your pod."

Sirena's heart fell, and she looked at Desde for a moment longer before turning to leave.

"Come and visit anytime," Desde smirked, but Sirena felt a sense of sincerity to her words.

As Sirena turned to go, she felt Desde move slightly closer to her. She turned to look at the undead leader, raising an eyebrow as they made contact.

"For what it's worth to you, Alcie, I'm proud of the mermaid you've become," Desde said.

Chapter 34

Sirena

Sirena exited the cave, looking left to right, not seeing what she was looking for.

Xan came out of nowhere, grabbing her by the shoulder. "It worked!"

Nova let out a squeal and threw her arms around her friend.

There were a few Rusalka wandering around, but they no longer seemed to pose a threat to the pod. Sirena searched their faces, looking for Asterios.

"How did you do it?" Xan asked her.

"The coin. It was Bia," Sirena said distractedly, noticing that someone was missing. "Where's Kassia?"

Theo choked and sunk to the ground. Sirena's eyes widened, shock shaking her body.

"No, no, no…"

Xan wrapped his arms around her, and Nova let her sobs loose.

"What… what happened?" Sirena forced the words out.

Neo cleared his throat and spoke up. "When we caused the distraction, nothing happened for a while. The four of us moved closer together and were deciding our next move when a Rusalka stabbed her."

"I haven't seen her yet; she must be here…" Theo trailed off.

Sirena felt her heart tighten in her chest. "She might not be. It's a long story, but I didn't enact the same curse. I gave the souls a choice. A choice to choose their fate. They can either stay and roam free or they can choose to move on." Sirena trailed off.

Theo said nothing, but lowered his eyes. "She would choose to move on. She wouldn't have wanted to stay here."

"Maybe she would. She knew you were here," Xan offered gently.

Theo stared into the distance, not moving or speaking.

Xan turned to Sirena. "What did you mean, she moved on? What choice did you give them?"

"I struck a bargain with Desdemona. We didn't reinstate the original curse. Desdemona explained her original curse, and it wasn't what we thought it was," Sirena said.

The pod appeared to stop breathing, staring intently at Sirena.

"We're going to need more information than that," Xan said sternly. He was watching Sirena cautiously.

Sirena sighed, her gills struggling against the anxiety that had built up in her over these last several days.

"We were right and Desde wasn't involved with the curse breaking. I don't believe she was, anyway. She told me about the original curse that she placed and it wasn't a curse necessarily. She gave souls a choice. They could move on or they could remain in the world as a Rusalka. However, my mother bound souls to the territory, and she used Bia to place the curse. She took away their choice to move on or remain, forcing them to stay here. Prior to the curse, they roamed the oceans like us." Sirena paused and looked at the members of her pod for acceptance. She wasn't receiving it.

"What did you do, Sirena?" Xan asked.

Sirena bit her bottom lip and hesitated for a moment before answering. "I had Bia reinstate their choice. Souls can choose if they stay or go, and… they can roam the oceans as they did before."

As the pod absorbed what she said, Sirena felt a wave of guilt and regret flow through her. Had she made the right decision?

Stuttering, Xan said, "Is that the right call? What will stop them from killing the rest of us?"

"Desde said we lived together before without issues. There had been a few incidents, and she had agreed that something needed to be done, but binding them to the territory without a chance to choose their fate was wrong," Sirena defended herself. "If even one Rusalka hurts a living merperson, the borders go back up. Even then, they get the right to choose."

Sirena watched as her pod thought through the situation. Finally, Neo spoke.

"We said we needed to undo what the previous leaders had done. If you had put the borders back, you would not differ from your parents," Neo assured her.

Xan nodded. Theo looked off into the distance but interjected his thoughts. "Who did your mother kill?"

Sirena couldn't hide her shock. "I don't know. Desde wouldn't tell me."

"How many Rusalka attacks were there before your mother put up the borders?" Xan asked.

"Not that many. Desde said unprovoked attacks were uncommon. She said that most of the attacks were Rusalka attacking those who had ended their lives," Sirena answered quietly.

"This makes me nervous," Xan said.

Sirena nodded and took in a deep breath. "Me too. Desde agreed that there should be rules and proposed reinstating the borders if there is one attack. Hopefully that is enough of a deterrent."

The pod didn't speak, processing what Sirena had told them and what this might mean for them. Rusalka would now swim alongside them, along with the nightmares that lurked in the Midnight Zone. There would be danger behind every rock.

Sirena waited a few minutes before she spoke. She looked at Catalina. "Where did my father go?"

Shock registered on Nova's face as she absorbed what Sirena had said. She looked at Cat as well, eager for the answer.

"Well, based on what you said, I think he moved on," Cat whispered.

Sirena's eyes burned, and she closed them, crushing her emotions behind her lids. Of course, he would choose to move on. She had wanted answers. To see her father one more time. She couldn't hold it against him, wanting to move on. Though she didn't know that she would move on under the terms of her new agreement with Desde.

As Sirena looked at her sad and exhausted pod, grief overwhelmed her. "Desde said Apollo isn't here."

Xan nodded and pulled her close. "Let's find Orinn and go home."

"Do we have to find her?" Nova asked.

Sirena laughed softly and led her pod carefully through the rocks of the Rusalka territory.

Chapter 35

Apollo

"We need to move him again. We've been here too long."

Apollo woke to the sounds of his captors talking.

Water blanketed him again, and he was deep in the ocean. The blindfold was gone. The cave that he had awoken in the first time surrounded him again.

Gasping and struggling against the chains, he looked at the two hooded figures that sat flanking the entrance.

"You brought me here? Why?"

The guards started laughing. They looked at each other, their hoods still covering their faces, but this time, he could see the black fins of the Undines.

"What are you doing? Where am I and what kind of game is this?" Keep yourself calm, he reminded himself.

"Keep your mouth shut." The laughter continued, more subdued, but still it continued. Taunting him.

Apollo willed his magic to come to him. Begged for it. He pleaded with his energy to find its way to him. Remaining motionless and letting the guards laugh at his expense, he summoned every ounce of strength he had. One shackle. Get one shackle off one wrist and he could pull the other off.

No magic? Fine. He was still one of the strongest mermen alive.

Not caring if the guards saw him, he pulled with all of his might on the cuff around his wrist. His fingers aching and bleeding against the sharp edges. The laughter from the guards increased as they watched him try to break free. Still, he pulled on the cuff.

There was dim sunlight filtering in through the cave and he watched it dance across the iron that held him. No seams that he could see. Magic held them in place. The Undines had helped in holding him; they weren't capable of magic. Pounding the cuff against the edge of the rock ledge next to him, if he could damage it enough, the magic might let loose.

The Undines roared.

A quick glance in their direction and he noticed the tipped hood of the closest guard. An Undine, no doubt, but not one that he recognized. Hired hands to take him and hold him captive.

The magic on the cuffs was strong, but sparks flew with every hit. Since Undines lacked magic and couldn't create magical cuffs, it implied that someone enchanted these cuffs. One could break enchantments with force. If Undines were smarter, they would have realized that he could absolutely escape.

Blood flew as he pounded his wrist against the wall again and again. Debris fell from the wall and hit him in the eyes and his face, but still he pounded the cuff against the wall.

Would his magic return if he got one hand free? He didn't have to wait long to find out.

The cuff fell from his wrist, and he paused for a moment in disbelief. The Undines, still roaring and talking, didn't notice immediately that the clanking stopped. It was long enough for him to channel his magic into his free hand.

Glowing fingertips caught the attention of the Undine facing him, and Apollo had to make a quick decision. Blast off the other cuff or hit the Undines.

He shot energy across the cave, navigating the length of the cave with ease. Both Undines slumped to the floor. Shock spread throughout him, but it didn't last long. He popped the other cuff off easily with his free hand and his bloody and broken hand immediately healed.

A quick glance at his fin and it had healed, although there was a thick scar.

Apollo dropped to the cave floor and pulled the hoods off the faces of the guards that had held him. He didn't recognize either of them. Searching their cloaks turned up nothing. There was nothing on them.

Both dead, their bodies melted into the cave floor and he leaned up against the wall and watched them slowly disappear until nothing remained but a sticky gray puddle. Satisfaction spread throughout him.

He exited the cave to find the rows upon rows of rock formations that the Undines had dragged him through before. A sinking feeling hit his stomach and the hopelessness that he had felt during his captivity hit him again. Maybe this time would be different, since there would be no one to blindfold him, but he did not know where he was. None of this was familiar, and he had traveled the oceans his entire life.

Confused and frustrated, he looked around him. The rock formations formed a wall on either side of him. Without the two

Undines on either side of him, the space seemed slightly larger, but it was still a narrow, never-ending passageway. Rocks lined both sides and the ceiling. The floor, well, that was a problem. There wasn't one. Blackness blanketed the space underneath him where he was floating in place.

There was no way he could sink below into the darkness; his nerves wouldn't allow it. He had to make it out of the formations before he tired or he'd sink into the unknown and something told him death awaited him there. The Undines had stayed above the blackness and blindfolded him before they reached the end. He made it out once so he could do it again.

Sirena and the rest of the Sirens were on the other side of this obstacle, and he was going to make it out. If Sirena wasn't alive, as the last living royal, he was the king of the Sirens, and his people were in trouble.

Chapter 36

Sirena

Exhausted from days of travel and fighting with the Rusalka, Sirena surveyed her pod of merpeople. They looked as weary as she felt. Theo and Xan were the only ones that seemed able to stay upright without a struggle. Though Theo was a shell of himself and she didn't know if he'd ever be the same. They weren't far from their own territory, maybe only a day's worth of swimming left.

She felt tired, but she also felt overwhelming gratitude. Gratitude that her father's and sister's spirits were at rest and no longer forced to wander the Rusalka territory. Gratitude for her friends and advisors that had fought alongside her. She thought she might feel gratitude for Neo too, for the recent addition to her pod.

There was still the Apollo issue and who had him? Her mind drew a blank when she thought about who was doing this and why. He wasn't next in line to rule after Maia, as the next oldest mermaid, she was. There was urgency to find her last living family member, but she felt dread when she realized that if the Rusalka didn't have him, there were others working against her and the Sirens. In a world that felt like it was closing in on her, it seemed even smaller knowing that there was more than one enemy lurking. Cat's words stuck with her as well, though she didn't want to admit it to herself. She couldn't let herself consider the possibility that Apollo was involved. No, Apollo wasn't involved, but she was positive that Aiko was. Aiko was the only one that made sense.

For someone that never wanted to be the ruler of the Sirens, she had ended up responsible for this latest disaster that they found themselves in. Resentment, panic and despair fought to take hold of her thoughts. She took a deep breath to quiet her emotions and compose herself.

The group of merpeople she had taken this journey with looked older than they had days before. It felt like it had been months since Sirena had lost Maia and Apollo, but she had a feeling it had been less than a week. She planned to ask Sophie when they returned home. She was too disoriented to have a concept of time.

"Let's rest here," Sirena turned and looked at the rest of the merpeople following her lead.

"I won't argue with that," Cat said cheerfully, coming to an abrupt halt.

"Me either," Xan added.

"There are a few caves to our right. We'll have to double up or maybe triple up," she glanced at the rocks and cliffs at her side.

Letting her merpeople choose where they were going to rest for the next few hours, she waited to settle into a resting spot until they were all tucked away somewhere safe. Theo, Xan and Neo had taken shelter under a ledge, while Cat and Nova had taken the smallest of the two caves above the ledge that the boys were under. Orinn was in the opening of the second. Sirena nodded and moved up to the top cave by Orinn, telling the tired mermen to get some rest and giving Nova a half hug on her way to her own resting spot.

Resting up against the side of the cave, Sirena felt some of the tension leave her body. It felt good to not move and to close her eyes. There were soft whispers of voices coming from the mermaids next to her and she smiled as she heard their conversation slowly pitter out as they gave into their exhaustion.

Her own resting spot was quiet as Orinn seemed to have settled in without so much as a word. One last glance around the cave and she saw some slight vegetation on the walls and a few rocks littered the floor. Similar to what she was living in at their territory. When she closed her eyes, she often let herself think about the plants and fish that adorned their previous home. The Siren's previous territory contained beautiful stone structures that the Sirens had built over the years. She made a silent promise to make the rest of the Sirens at home as best she could. It may not be their beautiful palaces and caves but, she could make it slightly better. Anything would be better than what they were doing. Sheltering in fear. They would not remain in the Midnight Zone a moment longer than they had to.

Sirena listened for sounds coming from the mermen below them and when she heard nothing, she gave herself permission to drift off to sleep.

"We need to talk," Orinn spoke coldly, pulling Sirena back from the brink of sleep.

"About?" Sirena was groggy, fighting to stay awake.

"The future of the Sirens. Who's going to take over the Queen role for the long term? You can't honestly think that we're going to leave you as the ruler of all the merpeople."

Despite her reluctance to be the leader, Sirena felt a sudden sensation of being slapped in the face. She was wide awake now and staring at a fuming and intense Orinn.

"Explain yourself."

"You are not qualified to rule over the Sirens, and especially not over all the clans. Sophie and I are the elders and we'll need to pull in the leaders of the other clans and decide our future. We cannot leave our future in the hands of a young, immature mermaid."

"Then who do you propose should take over?" Sirena kept her anger in check and tried to exhibit authority over Orinn.

"If the royal family loses its ability to rule or gets exterminated, then the eldest advisor assumes the role of the clan's ruler." Orinn crossed her arms and dared Sirena to argue.

"You are the eldest Siren advisor. You want to take control."

"Yes, it would be me."

"The only problem with your plan is that I am very much alive and, as far as we know, so is Apollo."

"Well, we truly don't know about Apollo and you. That's something I can take care of."

"Excuse me?"

"You were never supposed to make it out of the Rusalka territory."

Orinn's voice had gone from cold to pure rage. Sirena noted her blackened eyes, her claws making their way out from her fingertips. Orinn's face twisted and rows of jagged, sharp Siren teeth formed where her mouth should be.

Sirena tried to remain calm.

"I made it out of the Rusalka territory. Still alive, I'm sorry to disappoint you. I will agree that I am most likely not the ruler that the merpeople want, but I'm what we have for now. I will find Apollo and I will hand over the rulership to him if that's what is best for our people but you will not remove me from my responsibility. Not like this."

Orinn's eyes flashed again, and she snarled at Sirena, jumping at her.

Sirena felt Orinn's claws digging into her upper arms as she fought against her crushing force. She felt the side of her head hit the wall of the cave behind her, and the sudden shock to her skull made her eyes sting. She tried to regain her eyesight against the already dark cave, while holding Orinn away as best she could.

"You have no right to lead. You are a child! I am the rightful ruler of the merpeople and I shall take my place," Orinn hissed in Sirena's ear.

Orinn was strong and even though she had adrenaline pumping through her and this newfound power, Sirena felt weak against Orinn. The days of endless travel with little rest had exhausted her. She pushed her weight into Orinn and brought her fin up with a quick, jerking motion between them to push Orinn away from her.

Her tail push worked, but Orinn's claws dug through the flesh on her arms and Sirena looked down to see claw marks in her arms. She yelled as her arms went hot with pain and she tried to send magic down her arms to heal. The reprieve was short-lived as Orinn was on top of her, clawing at her face and digging her fangs into Sirena's shoulder. Sirena screamed again as she tried to shove Orinn off of her, or at the very least, get her shoulder out of Orinn's reach.

She flipped her tail and brought out her own claws, shredding Orinn's face and tearing at her cheeks. Orinn howled in pain, but didn't let go of Sirena.

Anger took the place of her fear and shock. She had gone head-to-head with three other clan leaders in the last few days and lived to tell about it. She would not die at the hands of her own advisor. Her claws glowed as she let her rage fuel her magic. Sparks flew from the tips of her fingers and she dug her claws deep into Orinn's arms.

Relief flooded her body as Orinn finally let go of the hold she had on Sirena's shoulder. Orinn slumped forward on top of her, and Sirena pulled her claws from Orinn and pushed her to the floor of the cave. Orinn whirled around, fury in her eyes as she prepared to attack again.

Sirena was panting, and she could feel blood flowing down her shoulder. Mermaids weren't supposed to fight for this long without rest. Her body and her magic were weak, and she tried to take control of her breathing. Lifting her arms to defend herself again, she noticed a shadow move in front of the cave.

"Everything ok here?" Neo looked at Sirena.

Orinn roared with rage and set off after Neo.

Neo whipped his fin at her, spinning himself around and throwing Orinn into the rock wall of the cave. Orinn slid to the bottom of the cave and, though dazed, began moving upright.

"Nah, I don't think so." Neo moved quickly to pin Orinn to her spot on the floor.

Orinn kicked and bit at Neo, her hands trying to fight against Neo's hold.

"I can't hold her forever. She's strong." Neo's voice had taken on a higher pitch and he was looking at Sirena expectantly.

"Oh, right," shaking herself out of her daze, Sirena sent streaks of white-hot magic through Orinn's body, tearing her in half.

The Siren's body shuddered and her Siren form dissipated, leaving the intact bottom half of the mermaid but shreds of a torso.

"Whew! That was close! I thought she was going to take you out!" Neo ran a hand through his curly hair and looked from Orinn to Sirena.

Speechless, Sirena stared at him for a minute before responding.

"I had it under control. She caught me off guard and my magic was weak from overexertion the last few days. She would take no one out."

"Right, yeah. I mean, she was in it to win it. Her eyes and those teeth, eek."

"Are you mocking me?"

"Quite the opposite. You totally had it under control. Yeah, totally. I meant she was angry. She wanted to be the Queen and you to die. Scary," Neo was slightly smiling at her.

Sirena stared at him again. She didn't know how to take him. This is the reason that Leander tossed him off to her. He was a lot to take in at this moment.

"Hey, I'm sorry. I was trying to lighten up the mood here. It must have been a real shock to have your advisor trying to kill you," Neo spoke softly and reached out a hand to the wound in Sirena's shoulder that wasn't healing.

Sirena matched Neo's quiet tone. She winced as he came into contact with her shoulder. "Yes, it was. I didn't see it coming."

Looking down, she could see the blood still pouring from the wound.

"Will you let me heal that for you?" Neo touched her shoulder again.

She managed a slight nod and let him put his hand over her shoulder. Warmth flooded her body, and she felt her skin closing over the wound. Within a few seconds, her shoulder had healed.

Looking incredibly proud of himself, he beamed at her. "See? All better."

"Thank you."

"Don't mention it. Where is everyone else?" Neo looked over his shoulder.

"What do you mean?"

"Uh, you two were loud. I would have thought that Theo and Xan would have woken up." Neo was at the entrance of the cave.

Sirena followed him out and looked under the ledge of the cave to see Theo and Xan still sleeping. She looked to where the mermaids slept in the cave next to them in time to see Nova sticking her head out.

"What happened?" Nova's eyes were wide as she looked from Neo to Sirena.

“Orinn decided she was going to be the ruler of the merpeople and tried to take out Sirena. I stopped her.” Neo winked at Sirena.

Before Sirena could protest and set the story straight, Neo spoke again.

“Well, it was more like, I knocked her off guard so that Sirena could take care of the situation, you know,” he spoke slowly when he said the situation, dragging out the word and winking at Nova.

“So Orinn is gone?” Nova looked at Sirena inquisitively.

“Yes,” Sirena said solemnly. How was she going to explain this to Sophie? Or to the rest of the clan leaders?

“I saw the whole thing go down. I’ve got your back,” Neo punched Sirena in her newly healed shoulder lightly.

“Good riddance, and good night.” Nova gave an odd look at Neo and then looked at Sirena with another strange look before turning into the cave.

“Nova has the right idea. That’s enough excitement for a lifetime.” Neo turned and moved into Sirena’s cave.

“Ah, I don’t think so,” Sirena said firmly.

He poked his head out as he flipped the remnants of Orinn out into the open. Merpeople’s remains dissipated quickly after death, but there were still parts of her left.

"You want to cuddle with this or what? I'm only helping," he shrugged at her.

"Oh… thanks again," her face felt warm, and she remained where she was, not sure what to do with herself.

"I'm on your side. I've seen what you're up against. Leander sent me with you to get rid of me, but, for real, I'm here to help you. I realize you may have some trust issues and I want you to understand that I'm looking out for you. My intentions are pure."

He had given her no reason not to believe him, but the over reassurance that she could trust him left her skeptical. Sirena searched Neo's face for sincerity and found it as he stared into her eyes. Neo was a little intense, but he helped her when he could have let Orinn kill her. Adrenaline was still racing through her and she imagined he was experiencing the same.

"And I mean it too. Thank you." She brushed his arm with her fingertips as she moved past him and into her cave.

"Sirena," Neo stopped her.

She looked at him and tilted her head, encouraging him to continue.

"What did Desde say to you when you spoke to her? It's none of my business, but your face was white when you came out of her den."

A long moment passed before she muttered. "She told me there was a traitor in my pod."

"Oh," his eyes were wide. "Ohh, Sirena. I'm so sorry but you found her. She showed herself quickly. It's over."

"Is it though?" Sirena looked at him with despair lingering in her eyes.

"It is. Orinn is gone. Sometimes it's that easy."

"She's gone, but along with that, so is my trust. Nothing is ever that easy."

He nodded at her. Hurt filling his eyes as if she directed the comment at him. She hadn't meant him, but she didn't correct it either. Entering the cave, she sat down in the center, hugging her arms around herself as she sat alone.

She felt him look after her for a few more moments before he moved to the lower ledge beneath her cave.

Unease settled into her. Orinn was gone, but she had never considered Orinn to be a member of her pod.

Chapter 37

Sirena

Approaching the Siren's territory, Sirena knew she should feel relieved that they were home. But this wasn't home. The darkness, the cold, the creatures that lived here, they were temporary. With the Rusalka threat mitigated, her next task was to find Apollo and put an end to the internal merpeople fighting.

Xan to one side of her and Nova to the other. They entered the circle of caves and caverns that the Sirens were hiding in. She could feel the eyes peering out at her from the caves and she shook off their questioning gazes. They could see Apollo wasn't with her and she could hear the whispers, "*where was Orinn?*"

Her pod was safe and to Hades with Orinn. She had never cared for her, anyway. Maybe it was time for some changes in leadership among the council. Drawing from Neo's tales about Ajax and her own firsthand experiences with Sophie and Orinn, she was convinced that a change of leadership was needed. These blasted advisors were the ones that left them stuck in a battle with humans for a hundred years. *One hundred years.* Double her lifetime. These people have fought and hid and been fearful. Feeling a surge of confidence from her journey over the last few days, she believed that she and her pod could take on the humans. Right the wrongs.

Last night, after she fought with Orinn, she knew in her heart that letting Xan and Theo return to rescue missions was the right thing to do. They were fighters, and they were determined to find her people and the merfolk that were forgotten on the surface, left to die in circuses, zoos, and private exhibits. She'd tell them today, and she'd appoint Theo and Xan as advisors until she found Apollo. Maybe she'd toss out Sophie too. The old betta had been a member of the council for too long and she'd made too many mistakes.

Her friends didn't know her thoughts, but Nova looked over at her as if she had heard her thinking and gave her a reassuring smile and nod. Catalina started squealing at the sight of a few Sirens sitting out on ledges and rocks in the center of their new home, obviously happy to see the merfolk. Sirena fed off the energy from her pod and felt a moment of peace, the quiet of the water calming her thoughts.

Sophie was in the center of the territory, awaiting their return. "Looks as though you're a few merfolk short." Her voice was bitter, accusing.

"There were some… difficulties, yes," Sirena said quietly.

"So, I heard."

Sirena stopped dead in her tracks. Sophie knew already?

"Ozara paid me a visit this morning."

"Ocean nymphs, meddling little barnacles. Every one of them," Neo mumbled under his breath.

Sophie cast a glance in his direction, no look of recognition as she sized him up. "I've been patiently waiting for your version of the events. I'd love to know how you plan to explain away your murder of our eldest advisor and longest serving member of the mercouncil."

"Orinn would have killed me had I not killed her. *She* attacked me." Sirena matched Sophie's tone. "And Kassia…" Sirena cast her eyes downward, her voice choking in her throat.

Neo had pushed himself up to her side. She could feel his arm brush up against hers. He had gently nudged Xan to the side to hover next to her. "I can confirm Sirena's story. I was there. Had I not intervened, Sirena would not be here."

Sirena brushed off the annoyance at his attempt to claim he had saved her life, but she was also grateful that there had been a witness that wasn't intimidated by Sophie.

"Nova heard the tail end of the altercation as well. I didn't attack her," Sirena stated firmly.

"Yes, that's true," Nova confirmed loudly. Sirena cringed at how loud Nova had shouted in her ear, her anxiousness causing her to raise her voice. "Sorry," she whispered, looking embarrassed.

"Anyone else see this tangle?" Sophie looked around at the rest of the pod.

Xan, Theo, and Catalina all shook their heads slowly. The brothers looked embarrassed, while Catalina shot a defiant look at Sophie. Xan finally said, "We'd been swimming for days. We battled the Rusalka and broke multiple wards in the Mami Wata territory. I was dead asleep. I don't think I would have moved if Orinn had attacked *me*."

"Kassia was a casualty of the battle with the Rusalka. Neo tried to save her, but it was too late. They said a Rusalka speared her." Nova's guilt was clear, and she looked at Sirena and the others. Theo didn't even lift his head, his arms hanging limply by his side.

Sirena pulled at the confidence she had felt moments ago. An ancient mermaid, who, for all she knew, had been in on

Orinn's plot to kill her, would not push Sirena around. No, it was time for her to make some changes.

"Sophie, after the events that occurred with Orinn, I believe it is best if there is a change in leadership for the Sirens."

Sophie looked shocked but also relieved, not so much as breathing. Sirena lifted her eyebrows as she realized Sophie thought she was stepping down as Queen and continued on. "I'm relieving you from your duties as advisor to the Sirens and as a member of the mercouncil. With the events of the last one hundred years and the issues that we've experienced with our inner council, I believe it is best that I have my own advisors appointed to the council." Sophie's face had gone white, and she looked as though Sirena had slapped her. She had arched away from Sirena, her pale green tinted, black finds fins bobbing in the water as she took in Sirena's words.

Continuing on, gaining momentum as she spoke, "I am appointing Xan and Theo as my advisors. When Apollo is located, we'll make any necessary adjustments."

Xan and Theo stood firm, but she could feel Theo flinch slightly. Cali looked shocked and slightly hurt from where she hovered behind Sophie. She loved Cali, but she had remained here with Sophie while the rest of the pod was out searching for Apollo and dealing with the Rusalka. The two were friends and she couldn't take the risk. Her nerves prickled at her as she looked at

Sophie and Cali. Sirena was closer to Kassia than Cali and while Cali and Kassia were inseparable, Cali was still close with Sophie. She needed to choose Sirens that she knew were on her side and that meant Xan and Theo.

No one spoke for several minutes.

"What are you going to do with all of your free time, Sophie? Take up basket weaving? Collect seashells?" Neo broke the silence with his ill-timed humor.

Sophie huffed and turned away from the pod, swimming off to wherever an old betta swims off to, but not without a glance and an obscene gesture to them.

"Go fluke yourself too!" Neo yelled cheerfully out across the water with an exaggerated wave.

Sirena felt a small smile tug at her lips as she risked a side-eyed glance at Neo. He was grinning from ear to ear.

"Nice one!" Xan clapped him on the shoulder.

"I'd had enough of that. She can pound coral. Judging when she wasn't there and didn't see what we saw," Neo had a slight hint of anger in his voice, and Sirena felt a bit of surprise. She hadn't heard him express that kind of anger yet. Other than when he had talked about Leander. Sirena nodded to herself, his emotions making sense to her in that moment.

Theo cleared his throat. Sirena turned to him. "Thanks for the appointment but, we do not know what we're doing."

"And I do? We're going to figure it out together. This pod is going to change the way things have always been done. We are in the Midnight Zone, for *tail's sake*. Our council let us suffer and die for a hundred years. We're not doing this anymore. Our mission is to find Apollo and bring our people home. Put an end to the Human Wars once and for all."

Xan looked giddy. "And…" he waited expectantly.

"*And* we can resume our rescue missions with you two leading the charge," she said. Xan erupted into a celebration before she had even completed her statement.

Theo turned to Neo. "What will you do? Return to your territory?"

Neo bit his bottom lip for a second, thinking about his response. "I was thinking maybe I'd stay here with all of you. If that's ok, I mean…"

"Our home is your home," Sirena stated, opening her arms and gesturing at the Siren's sad unfamiliar territory.

Neo's eyes sparkled as he smiled at her gratefully. He reached out to pat her on the arm as Xan began his celebrations.

"We reinstated rescue missions!" Xan swirled around, still basking in their win and excited about what these changes meant for their future.

Sirena allowed herself to laugh as her new advisor swirled, doing flips and spins. The rest of the pod joined in and she breathed a sigh of relief. The immediate threat was over and they would tackle the larger problems together. Starting tomorrow.

Chapter 38

Alanna

Alanna looked over at Orla as her thoughts became a jumbled mess. A few kilometers left until they were in front of Sirena and her clan of Sirens. Alanna could feel her heart race. It was taking everything she had in her to keep her hair and tail in check. As her emotions soared, she felt the roots of hair tingle, begging to turn black.

Shoving her emotions deep into the pit of her stomach the best she could, she turned her head away from Orla and continued on their path. Orla had a slight smile and was almost giddy about seeing the Sirens. She was a mermaid in love and nothing else mattered to her. To really think that the Sirens were going to grant her the gift of legs and send her to the surface, Alanna could only shake her head.

When she really thought about it, had she known that Maia was going to be killed and that Apollo would be missing, she would have stayed in their home territory. This wasn't the time to be trying to broker deals with the Sirens, but here she was and how would she convince Orla to turn around?

Alanna thought about the last several years and the times that Orla had stood by her side while the Merrows berated her and threatened her. They had not accepted her as their leader willingly; they didn't want her. The Merrows loved and respected Orla because she was like them. Her falling in love with a human only proved that. That was a feeling and emotion that Alanna would never understand.

She still didn't know what she was going to say to Sirena and the rest of the Sirens. Surely the advisors would be there too. Staring at her with their hatred for her and the rest of the Merrows. As if she could read her mind, Orla interrupted her thoughts.

"How do you think this is going to go?" she asked timidly.

"I don't have even the slightest idea."

"Sirena is a new ruler, and so are you. Maybe she'll understand and want to start fresh? New rulers of both territories?" Orla showed the first signs of hesitation, with the slightest tick of intonation in her voice.

"I'm not that new, and she has no reason to believe anything I say. She could strike us both dead the moment we enter the Siren's lair. I would understand if she did." Alanna stared straight ahead, still struggling to control her emotions.

"You what? You would understand if she killed us?" Orla almost yelped with surprise.

"I'd understand being a new leader, having enormous problems like rogue Rusalka, a dead sister, another royal family member missing and being annoyed that two Merrows who started the biggest war in our species' history showed up at my home asking for favors. I'd understand having rage and frustration and wanting to take it out on someone and if I were her, it would be us. So, yes Orla, I'd understand if she wanted us dead," Alanna maintained her composure, her head throbbing from fighting her true form.

Orla was silent for a minute, staring down at the darkness below them. They had stopped moving, and Alanna was staring at Orla.

Finally, she spoke.

"I'm sure whatever you say to her will be perfect. It will come from your heart. She'll understand."

Alanna felt her body shake with rage and she gave a short, haughty laugh. The absolute naivety of Orla was frustrating, although not completely shocking. She was a terrible leader and why the Sirens had forced her out of her position.

They were fortunate that they even appointed Alanna instead of erasing their clan from existence. Still seething, Alanna closed her eyes briefly and tried to calm her racing heart. After a few seconds, she felt calm enough to keep moving.

She could see the Sirens, Sirena in particular. They were within eyesight. While most of the Sirens were in their caverns and lairs, a small group of merpeople were in the center of the territory.

Their new home was nothing like what they had before. Before the wars.

In the past, they had elaborate sculptures, and human items that people threw into the sea. There used to be beautiful foliage and plants and schools of fish. The Sirens used to sing and swim about. There would be streams of sunshine from the surface that highlighted the beautiful creatures and their caves and dwellings.

She saw eyes staring at her from under ledges, rocks and cliffs. The plants in the depths of the ocean were dark and dreary. Nothing extravagant or luxurious. The Sirens, the rulers of all merpeople, lived like the rest of the clans. In the dark and afraid of their surroundings.

Alanna felt her heart clench and her stomach go cold. If Sirena didn't kill them, these haunting sets of eyes in the caves would.

Her people had caused this. They had caused so much pain.

She felt a cold tingle run through her body, as she was only a few meters from Sirena and the group of Sirens. She recognized Sirena, of course, and there was one other mermaid that looked familiar. Another Merrow maybe? Was that even possible?

Alanna felt her body fail her, and she began to shake and quiver. Her ability to control her true form was waning. The thoughts racing through her head made it hard for her to even speak. If the Sirens were paying attention, they could hear or see her.

Her voice failed her. She opened her mouth several times, but there was no sound.

Hovering in place, staring at the Sirens, mouth opened. Orla looked at Alanna and then to the Sirens.

"Sirena, we want to talk to you," Orla caught their attention.

Alanna went cold. She hadn't been ready, and she felt Orla staring at her, willing her to talk.

Sirena turned around and stared at them with a look of disbelief. The other merpeople tensed as they looked at the two Merrows floating in front of them.

"Who are you and what are you doing here?" a male spoke up and moved towards them. Alanna didn't recognize him and he didn't look like a Siren. She felt herself flinch slightly.

Sirena held her hand up to him to silence him. He retreated slightly behind her, but remained close to her side.

"I know who you are, but I have the same question as Neo. What are you doing here?" Sirena's voice was flat and void of emotion. She looked tired and still on edge from whatever had happened with the Rusalka. If Alanna lived through this, she'd be sure to ask the Oceanids what actually happened.

Alanna's voice cracked, but she regained her composure quickly. She pinched her shoulder blades together and tried to appear confident. As she looked at Sirena, she couldn't help but notice their similarities.

"We came to talk to you. About the Merrows rejoining the rest of the merpeople. With what happened with the Rusalka and to Maia, we can help. We should unite and no longer be divided. Let us rejoin, and we can help you."

"Our issues with the Rusalka are over. It's done. You're too…late." Sirena dragged out her last couple of words. Her eyes were cold, but not cruel.

"I know, and I'm sorry for that. We're on the outside. By the time that we found the river and sea nymphs and learned about Maia, they told us you were most likely on your way here."

Alanna knew she was begging. She could hear the pleading in her voice, and it made her cringe. All the time she had spent rehearsing this in her head on their way here, and none of that was coming out of her mouth. She had only made pitiful pleas for a reunion. She knew how dumb she sounded.

"Sounds like you heard Maia was gone and you hoped for a fresh start," Catalina spoke to Alanna but was looking at Sirena.

Sirena didn't move and continued to look at Alanna, searching for answers.

"Although I understand why you might think that, I want to assure you I am here to correct the mistakes my clan has made towards you, the Sirens, and the other merpeople. Having full knowledge of what we did and the impact it had on everyone, I want to make this right," Alanna's voice was growing firmer, and she maintained fierce eye contact with Sirena.

"Our clan is dying. They're being taken advantage of by the Finfolk. Attempts to go to the surface are being facilitated by the Finfolk, but it's harmful. I don't know how the Finfolk are doing it but they are. Merrows go to the surface with their new legs but they don't last and they're dying up there! They are being captured and the wars are still going strong above the surface. If you let us into the fold, we can help you and you can help us." Orla's said hopefully.

"Ah, there it is. There's always a catch. Tsk, tsk," Neo smirked and waved a finger at Orla.

Sirena's eyes blackened, and her face distorted. Her Siren form was going to emerge any second. Alanna could see the corners of her mouth twitching and she didn't need to see Siren fangs today.

Alanna felt her own rage surge through her and she lost control of her emotions. Her hair turned black, with streaks of red and blue. She looked down at her tail to see it too was jet black. Streaks of color were swirling through her tail. She felt fangs breaking through her gums.

She turned to Orla.

"I love you, sister," her voice was crisp and without feeling as she spoke the empty words.

Confusion filled Orla's face, replaced quickly with terror. Orla looked Alanna up and down at her true form.

Alanna let her fangs break through. She heard a few gasps from the Sirens, but Sirena didn't move. She didn't even blink. Sirena was staring at Alanna, waiting to see what she was going to do next.

"I promise you, Sirena, that I will kill every Merrow that tries to go to the surface for a human."

Alanna grabbed Orla by the shoulders and with one last look into those terrified eyes, tore her fangs through Orla's throat.

Staring at Sirena, with her sister's blood dripping from her face and filling the surrounding water, she dropped Orla's body into the ocean.

Sirena's face filled with confusion, and her words were barely audible. Her face drained of color and she held firm eye contact with Alanna as she whispered,

"You're a Siren?"

The Merpeople Dictionary

Aicaya (A - i - Caya)

In the Caribbean, the Aicaya are mermaids who have lost their families. The Aicaya are mermaids who have lost their families, not banished to sea as people believe, but rather abandoned by their families or shunned by their clans. They are accepting of all and have become a safe place for merpeople of all kinds.

Ceasgs (Kee- Ahsk)

The Ceasgs are Scottish mermaids with human upper halves and salmon and gold-colored bottom halves. They bring fortune and good luck to those around them. Because of their good fortune, people heavily targeted the Ceasgs during the Human Wars. They are dangerously low in numbers and the clan struggles for survival. They have moved out of the waters that they called home and are deep in the oceans off of North America.

Encantados

Shapeshifter mermaids with their true form being dolphins. Historically, they have been located off the coasts of Southern America, but most of their clan lived their lives as dolphins during the Human Wars. Those mermaids who remained in their mermaid form are dispersed throughout the oceans, living as part of the

Aicaya clan. Encantados favor pink in their tails and hair. Prior to the wars, they could control weather and create storms. They previously could cause sudden illness or insanity in their victims.

Finfolk

People know the Finfolk as the leprechauns of the sea. They love shiny jewels, metals and anything that sparkles. Financial wealth highly motivated Finfolk and they entrapped humans to steal their treasures. They are in the North but travel at will to gain treasures. The Finfolk can shapeshift into plants or foliage, but their skin tone limits them. Their skin is green hued and their tails are dark green and black.

Kelpies

Kelpies are from the coasts of Scotland but had to move to the depths of the ocean off of North America to survive. They are the rarest form of mermaids. They are shapeshifters and often mirror their image to the likeness of other mermaids; however, their true form is that of a hippo. Their shapeshifting abilities allow them to shift to plants, other sea creatures, or even that of other mermaids.

Mami Wata

The Mami Wata derive their name from their deity and they function as sea witches. They can bring wealth and fame to those they choose to help. Unlike the Ceasgs that bring fortune to those around them, the Mami Wata can channel their luck to their own benefit. They sunk their clan to the depths of the ocean during the wars and could maintain the size of their population.

Merrows

The Merrows are in the oceans of Ireland and caused the Human Wars. Merrows easily fall in love with humans, much unlike the Sirens and other merpeople who resent humans. Asterios and Malee banished the Merrows from the council and the Sirens no longer offer their protection for the Merrow clan. Merrows are usually fair skinned with blonde or red hair however, a few can change their appearance at will.

Morgens

Morgens are the closest of kin to the Sirens, although their magic and shapeshifting abilities are weaker than the Sirens. The Morgens, a dangerous clan, have a reputation for drowning fishers or flooding villages and destroying crops. People know Morgens for their long hair and their ability to sing. While originally from Greece, they have migrated to North and South America throughout the course of the wars, seeking safety.

Ningyo

The Ningyo takes up the Eastern territory. They are beautiful, seductive but very dangerous merfolk. They can cast curses on those that wrong them and they cry pearls. People captured them for their pearls during the Human Wars. Their natural form is that of a large fish with fangs and many eyes.

Rusalka (Roo-saal-kuh)

In Russia, the Rusalka are ghost mermaids. They are mermaids that have met tragic ends and their souls banished to the depths of the icy waters. These mermaids are bitter, filled with rage and will kill humans or other merpeople with little to no notice. The longer they have been dead, the more violent they become. Sirens have long used the Rusalka territory as punishment for merpeople who have harmed others. Rusalka cannot leave their territory but the Sirens have tossed merpeople into the Rusalka territory for undisclosed time periods as punishment.

Selkies

Selkies were previously in the waters of Iceland. They traveled to the waters off of North America with the Kelpies and Ceasgs to avoid extermination from the humans. Because of their ability to shapeshift, they would shape into their natural form of seals to avoid humans. However, when humans learned that seals that reacted negatively to silver were, in fact, mermaids, they caught seals as sport. Selkies revealed themselves as mermaids when in contact with silver and humans held them in captivity, placing them in zoos and sideshows.

Sirens

Legends say that the oldest mermaids, the Sirens, enticed sailors to their death with their enchanting songs. The Human Wars have diminished the Siren population and because of their descent to the Bathypelagic Zone, above the abyss, they no longer travel to the surface. Their ability to sing is lost, and the clan prioritizes survival. The Sirens are the governing body of the merpeople. They were originally in Greece but they hide in the lowest levels of caverns in Greenland.

Undines

The Undines are soulless mermaids who dwell in lakes and rivers. Their natural forms are that of beautiful mermaids; however, because of the wars and their evolution to remain safe, they resemble swamp monsters. Their skin is a ghostly, sticky looking white and their facial features resemble melted wax. Where their hair once existed, they sport blackened stumps of hair. Their tongues are dart shaped and they can transmit their poison to their victims simply by blowing the spores or through a bite.

Water Nymphs

Water nymphs are the guardians of the waters. They are located globally and are the only species that is completely female. Water nymphs are referred to as water sprites sometimes, as they are the smallest species of merpeople. They are loving, empathetic and immortal, so long as they are not removed from water. Without water, they will die within minutes.

The Mercharacters Dictionary

Aiko (Ningyo) Pronounced- Eye-Co: Aiko is the leader of the Ningyo. She is a slow speaker and methodical in her interactions. Despite being a cold- hearted mermaid, she cares deeply about two things, the Ningyo and her magic. She has a long, narrow face with dark hair. Her tail is black, blue and gold and it sparkles when she's deploying her magic.

Ajax (Morgen): Second in command for the Morgens. He is Leander's senior advisor and among the oldest living mermen. Ajax is white-haired with a deep blue tail. He does, however, shift often to appear younger than he is.

Alanna (Merrow): Leader of the Merrows and sister to Orla. She has a heart-shaped, pale face. Her natural form is black-haired with streaks of red and blue and a black tail with blue, purple and green swirling streaks. Alanna hides her true form though and shifts to the more common red hair and a deep blue tail that is the usual form for the Merrows. When she experiences powerful emotions, however, she cannot hide her true form.

Apollo (Siren): The middle child of the royal family. Apollo is a very tall and athletic merman. He has medium length, dark brown hair and well-defined features. He has deep blue eyes that complement the blue shimmers in his black tail.

Asterios (Siren): Asterios was the husband of Malee, king of the Sirens and father to Maia, Apollo and Sirena. He is olive skinned with dark brown hair, much longer than Apollo's. His tail is a deep blue and green.

Bia (Mami Wata): The leader of the Mami Wata, Bia, has protected her people by driving them down to the abyss layer of the ocean. Bia is an original mermaid and has long, curly, black hair that compliments her black and gray tail. Her magic is mature, making her one of the most powerful mermaids alive.

Cali (Siren): Cali is an older siren and likes to observe whatever drama is happening from afar, as she's not one to get involved. She has, in true form, a deep blue and green tail with jet black hair but changes her skin, hair and tail to suit her mood.

Cara (Ocean Nymph): Cara is the sister to Ozara and aunt to Yara. She is younger than Ozara and follows her sister's lead. Cara has a peach tone color to her skin but the same blue hair as her sister and niece. Her tail is deep shades of blue and green.

Catalina (Encantado), "Cat": Cat is the closest friend of Sirena. Sirena and Cat met as children and Sirena insisted that Cat come home with them after humans captured and killed her parents. Catalina is a short but stockier mermaid, with dark hair and tanned skin. Her tail is a beautiful shade of deep purple with hints of blue iridescence.

Desdemona (Rusalka, "Desde"): Desdemona is another original mermaid, now a ghost mermaid. Her hair is a chalky white-black, and she looks like a true Rusalka- ghostly white from head to fin.

Eevie (Finfolk): Leader of the Finfolk. Eevie is a short and plump mermaid. She has the typical green tinted skin of the Finfolk with deep brown hair. Her tail is a dark green with accents of lighter shades of green and black fins.

Kassia (Siren): Kassia is Cali's closest friend. She is a blonde-haired, blue-eyed Siren by choice and stands out from the rest of the darker-haired Sirens. Her tail is a deep fuchsia with bits of orange and cherry colors working into her fin.

Leander (Morgen): Leader of the Morgens. Leander has strong, well-defined features. He is a tall and incredibly muscular merman. Sirena describes him as looking as a stereotypical Greek god. He has long, wavy dark hair and a deep blue tail.

Maia (Siren): Sister to Apollo and Sirena. Leader of the Sirens for only a few short weeks, ascending to throne after her parents were both killed during the Human Wars.

Malee (Siren): Former Queen of the Sirens and merpeople. An unknown assailant killed Malee during the Human Wars, resulting in Maia taking over the throne. She is an average sized mermaid with jet black hair and pale skin. Sirena describes her mother's tail to be the most beautiful to have ever existed. Her tail was jet black, with swirls of ruby red and gold throughout.

Naiya (Sea Nymph): Eldest of the sea nymph triplets. She is friendly, outgoing and has a vibrant personality. Naiya's tail is a brilliant shade of sparkling yellow. Her matching gold hair beautifully accents her darker skin.

Neo (Morgen): Neo is the cousin of Leander. Neo's parents got captured in the midst of the Human Wars, and despite Leander's intention to send him to the Aicaya, he remained true to his promise to his family by keeping Neo with the Morgens. Neo is an average height merman with curly brown hair and a vibrant green tail with accents of dark and medium shades of blue.

Nerissa (Sea Nymph): Middle of the sea nymph triplets. Nerissa is a more subdued personality than her older sister. She still sports the gold hair and tail that is typical of sea nymphs but has a more matte appearance to her tail.

Nori (Sea Nymph): The youngest of the sea nymph triplets. She often defers decisions to her older sisters, but is the comic relief in times of difficulty. Nori is the youngest and smallest of the triplets and while they are identical; she has a small, gold colored, heart-shaped birthmark on her cheek.

Nova (Merrow): Nova is a lost mermaid, having lost her memory during the Human Wars. Her pale skin and orange/red hair, characteristics of the Merrows, suggest that she is a Merrow. Her tail is deep blue, green and aqua, with the tips of her fins in the darkest shade of blue. Nova is stunningly beautiful.

Orinn (Siren): As the senior advisor to the royal Siren family, Orinn is next in line if the royal family ceases to exist. She is thin with an athletic build and her skin is ghostly white, almost as pale as the Rusalka. Her tail is a deep black with red streaks running vertically, with the red meeting at the center tips of her fins.

Orla (Merrow): The former leader of the Merrows, removed from power by Malee and Asterios during the Human Wars. Orla looks like a typical Merrow mermaid, with red hair and a tail of deep shades of blue, green, and purple.

Ozara (Ocean Nymph): Leader of the Ocean Nymphs. She is a small sprite of a nymph with blue tinted skin and deep blue hair. Her tail is fuchsia pink and royal blue and she is the most recognizable creature in the ocean.

Rain (Freshwater Nymph): The leader of the Freshwater Nymphs, Rain is a black and white protector of the Freshwater. She is a rule follower and maintains the order set by the Sirens and the rest of the council. She has the typical glow of a nymph who gets plenty of sun and her dark emerald green hair and tail are a perfect matching set.

Rian (Freshwater Nymph): The surviving twin and sister to Rina. Rian and Rina were two of the original Freshwater Nymphs before Rina was killed. She has a sun kissed glow from being in the open freshwater and her tail is a vibrant emerald green. She has mint green hair that is the only similarity that she shares with Rina.

Rina (Rusalka): Former twin of the Freshwater Nymph, Rian. Rina met a tragic end and has found herself as part of the Rusalka rather than protecting the open waters. She looks like the other Rusalka's now, despite being the sprite size of the nymphs. Her skin is ghostly white and shades of gray mute her green tail.

Ripley (Freshwater Nymph): Ripley is the newest nymph, having taken over after Rina passed. She is determined to show her strength and prove her worth. She has the same green hair and tail as the other Freshwater Nymphs but has gold accents in her hair.

Sakura (Ningyo) Pronounced Sah- kr- ah: Sakura is the significant other and second in command for the Ningyo. She had dark, long hair with streaks of red that match her blood red tail.

Sirena (Siren): The newest Queen of the Sirens and ruler of the merpeople. She is the youngest sibling in the royal family. Sirena has a round face with black hair, much like her mother. Her tail is black with swirls of gold and the tips of her fins look as though they are brushed with gold. She is a smaller than average mermaid and believes her size is a benefit to her.

Sophie (Siren): Sophie is an older mermaid and was an advisor to Malee and Asterios. She has a heart-shaped face, pale skin and long, chocolate brown hair. Her tail is a deep shade of green with lighter green accents on her fins.

Theo (Siren): Older brother of Xan. Theo and Xan were fighters during the Human Wars and saved thousands of merpeople. He has multiple battle wounds he wasn't able to heal, with scars throughout his tail and a nipped fin. His tail is a silver gray with black fins and he is an athletic merman.

Xan (Siren): Younger brother of Theo. Xan and Theo were a large part of the Human Wars and fought tirelessly to save other merpeople. He can be somewhat immature, despite being a war hero. He is dark and his tail is black with gray fins.

Yara (Ocean Nymph): The youngest of the Ocean Nymphs, she is Ozara's daughter. Yara has
the blue hair and skin tone of her mother but has a solid, shimmering blue tail.

Acknowledgements

A huge thank you to my friends and family that supported me in this endeavor. Thank you for talking me off ledges, listening to fear-stricken rants and for tolerating everything that comes with being my friend.

Thank you to Dave Kippen for making the pictures inside my head come alive!

A special thank you to my husband who had to listen to countless story ideas, re-writes and edits about mermaids. Thank you for putting up with the absolute chaotic world that I surround us in.

About Jayelle

Jayelle is a mermaid living in Green Bay. When she's not writing or reading, you can find her teaching Barre or Yoga. She is a proud husky mama to Mika Quinn and Kiki Pancake.

Made in the USA
Middletown, DE
10 September 2024

60146506R00210